Stan Hey is a long-established writer for television, with such programmes as *Auf Weidersehen, Pet* and *Spender* to his name. His most recent credits include *The Manageress* and *All in the Game*. He lives in Wiltshire with his family.

SCARE STORY

When Frank Brennan's interlude of back-seat passion with his wife, Janet, is disturbed by a fast-moving convoy of army trucks on a minor road over Salisbury Plain, he decides to investigate. Turned away by army troops at a road block, he succeeds in breaching the security cordon and witnesses a chilling sight: in the glare of floodlights, soldiers in biological warfare suits are blue-bagging the heads of dead cattle — a signal that a chemical or biological attack has just taken place. And the government's research establishment at Porton Down is only a few miles away . . .

STAN HEY

◆

SCARE STORY

Complete and Unabridged

ULVERSCROFT
Leicester

First published in Great Britain in 1999 by
Hodder and Stoughton
a division of Hodder Headline
London

First Large Print Edition
published 2001
by arrangement with
Hodder and Stoughton
a division of Hodder Headline
London

The moral right of the author has been asserted

British Library CIP Data

Hey, Stan
    Scare story.—Large print ed.—
    Ulverscroft large print series: mystery
    1. Biological weapons—Great Britain—Fiction
    2. Detective and mystery stories 3. Large type books
    I. Title
    823.9′14 [F]

    ISBN 0–7089–4473–6

Published by
F. A. Thorpe (Publishing)
Anstey, Leicestershire
Set by Words & Graphics Ltd.
Anstey, Leicestershire
Printed and bound in Great Britain by
T. J. International Ltd., Padstow, Cornwall

This book is printed on acid-free paper

1

'What are you doing?' Brennan asked Janet.

She had slowed down the car and was now reversing it into the entrance to a field which, even at this time of the night, glowed with the golden colour of the oilseed rape that spread as far as the eye could see. A midsummer night's sky of deep indigo hung all around, like a velvet theatrical backcloth. Janet switched the Renault's engine off and listened to the absolute silence around them. Brennan had about three inches of his Havana cigar left to smoke: he was holding the smouldering stump out of the passenger window in token consideration of Janet's ban on tobacco within the confines of their personal spaces that, by mutual consent, included the car.

Brennan was a little bleary after the dinner they had shared at a classic Wiltshire manor-house restaurant, deep in the folding downland to the west of Salisbury. His semi-comatose condition stemmed not so much from the food, which had been modishly light, but from his solo burden of seeing off a bottle of vintage Côte Rotie with the meal, followed by a large Armagnac with the coffee.

'Bit late for a country walk, isn't it?' Brennan said.

His question was answered by the sight of Janet now unbuttoning her blouse. Brennan began to giggle stupidly.

'I think I must be in one of those Peugeot adverts . . .'

'I was trying to be romantic, Frank. You drink, I drive. You sit there, and I crawl all over you. Sounds like a good deal to me.'

'Yeah, but why not do it in the comfort of our own home, instead of trying to roll around in a ten-year-old estate car? We're not teenagers any more.'

'No. That's true. We're not.' Janet stopped undressing.

Pissed as he was, Brennan could still sense Janet's disappointment that her attempt at an apparently spontaneous moment had turned into a petty rejection. He could see that the look on her face was like that of a parent watching a child who had opened a parcel only to find a present it didn't want.

'I meant that *I* was too old, not 'we' as a couple,' Brennan offered as conciliation. 'I can tell you forty-five is a pretty depressing age to reach.'

'I have tried to make it a good birthday for you . . .'

'I know, and it has been. Great present.

Brilliant dinner. And now we can go back and do some fancy shagging all over the house.'

'Not in the car, then?'

'I don't think the insurance covers it,' Brennan said, waiting for, and receiving, the reward of a smile from Janet. He leant across and kissed her. Any hope Janet had of this developing was swiftly ended by a noise in the distance. Brennan broke away quickly.

'Relax, Frank. I doubt if the Wiltshire Vice Squad will be patrolling a B-road at this time of night.'

Brennan by now was leaning his head out of the window, registering the growing growl of a heavy-duty engine.

'Midnight ploughing?' he asked himself out loud.

As the sound of the engine reached a crescendo, a large camouflaged army truck swept down the road and past them. Brennan peered out and glimpsed the ends of two lines of soldiers sitting either side of the gangway in the back of the vehicle.

'Jesus Christ, did you see that?'

'Probably a night exercise on Salisbury Plain,' Janet said blandly.

'But didn't you see? They had masks on, chemical warfare things . . . '

'Frank, they do everything under the sun on that Plain.'

3

'How do *you* know?'

'Because our company made a documentary a few years back . . . I tried to show it to you once, but you weren't interested.'

Brennan eased himself out of the car.

'Where are you going?'

'Unless your map-reading was completely arse-over-tip, this isn't Salisbury Plain . . . '

Brennan strode off back towards the road.

'I'll be back in a sec . . . ' he called, before turning off down the road.

Brennan walked as far as the first bend. The noise of the lorry had ebbed away now, and he knew that in all probability Janet was right about it making its way onto the Plain for one of the seemingly endless exercises that had become part of the soundtrack to living in this part of Wiltshire. Hardly a night went by without the muffled *booms* of tank or artillery fire rippling over the ridge at Westbury and across to Bradford-on-Avon, followed by rushes of disturbed air that were often strong enough to rattle the windows. Added to these side effects of simulated combat was the regular drone of the Hercules transport planes from RAF Lyneham as they made their way over to the Plain, dropping equipment or soldiers into the pretend battlefield that it had been turned into over the past century. However, these disturbances

4

were nothing compared to the nights when a Chinook helicopter would scurry across the sky like a giant locust, with the heavy beat of its twin rotors creating a menacing bass note in the air. The noises and tremors of the army's exercises had become so familiar to Brennan after four years of Wiltshire life that they now passed almost as unnoticed as the police-car sirens had during his previous life in deepest Highbury. But tonight's sighting had not so much disturbed him as made him professionally curious. The instinct for the 'ambulance chasing' of his journalistic youth had never left him.

Brennan reached the first bend and scanned the horizon. Apart from the fields and the dark shadows of the rising hills, there was nothing. He cocked an ear. There were no mechanical noises, but he thought he could hear shouted voices carried on the air, like the distant sounds from a school playing field with a match in progress. But it could have been a car radio, or closing-time boisterousness from a pub car park. He promised himself he would return to Janet if the next bend in the road, a few hundred yards further on, didn't yield a change in the panorama. He walked on, slightly breathless now as the road curved uphill. He felt the first sensations of moisture in the small of his back and imagined that red wine would be seeping from his pores rather than ordinary perspiration.

Brennan crested the rise of the next bend and paused. Four or five hundred yards ahead, lights were playing across a field and he could make out the shape of the army truck, parked across the road. He could sense but not see the movement of the soldiers, fanning out across the field. Brennan instantly felt the beats of his pulse quicken. He moved away to the side of the road and crouched low against a drystone wall. His mind sifted out two immediate options. He could move closer and observe, knowing that if he were spotted he'd have no innocent excuse to fall back on. Or he could go back to the car and get Janet to drive on, so that they could stumble upon the scene as mere passers-by. The second option promised a better result, so he began to edge backwards. And then, from above, he heard the first drumbeat tones of a Chinook.

Brennan paused. The lights in the field were now being joined by two more powerful versions, arc lamps on stalks, wired to the lorry's battery and being carried on the shoulders of two soldiers in full chemical-weapons outfits. As the lamps were staked into the ground, the pool of luminescence revealed several dark shapes lying in the field. Brennan broke into a low-slung trot and moved along the road, clinging to the cover of the stone wall. The closer he came to the scene, the more its grotesque reality was revealed. About a dozen cows lay in the field, obviously dead, while the chemically-suited soldiers moved clumsily around in the stark light, taking it in turns to pull blue plastic bags over the heads of the deceased animals. Brennan had no deep knowledge of the physiognomy of cattle but even he could discern that the corpses were severely bloated, as though they had been inflated by air pumps. But, as the infernal drone of the Chinook grew louder and louder, it soon became clear that the soldiers were dealing with genuine carcasses and not some fairground novelty balloons.

Brennan watched as the Chinook moved overhead, with a circle of soldiers flashing their torches up into the night sky. Slowly, the giant helicopter lowered itself towards the field before landing gently about a hundred yards from the ring of dead animals. Four soldiers moved towards the open side doors of the Chinook and extracted a winch cable, which they pulled out as they walked to the nearest carcass. They tied the wire around the cow's body and signalled for the winch to be activated. The cable became taut and the gross body of the animal began to slither across the grass towards the helicopter, with the soldiers gathering around it finally to lever it up and inside the belly of the Chinook. They began to repeat the routine with the other carcasses.

By now, Brennan had seen enough to sate his curiosity. He paused to tie his handkerchief to a tangle of barbed wire on the drystone wall, and then retreated at a crouch down the road. Once he'd negotiated the first bend, with the field now out of sight, he broke into a gentle trot. He began to worry about Janet. The bizarre spectacle had distorted his sense of time and he became anxious that he'd left her alone for longer than was advisable. But, as he turned the second bend in the road, he could see Janet up ahead of him, anxiously pacing the tarmac.

'Where the bloody hell have you been, Frank?' she hissed.

'Not now,' he said breathlessly. 'We should get out of here. Quick. Back the way we came.'

Janet led him to the car and they clambered in, with the intended re-enactment of teenage passion now a remote memory of the night.

'Leave the lights off for a few hundred yards,' Brennan panted as Janet started the car and eased it out onto the road.

'What is it, Frank, a Martian landing? I heard a helicopter in the sky.'

'Chinook. Big bastard. Look, this'll come as no surprise, but I'm totally out of shape. Can we talk when I get my breath back?'

'Be about an hour, by the sound of it,' Janet said pointedly, in the tone that Brennan recognized from one of her 'ditch-the-cigars' lectures. She turned to look at his reddened, perspiring face and then moved the car off slowly, keeping her foot light on the accelerator. After a quarter of a mile of driving in the dark, during which Brennan had been looking continually through the car's rear screen, he turned back to tell her to put the lights on. His breathing was slowing now, and he groped for some paper tissues in the glove compartment to wipe the sweat from his face.

'If that was just an exercise I'm Brigadier Gerard . . . ' Brennan said as he dried his face.

'Who's he?'

'A famous racehorse with a military name.'

'For God's sake, tell me what you saw.'

Brennan took a deep breath and tried to order his thoughts, but they wouldn't fall into index formation.

'Lights. Soldiers moving around a field. Dead cows. All in these chemical-protection suits . . . '

'The cows or the soldiers?'

'Piss off, Janet. I'm trying to give you pictures here. The helicopter came down and they started loading the carcasses on board. Shipping them out.'

'Were the soldiers calm or agitated?'

'I wasn't that bloody close. Besides, they had these hoods on with blacked-out eyeglasses and air filters. That's another thing,' Brennan said as the images collided in his brain. 'They put blue plastic bags over the cows' heads: you know, just like laundry bags.'

Janet looked at him anxiously.

'How close did you get to all this?'

'Two, two hundred and fifty yards.'

'Christ, Frank, you really know how to walk into trouble, don't you? If you'd bothered to watch that documentary you'd have realized that the Army 'blue-bags' dead animals as a warning that they've been killed by a chemical or biological agent. And you've been poncing around in an Armani suit with a head full of red wine, breathing in any old shite that's in the air!'

'I was well away from the scene. And I didn't smell anything.'

10

'You're not supposed to — that's the point of using weapons like that. So, if it wasn't just an exercise, you have to go straight to a doctor's now and get checked over.'

'I've changed my mind — it must have been a stunt, OK?'

'What about my health, not just yours?'

'OK, OK — I'll call the night service when we get home. Oh, Christ, no!'

Brennan pointed through the windscreen to the junction ahead, where an army jeep was parked across the road and two armed soldiers in standard field uniform were patrolling.

They stepped forward as the car approached, flashing a red light urgently.

'Let me do the talking,' Brennan said grimly. 'Don't alarm the bastards, whatever you do.'

Janet slowed the car to a halt, and the two soldiers fanned out on either side of the car. Brennan poked his head out.

'Is there a problem, officer?' he asked, laying on a bit of a Wiltshire burr in his speech.

'This road is sealed off. How the hell did you get up here?'

'Well — me and my friend here, we turned off half an hour or so ago for a kiss an' a cuddle. Didn't see any no-entry signs or anything . . . if you'll forgive the pun.'

The soldier looked distinctly pun-resistant.

'This is a restricted area. How far up the road did you go?'

'Only about half a mile. Found an entrance to a farmer's field on the right.'

The other soldier was now talking into a walkie-talkie in incomprehensible military jargon, although Brennan was able to pick up on the word 'incursion'.

Janet waved anxiously.

'Look, mister — I don't know what we've done wrong, but can you please not report it? This man isn't my husband, see. I don't want to get into trouble, if you understand.'

The two soldiers moved well away from the car for what they would probably have called a 'confab', passing the walkie-talkie between them. Their words into this and the crackling response they received were now inaudible.

'Brilliant stroke, Jan. These lads will probably have us up for adultery now,' Brennan said quietly.

'I give good wench, don't you think? Why don't you just tell these bastards what you've seen and who you are?'

'If I do that we'll be banged up for several days while they sort out their story. Watch out, they're coming back . . . '

'Right, you two, bugger off home and be

12

more careful where you shag in future, OK?'
the older one of the pair said brusquely. The
younger soldier returned to the jeep and
reversed it to create a gap for Brennan's car.
Janet smiled and waved as she eased the
Renault past, and then turned off towards the
A36. Brennan checked behind as they moved
away.

'I think one of them is taking the car
registration. Should buy me a few days, I
hope.'

'To do what?'

'To find out what the hell was going on
back there before they have time to cover the
evidence.'

Janet looked at him knowingly.

'That's the best birthday present you could
have got, isn't it, Frank? A story . . . '

And Brennan smiled like a child.

*   *   *

By the time Janet had showered and come
back down to the kitchen, Brennan had
already spread his Ordnance Survey map for
'Salisbury & The Plain' across the table, and
he was staring at it intensely, marking it with
a yellow highlighter.

'Sorting your long barrows from your
tumuli?' Janet teased, knowing very well that

13

these features were one and the same.

'I'm retracing our route from earlier tonight.'

'Bear in mind that you were three parts pissed, Frank,'

Brennan's finger dabbed at the map. 'I think it happened here. Look — that would be the farm. There are Ministry of Defence 'Danger Areas' all around, but that's definitely not MoD land.'

'So?'

'So, they've got all these thousands of acres to do their war exercises on, but we find the army crawling all over private land. That says to me that it wasn't an exercise but a genuine emergency. And look — down here's Porton Down itself. What's the distance — two, maybe three miles between there and the field?'

'What are you suggesting, Frank?'

'Well, if it was a chemical or biological incident it almost certainly stemmed from something going on at Porton Down. That's where they do most of the research into the non-nuclear nasties of modern warfare.'

'But if there was a leak or something it would have affected the immediate area first, wouldn't it?'

'We don't know that it didn't.'

'Frank — there'd be news flashes and

warnings going out every thirty seconds if something ever got out from that place. The locals would know about it pretty soon.'

'Go on. Check on Ceefax, then,' Brennan said dismissively. 'Look for the story.'

'You've already done that, haven't you? Otherwise you wouldn't be so confident.'

Brennan gave her a deliberately smug smile.

'Have you called the doctor out yet?' Janet asked in retaliation.

'I'll make an appointment tomorrow morning. I felt fine, anyway. Am I foaming at the mouth or anything?'

'No more than usual. So, are we going to take advantage of Lester being away for the night?'

'You mean by having a go on his PlayStation?'

Janet turned away and headed for the stairs, tossing the towels away into the laundry basket to make a full display of her naked form.

'I'll be up in a few minutes, OK?' Brennan said without moving. As soon as Janet disappeared he returned to the map and began to circle all the military establishments he could find with his highlighter pen. Within ten minutes he'd marked out more than a dozen camps, barracks and airfields as well as over twenty sites designated as 'danger areas' that were for military use. Vast areas of Wiltshire were closed off for artillery or tank ranges, a scale of occupation that he had not envisaged despite living in the county. He thought that if recent roles had been reversed, with Serbia bombing Britain, then Wiltshire would have been blown off the map. Somewhere within this huge military complex there were people who would know all about tonight's incident but finding them and getting them to talk would require more than map-reading skills. Brennan yawned with weariness, the adrenalin rush of his escapade having drained away. He climbed the stairs to the bathroom and cleaned himself up before stripping off his sweat-stained clothes. In the bedroom, Janet had succumbed to sleep and, in contrast to her persistent denials, was snoring like a trooper. Brennan lay on his back next to her, retracing the night's events in orderly fashion.

He began to sift out a handful of possibilities to explain the incident. If it was an exercise, why had there been such nervousness, and why had it taken place on a non-military site? If it hadn't been an exercise, but a genuine emergency, what might have caused it? A stray shell, containing biological elements, from the artillery ranges?

An accidental leak from the Porton Down complex? Or a deliberate act of high-level vandalism involving dangerous elements that should have been under strict military control? Could it even have been a bizarre form of animal-rights protest against the experiments that were conducted with increasing frequency at Porton Down? Brennan suddenly found himself checking his body for signs of rashes or spots, but there were none. Reassured, he turned onto his stomach and quickly fell asleep.

★   ★   ★

Despite the night's exertions, Brennan woke early. Under normal circumstances he would sleep until after eight and then take up to an hour to become fully functional. Several cups of tea, a sugary intake of marmalade on toast or croissant, as much as he could take of the *Today* programme on Radio 4 before switching off in anger at the all-too-obvious news management, and a brief scan of the *Racing Post* for likely winners — these elements provided the template for a normal start to his day. But Brennan now found himself pacing the kitchen well before seven o'clock, listening to the local BBC station and slugging back several cups of black coffee to try and attain an early state of alertness. The local news consisted mainly of reports of further job cuts in manufacturing, a road accident on the A303, and the almost statutory details of several late-running or cancelled trains in the region. There was nothing about a field of dead cows.

Brennan crammed a banana into his mouth, hoping for an instant release of energy. He wandered across to the kitchen table where the Ordnance Survey map was still spread out and traced out again the route that he and Janet had taken last night. He listened. There was no sound of Janet stirring. She usually took the 9.10 a.m. train from Bradford-on-Avon into Bristol but, with Lester on a sleepover, there was a possibility that she'd have a lie-in for half an hour. Brennan crept back up the stairs and took a shower as quietly as he could. When he looked back into the bedroom, Janet was still fast asleep. Brennan tiptoed across to his chest of drawers and pulled out a sweatshirt and a pair of black jeans. He edged past the bottom the bed.

'Why are you creeping around, Frank?' Janet asked without opening her eyes.

'Didn't want to disturb you . . . '

'Like a child on Christmas morning, aren't you, Frank, once you've got the glimmer of a story? Awake, excited, giddy.'

'Is that praise or criticism?'

'Observation.'

'I thought I'd get back down to that field as soon as I could . . . you don't need the car, do you?'

'No. But you *will* go to the doctor's, won't you?'

'I feel fine. But yes, I'll go. Promise.'

'Don't build it up into something it isn't, Frank.'

'I was pissed but I know what I saw. If there's a simple explanation, that's the end of it.'

'You could call it 'The 6X Files',' Janet offered, referring to Wiltshire's most famous beer from Wadworth's brewery in Devizes.

'But I was on fine wines all night, remember?'

Brennan leant across the bed and kissed Janet's closed eyelids.

'Thanks for a nice night. And for my present,' he whispered. 'I'll have the bit I missed tonight, if that's OK.'

'What about now?'

'Don't tempt me, Jan. Look, I'll call you at the office later. Oh, and could you bring that videotape back tonight? I'll have a look at it.'

A smile spread across Janet's face as she fell back into sleep.

Brennan pulled on his jeans and hopped out onto the landing, pulling his sweatshirt over his head. He folded up the map, then scanned the kitchen, waiting for other objects to animate themselves and shout, 'Hey, Frank, you need to take me!' But none of them did.

Brennan left the house, closing the front door quietly. He paused for a moment to take in a few draughts of the sweet morning air. The long terrace of houses perched up on Tory enjoyed its own microclimate on most days. If, down below, Bradford was shrouded in a morning mist, then it could be guaranteed that Tory would be bathed in sunshine. Sometimes it would be raining in the town but dry up on Tory. Today was no exception. Brennan was able to enjoy a clear view right across to the Westbury Hills ten miles away while, a few hundred feet below, the River Avon and the town's bridge were both still wreathed in one of those ethereal summer-morning mists that had white swans moving magically through it. Brennan had, on a couple of occasions, tried to describe mornings such as these to city-confined friends in London as 'Arthurian', only to be asked what strength of dope he was on. No matter, it was their loss.

Brennan edged the car out from the small

parking area used by residents of Tory and its lower terrace, Middle Rank, and stayed in second gear while he negotiated the hills down to the town's centre. Five minutes later he was heading south on the A36, with the first wave of Bath's and Bristol's morning rush hour heading past him from the dozens of commuter villages on the Wiltshire-Somerset border. Brennan allowed himself a brief moment of pleasure at the contrast between their lives and his — they had offices to report to, bosses breathing down their necks, traffic jams to strain their patience, while he had just the glimmer of a possible story. There would be no interest, no deadlines and certainly no fees as yet, but right now he was at his happiest because it was the moment when he was most free.

★ ★ ★

The train driver thought at first that someone had simply left a coat in the shelter on the platform. But as his train, the 5.06 a.m. Virgin Cross-Country service out of Bristol Temple Meads, eased north through Filton Abbey Wood station on its journey up to Birmingham, the shadowy outline had become more illuminated by the lights from the building immediately behind the station.

Having brought the train to a complete halt, he was able to look back out of the window of his cab at the shelter and confirm what he had feared most. Dangling heavily from one of the structure's beams was the body of middle-aged man. After he had phoned back to Bristol to alert the police, the driver clambered out of his cab and crossed the track to the platform. He'd had two 'jumpers' in a twenty-five-year career: one off a bridge, the other from a station platform. There'd also been the brief glimpse in a train's lights of one bloke kneeling on the track before the thud of impact. So he'd seen enough messy deaths to make him curious rather than alarmed. He stayed well back from the body, knowing from past procedures that the Transport Police and maybe the CID would need to search the area. Even so, the driver could see that the dead man's face had bloated into a purple-coloured balloon and that the precise means of death had been his tie, tightened around his neck and looped over a strut of the shelter. Smartly dressed, the bloke was, really. Nice jacket, creases in the twill trousers, decent polished shoes. *No apparent reason why he should want to top himself*, was the driver's main thought.

And then four policemen emerged, running

down one of the flag-stoned pathways that connected the nearby building to the station. They shouted at the driver to bugger off back to his train. They didn't look like normal coppers. The uniforms were much plainer and their hats had no chequered trim. But then, as the driver returned to his cab and poured himself a cup of tea from his flask while he waited clearance to resume his journey, he saw that the fortified entrance to the building bore a sign that read: 'Keep Out — Ministry of Defence'.

2

Brennan parked the car in the same entrance to the field as the night before and allowed himself a brief moment of regret that he hadn't taken up Janet's offer of a bit of fun in the car. But then again, he would probably have got cramp or pulled a muscle. At forty-five years and one day old, Brennan knew that he had to leave adolescent fantasies in the past and just get on with the business of earning a living and being a good father and husband.

He set off down the narrow road in the direction he'd walked to follow the military lorries.

It was a bright, summery morning now, with bursts of birdsong up in the sky above him, while the wild flowers along the roadside hummed with flying insects. Whatever had passed off appeared not to have damaged the local ecology. Finding himself just short of breaking into song with 'Zip-a-Dee-Do-Dah', Brennan spotted his handkerchief, still knotted on a strand of barbed wire on the drystone wall.

Brennan paused, quietly chuffed that this

basic device had not only proved its worth but had also survived whatever 'clean-up' operation the army lads had conducted after they'd hoisted the dead cows away. But while the handkerchief confirmed that Brennan had found the right road again, the view this time round was entirely different. It wasn't just the comforting effect of bright light and warm sunshine contrasting with the claustrophobia of the previous night's darkness. Brennan couldn't square the picture in front of him now with what he remembered from last night. The most startling contrast was that, in the field where the stricken cows had lain, there now stood a small herd of a dozen or so identical animals quietly grazing and showing no sign of illness or distress. Brennan's euphoria became clouded by doubt. He would certainly have failed a breathalyser test last night, but had the drinking also distorted what he'd seen? Brennan reasoned to himself that he'd have needed to have been on something like absinthe to have generated an apocalyptic illusion involving a helicopter and dead cows that, along with the troops in their chemical-defence suits, were the key elements of what he had seen. Maybe he had understimated the intelligence of the soldiers clearing up after the operation — and, maybe, moving his handkerchief to another location in order to disorientate him?

Brennan watched the cows for several minutes before filling in the remaining geography of the site. Away to his left, about a quarter of a mile down a rough track, was a cluster of farm buildings, with sagging tiles or rusting sheets of corrugated metal for roofs. Brennan turned and headed back to his car. He brought it down to where the track began and turned in towards the farm. He knew that if the soldiers at the roadblock last night had done their job properly and forwarded the car's licence number to their command centre, then it would only be a matter of a day or two before Brennan's identity would be noted somewhere within the Ministry of Defence. Until that time, however, Brennan decided he would extract as much information as he could by playing the role of the 'busybody bystander', the sort of character who hangs around scenes of accidents and crimes for his own ghoulish relish but pretends that he's just being helpful.

'I hope you don't mind me dropping by,' Brennan said in the dullest voice he could summon to the man who looked like he was the farmer. 'But I was driving past last night and thought I noticed some sick cows in your field . . . '

The farmer straightened from the trailer he

was hooking up to his tractor and peered at Brennan with evident disdain.

'Know nothing about it, chum. Thanks for your concern, anyway.'

The farmer pulled himself up into the seat of the tractor.

'Only they were lying all over the field. Looked, well, dead to me . . . '

'I think you may have made a mistake,' the farmer said in a voice that didn't match his frayed and shabby clothes. He started the engine of the tractor. Brennan, who had parked his car directly across the tractor's path, moved closer.

'Didn't you see the helicopter, then?'

'What?'

'Helicopter! It landed in the field and some soldiers started to load up the dead bodies.'

Even above the howl of the tractor's engine, the farmer's laughter could be heard. He sat forward and turned off the engine.

'Look, mate. I think you should lay off the scrumpy, OK? You'll be seeing flying saucers next. Now, could you move your car, please?'

Brennan nodded.

'What's your name, then?'

'Why would you want to know that, mate?'

'I keep a diary,' Brennan said, with a simpleton's smile.

'OK. It's Tull. Jethro Tull.'

Brennan smiled and waved, before getting into his car. He reversed, allowing the tractor to pull out of the yard, and then headed back towards the road down the track. About halfway down, Brennan stopped and clambered out of the car. Without looking around, he climbed over the post-and-rail fence and walked out across the field, keeping one eye on the grazing cows. Without having to try too hard, Brennan found several long depressions in the grass where the carcasses had been dragged by the helicopter's winch and, where these marks converged towards one spot, several heavy indentations in the earth where the Chinook had put down.

Brennan began to prowl the perimeter of the field, looking for anything that might have been left behind in the clear-up operation. But, apart from the odd fragment of nylon rope and a few dog-ends, there was nothing. Brennan then heard the noise of the tractor growing closer. It was heading down the track towards his car. Brennan set off at a steady pace, preparing his defence to charges of trespassing.

The farmer parked his tractor right up behind Brennan's car and leaned out of the cab, waving.

'This isn't a footpath, mate. Now piss off out it, you nutter!'

Brennan looked up at the farmer as he stood on the tractor's steps like the hero in an old poster for a Soviet five-year agricultural plan.

'I'm not a nutter,' Brennan said, this time in his normal voice. 'And you're unlikely to be a real farmer if you're using the name of an eighteenth-century agriculturist or a Seventies rock group. That's too educated.'

'I was taking the piss,' the farmer said, with a brittle smile.

'What's your rank? Captain at least, I'd say. Grew up on a farm, or at least spent some time on one, so when last night's flap happened they get you to stand in and provide cover.'

'I think you should leave,' the man said firmly. 'Now'.

Brennan climbed over the fence, and jumped down next to his car.

'Some of your lads have already got my car number from last night. The name's Brennan. Want to tell me what happened?'

'I want you to leave my property.'

Brennan gave the 'farmer' one of his special 'wind-up' smiles before getting into the car and driving away. He paused on the way back to retrieve his handkerchief, a souvenir of his first little victory. Content that he had now alerted enough military personnel to his presence, Brennan returned to Bradford and had a quick cappuccino in the Dandy Lion, where he was able to flick through that morning's edition of the *Western Daily Press*. There was no mention of any alarums and excursions on or near Salisbury Plain. He bought himself a sandwich in the Spice of Life health-food store and walked back up Market Street to his house.

Janet had left a note asking him to ring her at work once he was back but, as it was gone one p.m., it was most likely that she would be out lunching at one of Bristol's trendy restaurants with her documentary-making colleagues. Brennan poured himself a glass of milk and climbed the stairs to his study on the top floor. He thought it was odd that while these companies were filling the airwaves with pictures of people's lives, from wheel-clampers to bin-men, they never allowed the fly-on-the-wall cameras to penetrate their own places of work and play. What fun viewing *that* would be, he thought, as black-clad researchers agonized over their organic-drink options and Pacific Rim designer dishes before drawing up lists of groovy ideas for future programmes about working-class life. Brennan unpacked his sandwich, and constructed an ad hoc lunch tray from his main birthday present, a wide-screen laptop computer that Janet had bought for him, instead of the box of twenty-five Hoyo de Monterrey Corona cigars he'd asked for. Pity, he could have saved her at least five hundred quid on the deal.

After he'd eaten his sandwich Brennan spread out his Ordnance Survey map of Salisbury Plain and taped it to the wall above his desk. He added the location of the dead cows to the splattering of markings he'd already made and stood back, hoping to see some pattern emerge. But none was apparent. The farm was listed as Breakheart Lodge, a somewhat melodramatic name that newspaper sub-editors would love if Brennan's story ever amounted to anything. Brennan scanned the vast acres of tumuli and other earthworks that were contained within the various military areas: had there truly been a peace dividend from the ending of the Cold War, these ancient sites would have been reopened for the people of Wiltshire to view. Instead, they remained sealed off, great treasure troves of English history commandeered by a military monolith that would probably never let the land return to civilian use.

Using a ruler, Brennan drew a line in black between Breakheart Lodge and Porton Down. As the crow flies, if it ever did in these parts without being shot down, there were about three or four miles between the two locations. It seemed highly unlikely that anything unpleasant leaking from Porton Down would have settled on this particular spot without affecting other properties, people and animals in between. With the artillery ranges several miles to the north, the possibility of stray shells with germ-laden warheads hitting the site looked non-existent. But *something* had brought those CBW-suited troops out in a panic: something credible, something real. Brennan fished out a copy of Yellow Pages from his crowded and unkempt shelves. And an hour later he had an appointment with the local vet.

Brennan sat in the vet's waiting room, the only person without a cat basket or a dog with a 'lampshade' protector around its neck. He'd thought of dropping by at the pet shop and buying a hamster as cover, but he couldn't see Lester welcoming the new arrival in the house. Lester was beyond pets now. So, when his name was called, Brennan ignored the nurse's impatient stare and scuttled straight into the consulting room, where a man in his late fifties sat, wearing a tweed jacket.

'What's so important that you couldn't discuss it over the phone with my staff, Mr Brennan?'

'Look, I'll pay you for your time, Dr Foster . . . '

'Mister Foster — we don't call ourselves doctors . . . '

'I want to know what would kill a small herd of maybe a dozen, fifteen cows, leaving the carcasses swollen . . . '

'I hope you're not planning another bloody vet series for television, Mr Brennan, because I'm bloody sick of them!'

'When I said I was a writer, I meant in the sense of newspapers, magazines. Truth, not fiction.'

'So this is not a hypothetical situation we're talking about . . . '

'No. It's for real. It happened last night. I came across it. And . . . '

'Your journalistic curiosity got the better of you?'

Brennan tried a self-mocking smile to defrost the room.

'I'm not so desperate that I chase animal carcasses. I would just like to know the range of possibilities, given the circumstances.'

'Which were?'

'A field. Ordinary dairy cows by the look of it, those black and white ones . . . '

'Friesians. And what else?'

'Nothing, really,' Brennan said guardedly.

'Well, cows are prone to many illnesses and

diseases. But if you're talking about something that might kill a dozen or so in one swoop, then it could be poisoning of some sort, most probably their water supply. It's less likely to be their feed unless it was something very dodgy, and most farmers don't do that any more after BSE.'

'But the swollen bodies, what might have caused that?'

'Well, that's consistent with anthrax . . . '

'Anthrax?' Brennan queried instantly, with a note in his voice that combined both alarm and interest.

The vet nodded calmly.

'It's fairly common for anthrax spores to be unearthed if there's any digging or drainage work done in a field. I probably get two or three cases a year.'

'And what would be the procedure if such a case occurred?'

'Well, if the cattle aren't already dead, they'd be killed and their bodies incinerated. And the farmer, or his vet, would have to notify the Ministry of Agriculture.'

'Would he graze new cattle on the same ground, knowing or suspecting what had happened?'

'Certainly not. The field would have to be isolated and detoxified, then left empty for at least six months. Does that fit in with what you saw?'

'Some of it does.'

'And what part doesn't?'

'Well — I went back to the scene this morning and there were new cattle grazing in the same spot.'

'That's highly irregular. And irresponsible. May I ask if this incident was local?'

'At least twenty miles away, so not your patch, I'd say.'

'I'm glad to hear it. If you want to take matters further, you should speak to the farmer and his vet. Failing that, you could shop them to the Min of Ag — though I didn't tell you that, if you understand?'

'I do. Thank you for your time, Mr Foster. Can I pay you for your advice?'

'I think I should keep out of this, Mr Brennan. And I'd be grateful if you didn't quote me if you do end up writing about this in any shape or form.'

'As you wish. Thanks.'

Brennan made his way out of the consulting room and passed through the line of anxious pet-owners with their stricken animals. He couldn't help thinking that if farmers had shown as much concern for their animals as the Great British Public feels for its domestic pets then none of the food scandals of recent times would have happened. The contrast between the cost-savings on battery-farmed animals for the nation's food chain and the millions of pounds spent on pet care was one of the more bizarre aspects of British life.

Did we really care more about the little furry things in the house than what we piled into our digestive systems? Brennan smiled to himself. He had started writing an 'intro' to his piece already without even knowing where it was headed.

★ ★ ★

'I think Frank should come and do some work for us,' Mark Beattie said as he sniffed the Calvados.

'He's not a team player,' Janet observed, sipping her espresso with caution.

'Doesn't have to be. We'd use him as our front-of-camera guy. The gung-ho reporter who won't take 'No' for an answer. A Roger Cook for the new Millennium. Six half-hours, for BBC West or HTV, with a chance of a network screening. I can pitch for that any time. What's he got on the stocks?'

Janet looked across the expanse of water outside the Bristol dockside brasserie, trying to think of a strategy. She had always known this moment would come, and while she welcomed the notion of Brennan getting more meaningful work, she knew that it would take a good deal of persuasion to get him onto a television screen as a 'personality' investigator.

'Something — but he's not letting on at the moment.'

'Chinese walls?' Mark said with a laugh. 'I see you borrowed the Porton Down film from our library this morning. If he's got a good story, I'll commission it myself, without even going to a broadcaster first. Frank could still have the publishing rights. That way he'd get paid twice.'

'I'll talk to him. But don't hold your breath, Mark.'

'Check, please,' Mark said, waving airily at a passing waiter.

* * *

'Bollocks. Double bollocks!' Brennan shouted in frustration as he sat at his desk.

'You all right, dad?' Lester asked from the landing.

Brennan turned in time to see his son's face appear around the door. It had been nearly thirty-six hours since he'd seen him but even in such a short span of time, Lester's features had changed to a degree that, admittedly, no microscope could detect. But the image retained on the parental retina from the last sighting immediately threw into relief the minuscule developments that had taken place in the absent offspring.

'You growing your sidies, then?'

'What?'

Brennan put an index finger to the base of his ear.

'They're longer than yesterday.'

Lester shrugged. 'I didn't bother shaving this morning, that's all. Good time last night?' he asked.

'Interesting rather than good.'

'What was all the shouting about?'

'This,' Brennan said, pointing at the laptop computer that sat unfolded and humming in front of him. An electronic prompt blinked on the screen.

'Least you've got it going,' Lester said, with a smirk. 'What's the problem?'

'I'm trying to get onto the Internet . . . '

Lester's face now broke into a huge smile of victory.

'Well, well — I just lost my bet, then.'

'What on, and with whom?' Brennan asked beadily.

'Mum. I bet her a CD that you'd never bother with the Net.'

'Right, well, that will teach you to make assumptions about my flexibility towards modern technology.'

'But you were one of those old print guys, weren't you? Hot metal, linotyping, ink-rollers, page-proofs . . . '

'How do you know about these?' Brennan asked patiently.

'General studies. The special subject this term is printing and journalism since 1950.'

Brennan's head hung.

'What's up?'

'Well, you're right, I happened to like the old style of newspaper-making. It was an assembly of crafts — thinking, writing, design, headline writing, and all that went into setting and printing the paper. It was a collaborative experience.'

'Yeah, but didn't the unions . . . ?'

'Don't start spinning me that Murdoch line, Lester. And if your teacher does, tell him to come and see me! It wasn't about politics, it was about labour costs — and driving them down. Machines like this enabled the owners and management to see what massive profits they could make. And that's *all* they see these days. Profit.'

'Sorry.'

'No, *I'm* sorry. It's just a bit disturbing for me to find a large and fairly recent part of my life being discussed in schools as industrial history.'

'You mean it makes you feel old?'

Brennan nodded. Then pointed to the screen of the computer.

'You going help me, then?'

Lester pulled up a chair alongside his father.

'What's the hitch, then?'

'I don't understand all this icon business. I'm a word man. I want computers to understand by words, not pictures.'

'You'll be able to voice-control them within a couple of years . . . '

Brennan put his hand to his brow. Lester tapped away at the keyboard and after less than a minute a brightly coloured logo was up on the screen, in the shape of a Grecian archway, with electronic music tinkling in the background.

'There's your portal. Now, what's your password?'

'Sorry?'

'You have to use a personal password to access the service in order to stop people like me going on-line for mucky pictures.'

'Well, I haven't got one, I don't think. Janet said the stuff . . . the CD or whatever . . . was already installed with all the software. All I had to do was switch on — that was the theory, anyway.'

Lester typed more information into the

computer and his finger whirled around the touch-pad as though he was stirring a cup of tea. A blank box now appeared between the soaring pillars of the arch.

'What do you want to use, then? As your password?'

'If it's supposed to be secret, why should I tell you?'

'All right, I can go out of the room while you type it in,' Lester offered with a touch of sarcasm.

'Teenoso . . . ' Brennan muttered.

'What?'

'Tee-double-ee-en-oh-ess-oh. 1983 Derby winner.'

'Yeah — ridden by that guy whose name you inflicted on me.'

Lester typed the password and awaited further prompts. The screen suddenly filled with a glowing billboard of text.

'Right. You're in. What do you want to look for?'

'Anything on Porton Down'.

'What's that, dad?'

'Well, let's type and learn . . . shall we?'

★ ★ ★

The three men waiting outside the pathologist's examination rooms were in broad

41

agreement that David Southwell's body couldn't have been found in a more inconvenient place. The station at Filton Abbey Wood was technically a Railtrack property but, with the Ministry of Defence's Arms Procurement Division adjacent to the purpose-built station, the MoD had an interest too, not least because Southwell had been one of their employees. Overriding both claims to jurisdiction, however, was that of the Avon and Somerset Police Force, who had first call on any death that had a hint of suspicion about it. So the three men — one from the Transport Police, one from MoD Security and the other from Avon CID — calmly assembled a pecking order for supervising the enquiry into Mr Southwell's death. Everything now depended on the pathologist's verdict that, in turn, would decide whether the Bristol Coroner drew the case to a close or insisted on a wider investigation.

The pathologist's masked face appeared in the glass panel of the steel door and his latex-gloved hand beckoned the three men inside.

'Sorry to have kept you waiting, gentlemen,' the pathologist said, disrobing.

'Better late than wrong,' the CID officer offered graciously.

42

'Right — I think you'll all be relieved to hear that the sole cause of Mr Southwell's demise was asphyxiation. His tie had been looped to form a classic slip-knot — he wasn't a navy man, was he?'

'Army,' said the MoD man. 'Before he joined us, that is.'

'Did you establish a time of death?' the Transport policeman asked.

'Between two-thirty and four in the morning, I'd say.'

'We had nothing running through the station during that time,' the Transport policeman said, happy to step out of the affair.

'Any marks or bruises on the body?' asked the CID officer.

'Nothing.'

'How did he actually do it, then — get himself up there without something to climb on?'

The pathologist smiled at the CID officer.

'Are you trying to complicate matters?'

The pathologist escorted the three men across to his desk, where the 'crime' scene photos were laid out. He pointed to the body hanging from the roof strut of the station's shelter.

'Mr Southwell was in good shape for a forty-three-year-old. His arms were well muscled. I think he attached the tie to the strut first, constructed the slip-knot, then pulled himself up, held on to the strut with one hand and put the loop over his head with the other. All he had to do then was let go and his body weight would have done the rest. The slip-knot tightens in an instant, and he's dead in less than a minute.'

'Sounds like a very organized suicide,' the CID officer suggested.

'The military mind,' the MoD man said proudly.

'Why there, though?' asked the Transport policeman suddenly. 'If you go to a railway station to commit suicide, you use a train.'

'You said there weren't any at that time of night!' the MoD official exclaimed, pleased with his deductive powers. 'Anyway, I think the reason he did it there was because he worked in the MoD building. It was his way of protesting.'

'About what?' asked the CID officer.

The MoD man paced the room.

'Look, we haven't found a note or anything else to suggest that Southwell definitely knew about this — but his name *was* on a list of redundancies that had been drawn up a fortnight or so earlier. Everybody who works at Abbey Wood had heard rumours there were some job cuts on the cards. My bet is

44

that he found out his number was up and, for some reason or other, it tipped him over the edge.'

'Was he in debt, then?' the CID sergeant asked.

'No. He'd have been in line for a decent pay-off, too. Thirty, forty grand, maybe.'

'So why top yourself? Not as though losing a job is an uncommon experience these days.'

'You don't understand the army, detective sergeant. It's a calling. A life. Southwell had been in the Mob since he was sixteen years old. For anyone like that to get the boot is . . . is, well, a humiliation. A total rejection.'

'Pity those who drew up the redundancy list didn't think about that before putting his name down,' the CID man said sharply.

The pathologist turned away to peel off his gloves, prior to washing his hands.

'I think we're getting a little over-excited, gentlemen, if I may say so,' he offered, over his shoulder. 'Did Southwell have any family?'

'Divorced ten years ago, and no kids,' the MoD official said.

'There you are, then,' the pathologist said, as he shook the water from his hands. 'The man had nothing to live for.'

*   *   *

After dinner, Lester had gone off to the Bradford-on-Avon Film Society's Friday-night screening — a short followed by one of the more refined movies of the distribution circuit — so Janet was able to commandeer the television set and show Brennan the tape she had borrowed. It had been, like most of Mark Beattie's programmes, a half-hour documentary made for BBC West in what was called, in trade terms, 'a regional opt-out' — that is, a programme specific to its immediate area, not meant for national broadcast. Despite the subject matter — what Porton Down was said to be doing to combat the alleged germ warfare threat from Iraqi-backed terrorism — the programme had failed to arouse much interest from the BBC in London. Mark, and Janet also to a certain extent, were convinced that this was a diluted version of state censorship.

'I think they were worried that it might be seen as alarmist,' Janet said by way of completing her introduction before inserting the tape into the video.

Brennan couldn't help smiling at this 'conspiracy theory'. The tape whirred into action and a wide-shot of the heavily secured main gate of the Porton Down site appeared with sepulchral music playing over it. A sombre, actorly voice-over began an opening

46

monologue that referred to the 'factory of death'. And then a reporter walked into shot wearing a gas mask. Brennan chuckled. Janet immediately hit the pause button.

'Problem?' she asked tersely.

'Sorry. I just found myself starting a 'Spot the television documentary cliché' count.'

'Is this professional jealousy, or just an instinct to rubbish the sort of area I choose to work in?'

'Jan — I'm reacting professionally, that's all. What I've just seen was the visual equivalent of the opening paragraph of a news story in the *Sun*.'

'You have to grab a television audience exactly the same way with a serious item, otherwise they'll be turning over to some celebrity chef's cookery programme. I mean, if you're such a smart-arse how would *you* convey the information that this place was working overtime to produce antidotes to a possible attack with nerve agents?'

'Well, I'd probably begin by saying that this was a nice bit of self-justification for Porton Down, who were only too happy to reassure the public about the work they were doing.'

Janet stood up and stomped towards the landing.

'You cynical bastard.'

'How did he get permission to film outside

there wearing a gas mask? It's a restricted zone. A stunt like that could only have been pre-agreed with the authorities, otherwise he'd have been arrested on the spot and charged.'

Janet said nothing, disappearing instead down the stairs to the kitchen and then loudly shoving pans into the dishwasher.

'I bet there's an official spokesman for Porton Down coming up on the film, isn't there?' Brennan shouted down the stairs.

'Just piss off, Frank!' Janet shouted back in retaliation.

Brennan decided to stand his ground, even though he knew there were elements at play other than just his distaste for the contemporary style of investigative documentaries. Having had Janet as his own researcher before they became lovers, and then husband and wife, he felt a lingering territorial claim on her services. Instinctively, he also felt that Janet remained under his tutelage, despite the fact that she'd developed her own career without him. And just edging into his consciousness was a spasm of jealousy, perhaps sexual, certainly financial, about Janet's relationship with her boss, Mark Beattie.

Brennan watched the remainder of the half-hour video with the remote control in his hand, fast-forwarding away from segments that he could tell would irritate him. There was the inevitable moment when a figure of authority, in this case a MoD policeman, was provoked into putting a hand over the camera lens in order to give the film a moral advantage. Soon there was also the cliché of clouds accelerating across the sky and a sun sinking fast, all achieved by stop-frame photography, signifying nothing more than that the director had run out of material. Finally came the apocalyptic conclusion, to the accompanying sound of Carl Orff's *Carmina Burana*, in which a retina-detaching sequence of library shots was jump-cut together to create a montage of lurid images of war and pestilence.

Brennan switched off brusquely and went downstairs, aware that he had to get out of the house before he said something more painful to Janet.

'I'm just popping down into town, to walk Lester back . . . ' he called, as he pulled on his jacket. Janet didn't reply. Brennan felt like completing this sequence by slamming the door, but settled on a quiet exit instead. He walked along the footpath that ran the length of Tory, the highest terrace of houses overlooking Bradford. The night was just beginning to chill, so he buttoned up his jacket. As he reached the plateau of Newtown, the lowest terrace, he paused. If he went left down Market Street, he could take in a quick drink at the Dandy Lion. If he went right, down the steep alley that tumbled into Church Street, he could take the footbridge over the river direct to the hall where Lester was watching the film.

The surly mood that had been generated by the video almost demanded a drink, but Brennan knew that if he indulged himself he'd feel cheap later. Besides, he wanted to take on Janet in a calm and sober mood when she retaliated about his reactions, and he knew that drink tended to fuel his sarcasm. So Brennan chose the alley as his route into town. Flanked by high stone walls, the path was well lit by a succession of street lamps. But, even so, not many people used it at night: indeed, it was claustrophobic at the best of times. Not many came up the alley, either, the climb being too steep for all but the fit and the keen. So when Brennan saw two men, hunched into dark leather jackets, coming up the hill towards him, he felt a touch of unease.

Brennan tried to rationalize this. He was responding just like a middle-aged *Daily Telegraph* reader who sees every younger male on the street as a mugger or a randomly violent psychopath. Brennan stood to one side of the path, determined to shake off this stereotype.

'Keep going, lads, nearly there,' he called, to show what a good, tolerant sport he was towards the young.

The two young men instantly pulled balaclavas down over their faces and lunged towards Brennan. He turned and tried to run back up the hill, but one of them grabbed his shoulders and spun him violently around, then slammed him back against the wall. The other produced a knife and held it in front of Brennan's face.

'When I last looked I had about ten quid in my wallet, and my credit card is well over the limit,' Brennan panted. The men made no move towards his jacket.

'This isn't about money, Mr Brennan . . .' the knife-holder said calmly. 'It's about you staying out of our business.'

'What would that be?' Brennan asked, almost relieved that this wasn't a standard-issue robbery but a pre-planned attack.

'We are the Salisbury Animal Militia,' the second man growled, without any hint of irony. 'Don't get in the way of what we're planning for Porton Down, or you'll get it too. Understand?'

The knife moved closer to Brennan's face. Though he could see that the hand holding it was trembling, and that the knife had more to do with carving wood than cutting throats,

Brennan took the safest option and nodded. Then both men grabbed him and shoved him down the slope, sending him tumbling onto the path. They ran up the steps at the top and as they reached the road on Newtown a white van braked sharply. They dived into the back and the van sped off with a melodramatic squeal of tyres.

Brennan laughed as the tension ebbed away. When violence was work-related, his ego would instantly translate such an act into a gesture of flattery, a signal that he was somehow getting up somebody's nose. Quite how he'd offended an animal rights group that had military pretensions he didn't yet know, but he was instantly grateful for their attention and for the unwitting momentum they'd given to his latest investigation. He pulled himself to his feet, using the metal handrail that ran along one wall. Had they installed it especially for the aid of stricken attack victims? he wondered to himself before he made his way down the alley.

As Brennan crossed the footbridge towards the hall where the film society had been meeting, he drew to a sudden halt. Leaning against a parked car was Lester, in an intense, shameless snogging session with a teenage girl.

3

'How old is she?'

'Fifteen,' Lester said, too quickly.

'She looked nearer fourteen to me,' Brennan objected as they walked up Market Street.

'All right — she'll be fifteen next month, how's that?'

'Are you sleeping with her, then?'

'Dad! Am I entitled to a private life, or what?'

Brennan paused. They were outside the Dandy Lion, its window seats filled with young drinkers enjoying their first legitimate experiences of pub life. Brennan looked at them and then at Lester. Lester could pass for seventeen, maybe eighteen already. But for the fact that the bar ran an ID scheme to discourage under-age drinkers, Brennan might have taken his son inside there and then.

'Look, I'm sorry,' Brennan said. 'I didn't have a proper girlfriend until I was seventeen. Never had sex till I left school. It was all a lot slower in my day. I sneaked into some backstreet pub in Hackney for my first pint when I was fourteen. And I was sick on the pavement outside. I didn't get my hand inside a bra until the fifth form. There doesn't seem to be any . . . delay or pause for thought for your generation. You just seem to go straight from being innocent kids to fully functioning adults.'

'Actually, it's not that different for me, dad. I mean, I can't legally go for a drink in there — wouldn't want to, to be honest. Don't like beer or tobacco smoke.'

'I suppose I've put you off both for life — one of my few successes as a parent.'

Lester smiled at him tolerantly.

'All my own decisions, actually. As is the one not to sleep with Jasmine.'

'Jasmine? Nice name. Does mum know about her?'

'Probably.'

'Meaning you haven't told her but you think she may have guessed?'

'Something like that.'

'I can hardly believe I'm saying this, but you won't go getting her pregnant, will you?'

'Who, *mum*?' Lester joked.

'Sorry. I shouldn't have said anything. Shouldn't have come down to the hall to meet you. Shouldn't have watched that bloody video.'

'What?'

'Your mother is trying to get me to do a

programme for her boss.'

'Cool.'

'I don't think so. Come on. Let's get home before she reports us missing.'

Brennan turned and ushered Lester under his outstretched arm, escorting him back up the hill as if he was a returning hostage. Brennan, in his darkest moments, could never forgive himself for going AWOL throughout a large part of Lester's time in London. The move to the West Country had allowed the family to come together again, but now Brennan faced almost daily reminders of how quickly his son had grown up, how he'd developed a life of his own — and, most painfully, how soon Lester might be away from him again.

* * *

'The Salisbury Animal Militia,' Janet repeated, with a hint of ridicule in her voice.

'That's what one of them said. I can't remember whether it was the guy with the knife or not. Well, it was a penknife, to be precise. One of those folding jobs that Boy Scouts use.'

Janet rolled onto her side in the bed, eyeing Brennan while trying to stifle a smile.

'Are you making this up to make me feel

55

less angry with you?'

'No, it really happened. I was there. And there's no need for you to be angry with me any more because I've decided that I *will* consider doing a documentary with your company.'

Janet climbed on top of Brennan in glee.

'What changed your mind?'

'Well — to be honest, the realization that I couldn't do any worse.'

Janet promptly pinned Brennan down by the wrists.

'Are you saying Mark's film is no good?'

'It's a ragbag of clichés. Well-intentioned, I'm sure, but the overall effect, from watching that video, is the sense of the audience being manipulated. The film has already made up its mind, and is determined that the viewers will have the same opinion.'

'How can it be otherwise in a documentary? You can't just stumble around, not saying what something means.'

'That's what I do . . . '

'But you can't compare written investigative journalism with filmed documentary.'

'Yes, I can,' Brennan insisted. 'It's the same method. You inquire. Follow leads, fruitful or otherwise. Only when you have enough facts do you reach a conclusion.'

'But, Frank, you're a one-man firm. You've

got the luxury of time on your side. If Mark's making a film, the first thing he has to consider is the budget. He can't afford to go off on wild-goose chases with a crew that's costing him seven or eight hundred quid a day! He has to know what he's trying to achieve with each sequence.'

'Exactly — which means operating with a closed mind. Finding out only the things that fit the story he's already constructed.'

Janet released her grip on Brennan's wrists and flopped onto the bed on her stomach.

'So how would you proceed, then — like Nick Broomfield?'

'Who?' Brennan asked, deliberately feigning ignorance.

'The guy who does all those documentaries on the hoof, with his earphones on and carrying his own sound equipment.'

'I know the one — gets results by hanging around and irritating people. Almost works.'

'Does the adverts for Volkswagen now, though, doesn't he?' Janet said, trying to goad Brennan.

'That says more about the state of British television documentaries than it does about him, sweetheart.'

'You really are one begrudging bastard, Frank. I give you the chance to broaden your range. You say 'No', and rubbish my company's work. Then you change your mind and say 'Yes', only now you rubbish *everybody*'s work!'

'That makes me choosy rather than begrudging.'

Janet slid out of the bed and headed for the bathroom for no other reason than to kill the conversation. Once inside she folded the toilet lid down, perched on it, and ran the washbasin taps to make it seem as though she was doing something purposeful. Unfortunately, the running water just made the tears that had been welling up burst their banks and stream down her face. When she reached for a towel, she saw that Brennan's hand had beaten her to it.

'Sorry,' he said quietly. 'If I didn't know any better I'd say I was just nervous. Intimidated, even. I can see the merits of getting into television, not least the money, but I'm frightened that I'd be a joke. An old dog conspicuously failing to learn new tricks.'

'*Refusing*, more like. Look, it's my fault, too. I'm pushing you into this, probably for selfish reasons.'

Brennan frowned. 'Why selfish?'

'I suppose it's because I think it would be a personal coup for me to get you to work for us. A boost for my professional esteem. Getting brownie points with Mark. That sort of thing.'

Janet paused and looked at the floor.

'I'd also feel more a part of you. Closer.'

Brennan reached out and pulled Janet gently up by the arms.

'There's always a part of you that's pushing me away, Frank. Like the other night. You made me stay in the car. It was your territory, your story, and suddenly I was made to feel like a trespasser.'

'That's just a newspaperman's instinct. It was in me even before I got a job. Always get there first, and never share what you find. Nothing personal in it, Jan. I *do* involve you as best I can. You can't deny that.'

Janet nodded.

'That's also one of the reasons that I've changed my view on meeting Mark. I need back-up on this one, intelligence rather than muscle. With a bit of luck, and goodwill, perhaps you and Mark can provide it.'

'You think he might have some knowledge of the Salisbury Animal Militia, don't you?'

'It crossed my mind. It's the sort of contact a regional docu-company would have. Fringe activists make good TV, don't they?'

'I'll ask,' Janet said teasingly. 'But you'll have to play fair with us. I can't have you just using us for information.'

'*Moi*? Exploiting? I don't think so.'

Janet pulled him towards her.

'Promise,' she whispered in the instant before her lips found his.

*   *   *

Brennan had made his request as vague and innocent as he could without making himself sound a halfwit. The switchboard operators on most regional newspapers, faced with someone asking to look through back numbers, are specifically trained to divert such a caller to the sales department in the hope of flogging them old copies of the paper or reprints of photos that have appeared in them. They are trained to expect nuisances or dotty pensioners asking about cake recipes, or people with stories about missing cats. However, a man claiming to be a student of the Open University who wants to go through back editions as part of his 'Media Studies course' receives a slightly more respectful response — and a call diverted to the news editor.

'Luke Barrs,' a crisp, young, male voice had answered. And Brennan had spun him his yarn that was duly met with a very cooperative response.

'Any day but Wednesdays would be fine, Mr Brennan, as that's our press day so it gets a bit hectic. I'm also the acting editor as well as the news editor, you see.'

'Then later today wouldn't be possible?' Brennan asked in his most humble manner.

'Well, yes — it might be. Is there any particular topic you're researching?'

'No, just general news presentation,' Brennan guessed off the top of his head.

'OK — say 2.30 and I'll be able to show you the backnumbering system. Do you know where we are in Salisbury?' Barrs asked.

'Yes, I looked you up . . . in the library,' Brennan replied.

'Fine. See you later. Just ask for Luke Barrs at reception.'

Brennan hoped the image of a rather earnest middle-aged late-achiever had been conveyed. Although the deception was a minor one, Brennan thought it worthwhile if it created for him and, more importantly, for his investigation a certain level of camouflage. It wasn't just the possibility that a local hack-on-the-make might sell the story, part-baked, to one of the national papers before Brennan could finely hone it himself. There was, too, a new etiquette to consider. Had he been attached to a paper, ideally one of the wedged-up tabloids, Brennan could have simply bought the co-operation of this small-scale Salisbury weekly and picked the journalists' brains to death over expense-account lunches. Lacking star status, not to mention money, Brennan had no chance of acquiring the information he wanted without incurring a potential liability. Nor could he trade on his 'name' — if today's papers truly ended up as lining for tomorrow's cat-litter trays, that didn't offer much in the way of posterity to a journalist who'd been out of the mainstream for nearly four years. 'Frank 'Cat-Shit' Brennan': what a byline that would be, he thought, if ever he got another full-time job.

It had just gone ten o'clock. The house was already empty, with Janet away into Bristol on the 9.50 train and Lester probably out walking the banks of the Avon, holding hands with Jasmine. Brennan reminisced, briefly, about his own teenage summer romances — the Fred Perry tennis shirts and desert boots he used to wear being enough of a fashion nightmare to blot out any memory of tender moments. He wandered up to the lounge and played Art Pepper's 'Straight Life' on the CD, just to get his blood pumping. The result of this musical infusion was the thought that he could pay a second visit to Breakheart Lodge on his way down to Salisbury. If the animal militia had genuinely been involved in the incident in the field, perhaps the young 'farmer', whoever he really was, would now be more forthcoming under precise questioning.

Brennan almost knew the route to the farm off pat by now. And the location had even assumed a warm place in his affections, given its key role in his investigation. As Brennan parked his car outside the large milking shed, affection rapidly diminished at the sight of a grizzled old farmhand wielding a shotgun as he walked towards the car.

'Good morning, sir,' Brennan tried as he stepped from the car. The farmer remained steadfastly grizzled, however.

'Piss off afore I shoots you . . . ' he growled as he stood his ground.

Brennan stood stock-still, carefully keeping his hands clear of his pockets, keeping his gaze fixed on the farmer just in case he looked nutty enough to open fire.

'I'm Frank Brennan. I'm a journalist.'

'Piss off out of it.'

'All right, I'm Frank Brennan of the European Community Agricultural Subsidy Committee . . . '

'Piss off even more quickly, then.'

'This isn't getting us anywhere, is it?'

'I don't want to go nowhere, so piss off.'

'Look. I'll say what I have to say and then pi — go. How's that?'

For once the farmer stayed silent, although

the shotgun remained levelled at Brennan's midriff.

'I want to know about the dead cows in that field the other night. The troops. The helicopter. I want to know if Porton Down had anything to do with it. Or maybe the animal rights mob from Salisbury. Can you help me with any of this?'

'Piss off.'

'I spoke to a younger man when I was here last. Is he your son? Or something to do with the army?'

'None of your business.'

Brennan smiled at the sudden outbreak of loquacity.

'Was it anything to do with an outbreak of anthrax in the cattle?'

The farmer's features darkened into a deep scowl.

'If you want to keep quiet about something that happened, shooting me won't be the best way to go about it, you know,' Brennan said, trying but failing to ease the tension. The farmer took two steps forward. Brennan suddenly sensed that sweet reason, or indeed gentle sarcasm, did not figure in his mental landscape.

'Look. I'll go now. I'm going to drop a card with my address and phone number on it out of the car window as I leave. If you want to talk, just give me a call. Any time.'

Brennan backed towards his car, opened the door and seated himself inside. An elegant three-point turn didn't seem the wisest option, so he gently reversed the vehicle out of the yard, pausing only to throw a business card from the car window. As Brennan accelerated on his reverse course down the drive, he saw the farmer advance to where the card had fallen and grind his cowshit-covered Wellington boot on top of it. It looked as though he'd have to revert to e-mail in future.

*　*　*

'He's coming round to the idea,' Janet said as she sipped her coffee.

'Terrific,' Mark responded instantly, flashing a genuine smile. 'He liked the tape on Porton Down, did he?'

'Not a hundred per cent, if I'm honest. I think he prefers to see himself as a lone-wolf investigator who may just happen to have a camera along with him.'

'Well, that may be one style worth considering. It has a lot of intimacy, the private video. Though, personally, I don't think it can be sustained without other footage. It comes over as too amateurish, too much the product of a geek with a gizmo. And Frank's not that kind of guy, is he?'

'Can barely open a tin of sardines without resorting to a hammer.'

Mark gave Janet a sly, private smile.

'You must have worked on him to get this change of heart . . . ?'

Janet ignored what she took to be a touch of sexual innuendo.

'I think what changed his mind was an encounter last night with two masked men claiming to be from the Salisbury Animal Militia.'

'You mean balaclavas?'

'From what he said. One of them waggled a penknife at him, too.'

'That would make a terrific scene to reconstruct . . . '

Janet frowned.

'Look, bear with me,' Mark persisted, noting the shadow of doubt as it crossed Janet's face. 'I'm getting a rough idea of how we present Frank to the viewing public — not in the overwrought style of a Roger Cook wrestling heavies on doorsteps. We film him going into situations, then he talks direct to camera afterwards, tells the audience what happened to him, what he's thinking. If we can pep this up with reconstructions, or even stuff that Frank films himself, I think we've got a terrific package to present to broadcasters. We could even go straight to one of the networks with this.'

'Look, do us all a favour and keep this between us, will you, Mark? If Frank thinks he's walked into something that we've already set up completely, he'll just walk out again. Let's hear how he wants to play it, let's cajole him — for one thing, I have to live with him.'

'OK. So how's he getting on with the story?'

'He's going to Salisbury this afternoon to do some research.'

'On?'

'Didn't say. I think he wants to follow up on this animal rights militia. Do we have anything in our archives or files?'

'I filmed a hunt saboteur unit a few years back, but they were based around Shaftesbury. There may be some names, or links in the files — have a dig around. You should tell Frank that these types may posture as secret squads but they just love publicity — I get one of their home-made videos three or four times a year. I bet you this Salisbury Militia would give him a filmed interview much quicker than anything they might do for a daily newspaper.'

'Thanks, I'll pass it on.'

Janet made her way back to her office,

trying not to look too pleased at the progress of the deal she was brokering between modern broadcast journalism and the scuffling 'gumshoe' otherwise known as her husband.

*　*　*

Brennan had passed through Salisbury several times on the train but had never stopped to visit. The sense of a small city that fancied itself rather a lot because it could boast an early thirteenth-century cathedral with a four-hundred-feet tall spire had rippled up to his northern corner of Wiltshire. This had not created outright resentment, more a sense that Salisbury was its own private corner and didn't relate much to the county around it. Brennan was therefore quietly amused to find that an infernal traffic system and a huge supermarket car park dominated the city's landscape almost as much as the cathedral itself.

Making his way back into the city centre itself, Brennan found a more pleasing combination of eighteenth-century relics and tasteful modern buildings. He liked the wide Market Square with its sense of mercantile bustle. And within the largely pedestrianized shopping area he could still make out the lineaments of an old market town with little alleys, water runs and ecclesiastical architecture.

On the western fringe of the centre, Brennan found the offices of the *Salisbury Gazette*. A modern smoked-glass reception area flanked by a fully computerized classified advertising section staffed by girls with the now-obligatory headsets quickly dispelled Brennan's preconceptions. He'd wanted to find an oak-panelled editorial office, with worn leather chairs and framed prints, a throwback to the small-town journalism in which he had started out. But everything had yielded to the power of the microchip now. What seemed odd to Brennan, however, was that local papers that used to be run with ease by half a dozen staff working a leisurely three-and-a-half-day week, now needed a similar number of people working full-time to produce just one weekly edition. The demand for local advertising had probably risen hugely, but Brennan also sensed that the new technology actually caused people to work harder than ever. The harassed girls in the classified section, electronically chained to their monitors and keyboards, were testament to that.

'Mr Brennan to see Mr Barrs, the editor,' Brennan announced to the pretty, uniformed receptionist who wore a slimmer telephone headset, modelled on the Madonna stage version. Brennan remembered the front desk of his first local paper that had been occupied by a formidable lantern-jawed spinster by the name of Miss Todhunter, who would simply continue with her knitting when a visitor arrived. Only when she had finished a row would this stern *tricoteuse* look up and ask, 'Yes, what do you want?' — whatever the visitor's status. So some things had changed for the better, at least.

'Mr Barrs will be right down to see you,' the receptionist trilled.

'Thank you'.

Brennan sauntered around the reception area, idly picking up a current copy of the paper. A thick section of classified advertising — houses, cars and domestic services — formed the backbone of the paper. Brennan could imagine punters extracting this and tossing away the news and features section. For a brief scan suggested no major innovations here, just the usual mixture of council news, Chamber of Commerce press releases and incidents from the police and the fire brigade. Brennan looked in vain for mentions of biochemical incidents or animal rights sabotage. Despite his own experiences, it had obviously been a quiet week in and around Salisbury.

'Mr Brennan.'

Luke Barrs was in his mid-twenties, tall and fresh-faced. He wore a smart pink button-down shirt and blue slacks. Editors got younger all the time, even acting ones. He offered Brennan his hand, almost as if he was greeting an exalted figure.

'Mr Barrs, thank you for letting me come in at such short notice,' Brennan said in a deliberately shy manner.

'No problem. Come on up,' Barrs said, standing to one side for Brennan. 'It's not every day we get somebody so well known dropping by our humble offices.'

Brennan laughed at the reference, trying to mask the puzzlement that this effusive welcome had created in him. They reached the first floor, where Barrs tapped a code into the door-entry system, then escorted Brennan through into the small but hi-tech newsroom. Barrs spread his arms over the empire in an ironic gesture.

'I'm sure this must be a bit of a comedown for you, but welcome, anyway.'

'So, this is what a newspaper office looks like,' Brennan offered, affecting a glazed expression.

Now it was Barrs who had puzzlement

71

written all over his face. He gave out a little embarrassed laugh and looked down at his shoes.

'Look, I'm sorry. But you are *the* Frank Brennan, aren't you?'

Brennan shrugged.

'I'm not sure who you mean.'

'Come on,' Barrs cajoled. 'I realize you must get pestered all the time, but you're among friends here. Well, one at least . . . '

Barrs stared at him expectantly.

'London College of Printing, autumn term, 1993?'

'I think you may be confusing me with . . . '

'You gave us a lecture. 'Fighting for the Truth in the Murdoch Age', remember?'

The realization that his petty disguise had been rumbled in an instant discombobulated Brennan for several moments. Barrs stepped in to fill the silence.

'It was a great speech. Inspired me an awful lot. But then, your work always was inspiring. I used to read you at school, you know.'

'Look, I'm sorry — you should have said on the phone and I wouldn't have bothered you . . . '

'*Bothered?* Mr Brennan, it's an honour to have you here. Though I'm surprised to hear that you're lecturing for the Open University. I suppose it was tough to get back into Fleet Street after your jail sentence?'

'Well, yes. But I'd already decided to pack it in, anyway. Do more writing from home. My new home down here, that is. Did I say I was lecturing?'

'Well, you said something about your Media Studies course, so I assumed you of all people wouldn't actually be on one ... ' Barrs said with a laugh.

Brennan scratched his head.

'Mr Barrs ... '

'*Luke*, please.'

'I'm afraid I'm here under false pretences, Luke. I'm actually researching a story, but I didn't want to, um ... '

'Pull rank?' Barrs offered.

'Something like that. Not that there's much rank to pull these days.'

'Come off it, Mr Brennan, there's no need for false modesty. So, how can we be of help to you?'

'Could we have a chat in your office?'

'Yes, of course.'

Barrs pointed to a glass-partitioned booth that overlooked the street outside and escorted Brennan towards it. As they walked, Brennan was aware of the glances he was getting from other staff in the office. Little smiles and nods that bordered on the obsequious. His arrival had obviously been well trumpeted by Luke Barrs. Brennan wondered whether or not he should just make his exit now, but he knew it would be seen as more than a little churlish by his one-man fan club.

Barrs closed the door and offered Brennan one of two chairs in front of his desk before he seated himself on a high-backed black leather number and leant back, drumming the desk with his fingers.

'Right. If you tell me what you're looking for, I'll pull out whatever you need. We only do fifty-two editions a year, so most of the news items we cover stick in the memory. And there's a dozen years or so stored on disk or microfilm.'

'Luke — I'm very grateful for your cooperation, but I have to say that what I'm working on is, in the first place, very sketchy at this stage. It may also cut across your paper's interests. In addition, I'm fairly anxious that nothing about it should get out.'

'OK. I've no problem with that. I'm happy to respect your professional privacy.'

'Well, it's not quite as simple as that. What I'm effectively asking you to do is provide me with information, perhaps even contacts, and then forget that I even came here.'

Brennan watched Barrs's open, youthful face, waiting for a sign of displeasure or concern, but there was no sign of anything other than boyish enthusiasm.

'All sounds a damn' sight more interesting than anything I normally cover,' Barrs said with hushed relish.

Brennan couldn't tell if the penny had yet dropped, or indeed if it ever would. So he leant forward slowly and spoke as clearly and firmly as he could without sounding like a patronizing git.

'The fact is, Luke, that what I'm about to mention is of the utmost confidentiality. Do you understand that?'

'Yes, of course,' Barrs said quickly — too quickly for Brennan's liking.

'OK. Can you tell me if you have had any reports or rumours in the past week of a serious incident either in or near Porton Down?'

For once, Barrs's expression darkened, and his demeanour instantly became more serious. He looked out beyond Brennan to the office to check that his reporters and sub-editors were all working.

'Please don't tell me that we've missed something big.'

'Well, I don't know yet. So, nothing's come through?'

Barrs shook his head.

'I'm afraid we have a very clearly defined relationship with Porton Down that's not just down to the Official Secrets Act. You know that it's been in the hands of something called the Defence Evaluation and Research Agency for several years now?'

'I thought it was all Ministry of Defence?'

'Well, it is, but DERA has a commercial dimension too. Some of the research there isn't just about chemical and biological warfare. There's battlefield weapons development, research into pharmaceutical products, and material science. They have strong links to the defence industry, too: joint development and so on.'

'So what you're saying is that some of these other elements can be exploited on the open market?'

'Absolutely. I mean, Porton Down for years was a one-task site — germ warfare. But since they changed its title from 'Chemical and Biological Defence Establishment' it's become more open, more commercially orientated. I've been to lunch there three or four times to talk to the Director and some of the scientists. It's all perfectly normal and rational.'

'May I ask why you went?'

'Well, nothing more than good relations,

really. DERA's a major employer in the Salisbury area and it obviously helps them to project that through the paper. They're also quite concerned to improve their image, from being known as a germ-war factory to being seen as a centre of general scientific excellence.'

Brennan was tempted to say 'Well, it obviously worked on you, mate', but limited himself to a wry smile.

'They're following the Sellafield route, then. Change of name. Accentuate the positive. Reassure the local population.'

'Yes, no doubt about it.'

'Forgive me for being difficult, Luke, but does this all mean that you'd be reluctant to print a negative story if you had one?'

Barrs shifted uncomfortably and gave a little, pained smile.

'Like being questioned by Torquemada, if you don't mind me saying so, Mr Brennan. Fortunately, I haven't had to face such a dilemma so far. But if I said I'd print, would you believe me?'

'Not sure. I can't see you betraying people you know, or to whom you feel obliged. Publishing the truth is often an act of treachery somewhere along the line.'

'So you won't tell me what this 'incident' at Porton Down involved?'

'If indeed there was one, either at or near DERA . . . '

'I haven't been much help, have I?'

'I don't know: you've saved me a lot of time searching through back numbers.'

'They have a public affairs officer on site, I've got his card somewhere . . . '

Barrs began to search through the right-hand drawer of his desk.

'I think they'll actually be in touch with me in due course,' Brennan said, a touch smugly.

Barrs pulled a business card from the drawer and handed it across to Brennan, who began to note down the name and telephone number.

'No, keep it, by all means,' Barrs said. Brennan pocketed the card and stood up.

'Thank you for your time, Luke.'

'No problem — it's great to meet you again.'

Brennan reached the door of the office before turning and faking the sudden onset of an idea.

'I'm cracking up. I completely forgot to ask you about the Salisbury Animal Militia.'

'Oh. Them. I *can* help you there a little. What do you need?'

'Anything — are they serious, for one, who are they, for another?'

'There's a hard core of about a dozen who

have been serial activists for years. Hunting, live exports, cosmetic testing — they held protests and rallies. But there was a split a year or so ago, with this 'militia' deciding on more menacing action. They claimed responsibility for releasing about five hundred mink from a farm last year, and I gather they're now threatening direct violence against local hunt members — burning stables down, that sort of thing.'

'Any names?'

'There's one called Joe Fletcher who I think got a suspended prison sentence a few months back. The rest, I don't know. They live completely outside normal life. Only the police would know about them. We wouldn't be among their natural supporters as a newspaper.'

'No — of course not. Can I buy you a drink or lunch sometime, Luke, as a thank-you?'

'You're going to hate me for this, but I'm teetotal — but, yes, I'd love to have lunch one day. Call me any time.'

'Thanks.'

'And good luck with your story, Mr Brennan . . . '

'*Frank*, please.'

Brennan tried hard, as he walked back to the car park, to recall talking at the London

College of Printing. He remembered visiting the building, but couldn't associate a date or an occasion with it. He guessed that he would, almost certainly, have been pissed at that stage of the decade, when his marriage had been heading onto the rocks. Whatever Brennan had managed to say in his lecture had plainly not made much long-term impact on Luke Barrs. It might have sounded good at the time, to youthful, rebellious ears. But journalism was now an industry that crushed individualism in every area, bar that of the celebrity columnist. Barrs might have done his formal training and made rapid progress up the provincial and editorial ladder. But Brennan guessed that the idealism, perhaps even the naivety, that had once made Barrs look on Brennan as a hero was now dissipated by an obligation to write for those who owned rather than for those who didn't.

Brennan strolled through the supermarket car park in a muted mood. He'd made no progress with the mad, monosyllabic farmer, and it was doubtful that Luke Barrs could offer him much help either. Brennan consoled himself with the fragment of information he'd gleaned on the animal rights militia. Further encouragement was almost instantly at hand, with the sight of a smashed quarter-light on his car. The damage itself was a pain in the arse. But the fact that nothing had been taken — not the radio, nor any cassettes, not even his single Havana cigar — despite what had been plainly a frantic search suggested to Brennan that there was somebody in Salisbury who was professionally interested in what he was doing. This was one crime he wouldn't be reporting to the police.

4

Brennan had stopped at Salisbury's council offices before his return home, and quickly found the names of the residents of Breakheart Lodge on the electoral roll. Only two were listed — Edgar and Nathaniel Gudgeon — both of which made 'Jethro Tull' sound attractive. Gudgeon senior, the monoglot with Tourette's Syndrome, and Gudgeon junior, the nervy sophisticate, made for an odd father-and-son pairing on the evidence so far. Brennan guessed that the son was probably the first in several generations of Gudgeons to complete a formal education, and might therefore be reluctantly detained at the farm by family loyalty. If Brennan could exploit that, he would certainly make more headway than standing around being sworn at by Gudgeon senior, who acted as though he was waiting for a *Monty Python* revival to come around.

Brennan had less luck with a search for 'Joe Fletcher' on the roll. Three Fletchers were listed as 'Josephs', but their addresses — one 'House' with a capital 'H', one 'Old Rectory' and one in Salisbury's Cathedral Close

— didn't scream out as the likely residences of militant animal rights activists. Brennan had noted them down anyway, as experience had taught him that disruptive citizens were just as likely to come from 'good' families as from 'bad'. Indeed, the animal rights people whom Brennan had often seen on television news reports seemed to be mostly middle-aged and articulate women, rather than bully boys in balaclavas with knives in their belts.

The drive home had therefore been a pleasant one for Brennan, relaxed rather than fretful, almost giving him the feeling that he had done a day's work. Brennan liked having names and being able to put faces to them. Knowing where these people lived also gave him a sense of being the hunter and not, for once, the hunted. It didn't necessarily follow that the people he knew about so far — the Gudgeons, Luke Barrs or Joe Fletcher — could be connected. But perhaps one of them, or more, would act as connections. The theory of 'six degrees of separation', proposed by American sociologists in the early 1990s, appealed to Brennan's style of investigation, not least because it always gave him hope. The suggestion that if two strangers each named a group of six close friends there would be at least one who was common to both had proved uncannily reliable. There was obviously some deep mathematical probability behind the reasoning, but Brennan just enjoyed the idea that all humans were creatures of habitual association, whose social and business circles intermingled at some point. It made the planet seem a smaller, friendlier place, at least to investigative journalists with leads to follow up.

Brennan's good mood lasted as far as the kitchen of his house, where Janet waited with a tense smile on her lips.

'What's up?' Brennan asked.

'There's an old friend upstairs waiting for you.'

Brennan could tell by her tone that the 'friend' in question was particular to Brennan and not to her.

'Not Stuart Gill?' Brennan said, briefly considering the image of his old editor, now a powerful man in the expanding television and newspaper interface, sprawled on Brennan's humble sofa with a ten-inch cigar alight and a sleek mobile phone glued to his right ear.

'He wouldn't have got past the door, would he?' Janet said with a hiss.

'So who is it?'

'Timmy.'

'Timmy Williams?'

'The same. At least he's sober.'

Brennan smiled, not at the prospects of

renewing the acquaintance but with the realization that he'd provoked one of the senior press officers at the Ministry of Defence into coming all the way down from London to see him.

'I'll see what he wants,' Brennan said as he headed for the stairs. Climbing quietly to the first-floor lounge, Brennan found Timmy running his gaze along a shelf of Brennan's jazz CDs.

'You got a warrant for this, Timmy?'

Williams turned and spread his arms in fraternal fashion.

'Frank! What a treat to see you!'

Brennan found himself on the receiving end of a manly hug, but he reacted more to the citrus smell of the aftershave and to the soft cashmere touch of Williams's suit.

'Very New Labour,' Brennan mumbled.

'Well, it's nice to see you, mate. Been too long. Still into the jazz, I see?'

'Helps keep me sane.'

'And Janet looks terrific. I'm really pleased you two got back together.'

'That's some statement, coming from the bloke who probably did most to drive us apart,' Brennan said, with only a hint of a smile.

'Frank, when you point the finger, take a look, old son — there's another three pointing back at yourself.'

Brennan couldn't help laughing. Timmy Williams had been spinning for governments in folksy fashion long before any of the New Labour whizz-kids had got into the business. He had always cajoled and charmed journalists with little homilies about how his 'old granny in Wigan' saw the world. One frustrated hack had even suggested at a press conference during the Gulf War that Timmy's 'granny' should put in an appearance herself, so useful was she at deflecting hostile media questions.

'Meaning what, Timmy? That I was a bigger piss-artist than you?'

'Of that there is no doubt, Frank. I merely accompanied you on your forays, to keep you out of harm's way. Although I could tell from Janet's face when I turned up that she still takes a contrary view.'

'Well, she rather likes me the way I am now, not the way I was when you knew me. Would you like a drink?'

Williams shook his head.

'I'm a bit of a changed man myself, Frank. Got a red card from BUPA about two years ago, so out went the beer and the ciggies, and in came two units of red wine and a walk each day.'

'Well, we can walk to my local and have a glass now.'

'I'll save it for our dinner.'

'Dinner?'

'I've booked us into a place near here — Homewood Park — at seven. Michelin star. Got to keep my expenses up, otherwise the client doesn't take me seriously,' Williams said as he self-consciously performed a touch of cuff-shooting.

Brennan frowned. It wasn't just Williams's presumption of Brennan's availability that needled him but also the use of a new terminology. 'Expenses' had never been mentioned in the past, because most of the time the journalist had paid the lunch bills in exchange for an accurate briefing on the story he was developing. Nor had the word 'client' ever figured in Williams's vocabulary. It had been simply 'the geezers upstairs'.

'You've changed, Timmy,' Brennan said suddenly, staring at, almost through, Williams.

'Don't make it sound like a betrayal, Frank. It's change or die, these days. You didn't, so you . . . ' Williams's voice tailed off without completing the insult.

'Ah, but I *did* change. Said goodbye to all the bullshit and the vanity. Nothing like a spell in prison to strip you of those.'

'Well, I couldn't afford to, Frank. Penny's given up work. I'm nearing fifty. The nearest decent school for the kids is an independent day-job costing me eight grand a year for both of them. Besides, I reckon I deserved a bit of gravy after so many years under the Tories.'

'So who are you with? The suit and the Michelin-starred restaurants tell me you're out of the Ministry.'

Williams reached inside his jacket and took out his wallet. From it he thumbed out a business card and handed it across, face up, to Brennan.

'Adcock & Williams, Public Relations Agency,' Brennan read out dutifully.

'We've had the DERA contract for nine months now. Which is why I'm here, of course.'

'I didn't think it was a social visit, Timmy. So what's the deal? You sell off your contacts to a slick agency in exchange for a partnership and then you charge the MoD twice as much as they would have paid you when you were one of its press officers?'

'A typically cynical Frank Brennan reading of a progressive development in how government now presents itself to the public, if I may say so. The truth is that the MoD, specifically DERA, gets access to my expertise in media relations, while I am allowed to develop a proactive stance on their behalf, something I would not have been allowed to do as a mere government hack. I can lobby, I can spin, and I can originate presentational policy. Better than a dull Q&A session over pie and chips in the Dog and Strumpet, eh, Frank?'

'Actually, I don't recall ever taking you to a mere pub on my exes, Timmy. You were very fond of Edwardian dining at Rules, with its well-hung game.'

'Well, now I can return past favours, so there's yet another improvement in the service. Come on, Frank. Get a tie on and we'll go and eat.'

★ ★ ★

Mary Ashton left work as usual, just after six, and took her traditional route along the B-roads to the north of Salisbury, looping round through Wilton and then into the West Wiltshire Downs. Her brick-and-flint cottage stood alone on a northern slope, with a stream running through the garden and down into the valley. On a late summer's evening, with the sun dissolving into a crimson wash on the western edge of Cranborne Chase, there was no finer place to be. As she parked her car, Mary simply sat still for a moment listening to the birdsong, letting it soothe away the accumulated stress of a working day. She eased out of the car and crossed the stone pathway towards the cottage's oak door. Lying among the potted geraniums was a brown-paper parcel, addressed to her by name only. She opened the door, then picked up the parcel and took it inside, dumping it and her bag onto the kitchen's waxed pine table.

The day had been a particularly strenuous one, with management in one of its stroppy moods, rampaging through the building looking for a scapegoat of one kind or another. Mary poured herself a large measure of gin, topped it up with tonic water, and sank three cubes of ice and a wedge of lime into the glass. She gave the drink a quick stir with her index finger, licking the bubbles off it as she pulled it out. After two generous mouthfuls she took one of the kitchen knives from its block and sliced open one end of the parcel. It was about the time of year when an old cousin in Devon dropped by with a large pot of clotted cream, but there was no note to this effect. As she stripped away the paper to reveal a small cardboard box, she held the box to her ear and gave it a little shake. The scratching noise of something on the move suggested jewellery, perhaps, or even a *pot pourri* of dried flowers.

She lifted the lid off the box. On top was a garish yellow sheet of paper, with a scrawled message written in red ink. It read: 'Stop Killing Animals — or, Boom! You're Dead!' Underneath the sheet of paper there was a tangle of wires, two 1.5-volt batteries taped together and what looked like a trip-switch. But there was no explosive — otherwise Mary would already have been spread all over her kitchen.

Mary finished her drink as calmly as she could. She'd always known that she would be found out one day. It was probably quite easy to follow her, or to note down the registration number of her car as it swept into Porton Down each morning. She decided that she wouldn't report this to management, because the damned MoD police would be around her twenty-four hours a day. Nor would she be scared out of her idyllic cottage. No, she would just call the bluff of these animal-rights people. If they were so concerned about the life of every creature on the planet, they could try putting hers first. In the meantime, she'd be careful and make sure that she looked under the car each morning and put any suspicious parcels into the garden's rainwater tub. She never ate her cousin's clotted cream, anyway.

Williams ordered a bottle of Santenay to go with the dishes that he and Brennan had chosen from Homewood Park's eye-catching menu. And because the evening was still warm, they took up the maître d'hôtel's offer of a table outside. This afforded a wonderful view out across the vale, where the white horse on Westbury Hills glowed like mercury in the sunset. Eating outside also guaranteed a level of confidentiality that Williams was obviously eager to establish.

Ordering completed, Williams leant forward across the table in businesslike fashion.

'Right, let's get this over with and we can enjoy our meal. What the hell were you doing at the scene of a joint DERA-army exercise?'

Had he been able to, Brennan would have raised a quizzical eyebrow at this opening salvo. The 'old' Timmy Williams would have been more circumspect, and would certainly not have attempted immediately to define his position.

'Suddenly we're playing — what is it you 'spin gurus' call it? — hardball. OK, well, firstly, I was at the scene of the incident because my wife fancied a shag in the car. Secondly, what I saw wasn't an exercise but a genuine emergency. A fact confirmed by your sudden arrival from London, when Porton Down has its own press officer.'

'It was referred upwards to me, Frank. Think yourself lucky that your name rang bells, otherwise you'd have been answering questions from inside a MoD Police cell. So come on, level with me. You were snooping. You'd been tipped off about something going on. People like you don't just 'happen' to be at events like this. You were there by design.'

Brennan took a long sip of his mineral water, dabbing his lips with the linen napkin before answering.

'Not true. I have the restaurant bill to prove it, not that I give a toss about making my case watertight for your benefit. So what was it, Timmy? An accident? Animal rights people playing silly buggers? A misunderstanding over where MoD land ends and private property begins?'

'Like I said, it was an exercise.'

'In what, covering up the leak of a pathogen from Porton Down?'

Williams bristled visibly.

'This is why I came down, you see, Frank. Because you're still a silly bastard who's ready to run off at the mouth with any old scare story, provided you can get it published.'

'I haven't written a word yet. Or

approached anyone. I was hoping you could help me compile an accurate account of what happened.'

'Forget that, Frank,' Williams scoffed, pushing a tiny vol-au-vent from the plate of *amuse-gueules* into his mouth. 'This isn't about cooperation. This is about you toeing the line. DERA has a very good record in being open with the public, both about its work now and what it's done in the past. It was my idea, for instance, to get them to come clean over the germ-warfare trials they did in Dorset in the 1960s and 1970s.'

'I must have missed the headlines.'

'They released micro-organisms off the Dorset coast to assess the threat a biological attack might have on Britain. They also released them into the London Underground system.'

'Jesus Christ, and you're sitting here telling *me* not to run a scare story. What happened?'

'It was all non-infectious. Nobody got hurt. But it was conducted in great secrecy. I persuaded DERA to place their files at the Public Record Office and to undertake a roadshow round Dorset, to tell people the truth and to restore their confidence.'

'A roadshow? Who are you working for, Timmy, Radio-fucking-One?'

The waiter arrived with their starters

— stuffed pig's trotters — so the discussion was silenced while Brennan and Williams cooed dutifully at the modish presentation. Once the waiter had departed, Williams resumed, pointing his fork at Brennan in order to emphasize his point.

'What I'm trying to get across, Frank, is that the place has cleaned up its act. It's a public-service industry and, while the details of the work have to be secret for obvious reasons, an awful lot of its business is out in the open. So if what you saw had been in any way dangerous, we'd have told people about it.'

'So what did I see, then? Spin it to me.'

'I repeat — it was an exercise, conducted with the complete cooperation of the farmer. A simulated clean-up operation after a biological attack.'

'Tim, correct me if I'm wrong, but I thought Porton Down had seven thousand acres of its own at its disposal.'

'True, but it's a contained site. Some of the tests and exercises are so specialized that they have to take place elsewhere in order to make them relevant.'

'OK — so what's so special about the recovery of a dozen or so dead cows? Why did that have to be set up outside Porton?'

'Because it was part of a larger exercise that

was happening on-site, simulating an attack on a rural location.'

'Right — so do you have advance information about a plot by Saddam Hussein to kill our cattle or something?'

Williams pushed his plate away, patting his chest as though Brennan had brought on an attack of indigestion.

'You probably don't know this, Frank, but during the Second World War scientists at Porton Down devised a way of infecting cattle cake with anthrax. The RAF were going to drop thousands of tons of the stuff onto German soil in order to kill the entire bovine population, thereby starving the Jerries into surrender.'

'So why didn't they do it?'

'Because it was considered unsporting, un-British. But that won't stop our enemies trying something similar on us one day. And we have to prepare for that eventuality. Ninety-nine per cent of DERA's work is on defence in the literal sense of the word. That's what the 'D' stands for, Frank.'

'OK, well, if what I saw is so routine and innocent, why don't I write about it now? I can probably flog a line to the *Sun* and let it make something out of nothing.'

'That would be highly irresponsible of you, as a professional journalist — it could create panic on the streets. That's why I'm asking you to go no further, Frank. If there was anything unusual behind all this, I'd tell you. Honest.'

'No, you wouldn't. But I'm going to tell you what I've got, so you can see things from my point of view. First, there're the dead cows and the chemical or biological alert, which takes place not on MoD land but on an ordinary dairy farm that just happens to be a mile or so from Porton Down. Next day, the cows have been very quickly replaced but neither of the farmers is keen to talk. The son tries to be clever, while the father threatens me with a gun. In between, I have a knife held to my throat by two masked youths claiming to be members of an animal rights militia. Their specific warning is 'Don't interfere with what we're planning for Porton Down'. To top it all, I get a sudden visit from Porton Down's *numero uno* PR man. So don't tell me there isn't something unusual going on.'

Williams finished the last scrap of his stuffed pig's trotter and slugged down a mouthful of the Santenay. With his napkin tucked into his shirt collar, Williams looked every inch the sybarite he no longer claimed to be. Brennan suddenly saw in him the

97

personification of the 1990s middle-class male corporate figure. Once an open, witty man, aware of the ironies and corruption of power, Williams was now effectively a paid-off lickspittle, happy to do what he was told by his bosses, and even happier to distance himself from his past.

'What happened to your granny, by the way, Tim?' Brennan asked out of the blue.

Williams looked back at him and shrugged.

'I made her up, Frank. My real granny died when I was six.'

Brennan excused himself and went inside the hotel for a pee. When he returned, Williams tried to steer the conversation towards the shared past, but Brennan declined the invitation. Well before they'd finished their meal and taken coffee and petits fours in the lounge, the two men had nothing left to say to each other.

* * *

The coroner's court in Bristol required only one morning session to consign the late David Southwell to history. Having decided not to summon a jury, the coroner was able to keep proceedings professionally brisk, with the standard parade of witnesses. The Home Office pathologist confirmed that Southwell's death had been brought about by asphyxiation, the precise mechanism being the slip-knot that the deceased had devised with his regimental tie. No marks or bruising had been seen on the body, other than the weals around his neck where the fatal ligature had done its worst.

Southwell's identity was confirmed by a Defence Procurement 'Human Resources Manager' who also stated that Southwell had indeed been on a shortlist for 'manpower rebalancing' due to the latest strategic defence review conducted by government and the ministry concerned. At this point the coroner made a plea for plain English, clarifying that 'manpower rebalancing' was corporate jargon for redundancy. Undeterred, the Defence Procurement man went on to express his belief that Southwell had become aware of his imminent 'career reorientation' through a slip-up in the department's internal e-mail facility, a lapse for which he had apologized at the time.

One of Southwell's colleagues in the ordnance provision section testified to the deceased's 'anxious and moody behaviour' in the weeks running up to his death. There had also been regular bouts of excessive drinking in this period, though these had been in a social rather than a working context.

The coroner asked if any notes or letters had been left behind, either in writing or in the computer at the deceased's workstation, but Southwell's solicitor confirmed that there had been none. A police search of the house where Southwell had lived alone had also yielded no clues or letters to indicate the reasons for the course of action that he had undertaken. The solicitor also revealed that Southwell had died intestate. He had no living relatives and attempts to trace his ex-wife, even by placing notices in newspapers, had failed to locate her. The solicitor had therefore applied for probate, so that Southwell's estate, amounting to nearly £90,000 with his army pension and house valuation, could be passed to the appropriate government department. The solicitor noted that Southwell had been an active contributor to an ex-services charity.

The coroner then heard from the train driver about his sighting of the body, and also from the MoD policemen who had attended the scene after the driver's alert. Mr Southwell had not been seen in the Abbey Wood complex since leaving at six the previous evening, his departure having been logged electronically by security staff in the complex's reception area. Southwell had made no attempt to re-enter the building during the night, and one of the policemen could only speculate that the place of Southwell's death was a melancholy gesture to the organization that was about to become his former employer.

The coroner then recalled the Home Office pathologist to ask about alcohol levels in the deceased's bloodstream. But, after consulting his notes, the pathologist stated that no traces of alcohol, nor indeed drugs of any nature, had been found. In his opinion, Southwell's death had been a sober affair influenced only by his presumed state of mind at the time. The coroner good-naturedly reminded the pathologist that speculation about the deceased's mental state was not his territory, and the pathologist apologized with a formal smile.

The coroner then adjourned the court for ten minutes before returning to announce the inevitable verdict of 'suicide'. He ordered the release of Southwell's body to the solicitor acting for him and then closed proceedings in time for lunch. Nobody was asked what Southwell's movements were prior to his death.

Two days later, Southwell's body was cremated at a ceremony on the outskirts of Bristol. Several former colleagues from the Defence Procurement office at Abbey Wood and a few regimental colleagues attended and left bouquets of flowers in his memory. They sang *Jerusalem* during the service, and then Southwell's closest colleague, who had testified at the inquest, read quietly from chapter twelve of the Book of Ecclesiastes:

'Remember now thy Creator in the days of thy youth, while the evil days come not, nor the years draw nigh, when thou shalt say, I have no pleasure in them; while the sun or the light, or the moon or the stars, be not darkened, nor the clouds return after the rain; in the days when the keepers of the house shall tremble and the strong men shall bow themselves, and the grinders cease because they are few, and those that look out of the windows be darkened. And the doors shall be shut in the streets, when the sound of the grinding is low, and he shall rise up at the voice of the bird, and all the daughters of musick shall be brought low. Also when they shall be afraid of that which is high, and fears shall be in the way, and the almond tree shall flourish, and the grasshopper shall be a burden, and desire shall fail; because man goeth to his long home and the mourners go about the streets; or ever the silver cord be loosened, or the golden bowl be broken, or the *pitcher be broken at the fountain, or the wheel broken at the cistern. Then shall the dust return to the earth as it was, and the spirit shall return unto God who gave it.'*

Only after the mourners had left the crematorium did the two dark-suited men who had sat at the back of the chamber wander out into the entrance hall and examine the cards that accompanied the bouquets. They made notes of all the senders' names before allowing the crematorium staff to take the flowers away for distribution to local hospitals.

5

Far from being downhearted by his evening with Timmy Williams, Brennan found himself readily assuming a sense of moral indignation. To a certain extent, Brennan needed no provocation to achieve this. Most of his working life had been based on the assumption that he was in the right while others were in the wrong but hadn't been found out yet. Indeed, it had become so much a part of his professional plumage that sometimes he wouldn't notice the transformation that had taken place. Janet always noticed, of course, and likened it jokily to the comic-strip moment when Clark Kent stepped into a phone box before emerging as Superman.

'I don't need to *become* arrogant, Jan — I started out that way,' Brennan said as he daubed his toast with a thick layer of marmalade. 'What you think you notice about me is not what's actually going on.'

'But you start sticking your jaw out and squaring up your shoulders,' Janet pointed out, dunking a piece of croissant into her coffee. 'It's a physical metamorphosis.'

Brennan shook his head, and then put a finger to his temple.

'It's up here where the change is. When I reach the point where I think a person, or especially a lot of people are lying to me, my brain starts to release those — what are they called?'

'Endorphins?'

'I thought it was more like pheromones. Whatever — it becomes like part of the old joke about the man banging his head against a brick wall for so long that he eventually gets to enjoy it. And I've just reached that stage.'

'What did Williams say to encourage you, then?'

'Well, he stuck rigidly to the line that what I saw was an exercise. I don't mind that so much, because it's so implausible as to be useful to me. What convinced me I was on the right track was his attitude. Tim used to be a civil servant who'd tell me about anything dodgy, on trust, because he believed in open government. Now there's contempt for the public in his tone, contempt for the press, too, a sense that they have no right to know what the governing elite is up to. Of course, he has to believe that because his business depends on it now.'

'But if you got nothing out of him, where does that leave you?'

'Travelling on the train with you to Bristol this morning,' Brennan said with a sudden smile. 'Always assuming I'm welcome, that is?'

★   ★   ★

Brennan and Janet walked together, a touch self-consciously, down through the town and across the bridge to Bradford's tiny station. They both hated cheesy, married-couple behaviour such as holding hands, or kissing on railway platforms because it impinged on the perception they had of their relationship. They wanted to be seen as two individuals making up a partnership rather than a single unit that had become utterly dependent on its two constituent elements clinging to each other. Equally, there was no doubt that they both enjoyed the novelty element of doing something ordinary together. They swapped papers at one point on the train journey, Brennan taking over Janet's copy of *The Independent* while she browsed through his *Racing Post* with wry amusement.

At Bristol Temple Meads station, Janet headed for the bus queue but was waved back by Brennan who had already decided to treat them to a taxi. Ten minutes later, Brennan was sitting in Janet's office for the very first time, exploring each detail with forensic intensity. He had deliberately excluded himself from her work, not because he didn't believe in it, but because he knew he wouldn't be able to stop himself being judgemental about it. The moment he stepped over the line, as when he had criticized the Porton Down programme, he knew Janet would react badly. So now here he was, an intimate stranger in her territory.

He noted the framed photos on her desk, one of Lester in his school uniform, one of all three of them on a day out in Dorset. There was a state-of-the-art desktop computer, complete with ergonomically curved key-board, and a plastic box full of floppy discs. It was all neat, high-intensity technology in complete contrast to Brennan's room at home, where the yellowing newspapers stood in Pisa-like towers and the residue of cigar smoke covered everything like the volcanic ash at Pompeii. The only discordant note struck in Janet's workspace was the large, glossy pin-up of George Clooney taped to one of the walls.

'Who's the geezer with the hooded eyes and dirty T-shirt?' Brennan asked innocently.

'A woman's allowed one little fantasy, even a feminist.'

Brennan laughed and wandered out into

the main office. 'Diatribe Films', a name so awful that Brennan could hardly bring himself to pronounce it silently let alone out loud, occupied the whole floor of a converted dockside warehouse. Nineteenth-century iron pillars still studded the room, but were now coated in silvery metallic paint while the bare-brick walls had been titivated with a shiny sealant. There were computers, racks of video-cassettes and television monitors everywhere, making the place look like the front window of Dixons'. As other staff — all in their twenties, Brennan noted with dismay — arrived, Brennan retreated into Janet's office and closed the door.

'They're all so young,' he whispered to Janet.

'Everybody wants to be in TV these days, Frank. Pity it took you so long to get round to it.'

'One thousand words will say more than thirty minutes of film.'

'Quite possibly, but they'll only earn you a tenth of what you'll get for making a documentary.'

Janet wandered out into the office and headed over to the coffee percolator that she'd filled on arrival. She poured two cups, chatted to the youngsters who were quickly forming a queue behind her, and came back.

Brennan suddenly saw his wife in a new light, as a respected senior professional rather than the junior assistant she'd been in the days when she had first been assigned to him on the paper. She was confident in this new environment, too, whereas Brennan had always felt her to be intimidated in the newspaper's offices, almost certainly because of the high percentage of boozy, leering men.

'Morning, morning, morning, everybody!' It was Mark Beattie arriving in a cheery bustle. He wore his dark suit, but it was offset by a retina-detaching lime green shirt. He carried a carton of coffee in one hand and an expensive leather briefcase in the other. As soon as he saw Brennan in Janet's office, he made a flamboyant detour from his own.

'I don't believe it. She actually got you to come in. Welcome at last, Frank.'

Brennan stepped forward to shake hands, trying not to show any reaction to the fact that Mark was black. Janet had never said anything, not that it mattered, but Brennan silently reprimanded himself for nurturing the image of Beattie as a flash white guy. And he realized that the reporter in the Porton Down video hadn't been Mark at all.

'Nice to meet you, Mark,' Brennan said, his smile as strong as his handshake.

'Let me just drop my stuff off and I'll be

right back,' Beattie said, as he made his way out and crossed to the other partitioned area on the floor, a space that was significantly bigger than Janet's.

'Why didn't you tell me he was black?' Brennan whispered to Janet.

'Does it matter?'

'No. Not at all. It's just that I'd have been prepared.'

'For what, Frank? The cultural shock?'

'No.'

'It is one for you, though, isn't it?'

'Based on my experience with newspapers, yes. But that's going back a while.'

'It hasn't changed that much since, actually. That's why the ethnic minorities are more drawn to broadcasting: it's much more open and democratic.'

'Spare me the Reith Lecture, will you?'

Beattie arrived back with a yellow legal pad in his hand, sipping his coffee on the move. He pulled out a chair and sat down, gesturing for Frank and Janet to do the same.

'Well, let me begin by saying, Frank, that I'd love you to make a film for us, if we're happy with the subject — and if you're happy with television.'

'I've been told that I should be,' Brennan said, with a sideways look at Janet. 'I can't pretend that I have much of a story as yet but

110

I may be getting somewhere.'

'OK — can you just outline what you think are the main elements? Janet has already told me about your fracas with two animal rights guys, by the way.'

'Well, that's one element. The other is Porton Down. The two are naturally linked by the experiments conducted on animals at the site, but I'm not sure if the incident I witnessed also brings them together.'

'Frank claims to have seen troops in biological-warfare suits taking dead cows off in a helicopter,' Janet said in an even tone. 'I wasn't actually with him when this happened so I can't back up his story, but it *is* what he told me at the time.'

'Did you note the use of the word 'claim' by my wife, just to underline her independence?'

Beattie laughed.

'I was just clarifying the situation for Mark's sake,' Janet protested with a smile. 'I could have told him that you'd also been drinking, but I didn't. I mean, it's perilously close to *Daily Sport* territory in the bare details, Frank.'

Brennan turned his gaze back to Mark and gave him an extravagant shrug.

'Janet's right, of course — but what makes it interesting, alarming even, is that it took place within a mile or so of Porton Down. The fact that a senior public relations man came out of his way to tell me it was all an 'exercise' only makes me more suspicious.'

'Who was that?'

'Tim Williams. He's got his own agency now, used to be a MoD press officer.'

'The person I dealt with when I filmed was a woman . . .'

Brennan took out the business card that Luke Barrs had given him on his visit to Salisbury.

'Kathy Green, Head of Corporate Affairs: that the one?'

'Yeah,' Beattie said with a nod. 'She was only too pleased to help when we started, but wasn't too happy when she saw the finished product.'

Brennan smiled sympathetically but said nothing.

'Do you think she knows about Tim coming to see you, Frank?' Janet asked, glimpsing the possibility of a power struggle.

'I'm pretty sure she must have done. It was probably all passed upwards direct from Porton Down. Tim's acquaintance with me made him the natural candidate to do the schmoozing.'

'Either way, we're unlikely to get much joy with a request to film there now, are we?'

Beattie concluded. 'So maybe we should veer more towards the animal rights angle?'

'I've been given a name in Salisbury — Joe Fletcher. Has an arrest to his name, and is reported to be part of the animal rights militia.'

'OK — let's find him then,' Beattie said in businesslike fashion. 'Janet and I will try and set up the interview as soon as possible, then you can go in and talk to him, Frank.'

'What about filming? We have to talk about this, but I don't think it's my style to have a crew hanging around with me.'

'I agree,' Beattie said with what seemed like surprising ease to Brennan. 'We'll get you a lightweight digital video camera, or even a Super 8. That way you're alone and you can film what you like, when you like.'

'Aren't there union rules about crewing levels?' Brennan asked with a frown. Janet and Beattie looked at one another as though someone who'd been cryogenically frozen for fifteen years had just been defrosted.

'Things have changed faster in television than they have in newspapers, Frank,' Janet said patiently. 'Does the term 'multi-skilling' mean anything to you?'

'No, but it sounds like the equivalent of getting all your Boy Scout badges.'

Beattie gestured around to the office

outside, where all the terminals and consoles were now occupied by his young staff. To Brennan it looked like an updated version of a Dickensian workshop.

'Everyone here is multi-skilled, Frank. Cameras have their own lights and sound recording now. You can just point and film. Then bring the cassette back here, or download the images to us by modem, and we'll get someone to edit pictures. Or you can have an edit machine with you, and do it yourself. If we linked you up with a digital relay system, you could broadcast what you're filming live to the nation. Even across the globe.'

Brennan nodded meekly, raising a hand in mock intervention.

'Forgive me, but there has to be something worth filming first, hasn't there?'

'Of course. The technology is all very well, but if there's no content, you're dead meat. Look at Channel 5. All that airtime just filled by conventional pap. It could have been a major breakthrough in ZOO-TV, but somebody lost their nerve.'

'I think you just lost *me* ... ' Brennan whispered. Beattie patted him on the shoulder as he stood up, and turned to Janet with a broad smile.

'Janet will sort you out, no prob. Catch you guys later.'

Beattie sauntered across to his own office, closed the door, and was instantly on the phone, spinning through a Rolodex as he dialled.

'Busy boy,' Brennan mused.

'Built up all this by himself. Started as a sixteen-year-old camera trainee and kept learning. Some people can just see the opportunities before they've even arrived.'

'My blind spot, I suppose. Technology. I mean, I can't figure out the attraction of a see-through vacuum cleaner. People can't really want to watch the shite they've left all over the house being sucked up, can they?'

'I'll get our hunt saboteur videos, let you spin through them,' Janet said as she stood, before crossing to the steel storage racks. Brennan felt as though it was the first day at school for him all over again. Indeed, the next two hours felt just like a lesson as he watched first the film that Mark Beattie had shot on hunt saboteurs and then some of the home-made videos that had been sent in by protesters in order to illustrate the purpose of their campaign. For the most part it was the usual frenetic hand-held footage, as the camera chased an incident or a provocative individual, with ugly fights breaking out between the 'sabs' and the hunt supporters.

Brennan fast-forwarded through much of

this, although his eye was taken by a banner at one demonstration — hand-painted across a white sheet was the logo 'Salisbury Animal Rights'. Brennan froze the frame. The group underneath the banner consisted mostly of women in woollies and wellies, but holding the supports at either end were two teenage youths in muddy anoraks. Brennan called Janet in and showed her the images.

'Could I get stills or printouts of those two boys, do you think?' he asked, dabbing a finger onto each face on the frozen picture.

'Yeah — I think so. I'll get one of the video editors onto it. You don't think they're the two who attacked you?'

'It's possible but unlikely. It's just a handy reference for when I get in among them. The news editor in Salisbury told me that the splinter faction from this group became the militia. I suppose it might have split along male-female lines, with the men endorsing the use of violence and the women preferring peaceful protest,' Brennan said with a knowing smile.

'I think you'll find that women can be equally violent when it comes to defending animals. Cruelty triggers our maternal reflexes.'

'Good job we don't have any pets at home, isn't it?' Brennan said as he stood and stretched. 'Right, I'll get back.'

'Not going to stay for lunch?' Janet asked.

'Am I welcome?'

'Well, we are working together. We can go to the River Station.'

'Let me guess, raw tuna with Thai lemon grass and coconut fritters?' Brennan asked with a pained expression.

'Actually, it's a lot better than that. *And* I can put you down on my expenses.'

'I'm doing well out of this story — free meal last night, another today. Just like the good old days of Fleet Street.'

Janet shook her head, but she needn't have bothered. Brennan knew the old days were long gone.

★   ★   ★

Mary Ashton had taken the same route as she always did to Porton Down that morning, the only difference to her usual routine having been a rather inelegant inspection of her car's undercarriage that she had undertaken in her pyjamas. Fortunately there had been nothing life-threatening, just a few spots of rust on the sill. Over morning coffee at work, it transpired that one of the other senior microbiologists had received a box of unassembled bomb-parts at his home. He'd reported it to security, and now there was to be a staff briefing at lunchtime for each section: Mary knew that it would go over the same ground again. Short of assigning individual guards to each Porton Down employee, there was no guarantee of complete security, apart from when they were all on site.

Mary genuinely didn't understand all the fuss about animal experimentation. She'd done it since her schooldays, with dead rats staked out on a board in biology classes, and all through her university career experiments had been conducted without hindrance or protest. But the growth in 'rights consciousness' during the past fifteen years had inevitably found its way into the thinking of those who protested against the very existence of Porton Down. These militant animal-rights supporters didn't seem to understand that sacrificing a very small number of animals was a price worth paying for the advances in medicine and science, especially in her own specialist field of developing antidotes to nerve or biological agents. What made it more galling for those working at Porton Down was the fact the animals used — the rats, rabbits, pigs, monkeys and cows — were all raised on the premises. It wasn't as though the scientists went out at night like Burke and Hare, culling victims from the streets or from domestic premises. These animals wouldn't have existed but for Porton Down's own breeding sheds and farms. If only these protesters knew how mercifully Mary killed her animals once their work was done. Their suffering was kept to a minimum, so that *human* suffering would never occur.

All these thoughts swirled through Mary's head as she carried a rabbit in a cage through to the site's Category Five isolation chamber, the most secure in the whole operation. She placed the animal's cage onto a stainless-steel block in one corner of the room, then pulled down the two overhead nozzles and positioned them directly above the cage. She opened the cage door to give the rabbit one last pat before closing up the cage's flap. Next, she retreated out through the chamber's double doors, which were then vacuum-sealed. Moving round to the triple-plated observation window, she gave the nod to the technician and he pushed one of the buttons on the console in front of him.

Mary watched as thin drizzle sprayed from the two nozzles. She'd given the rabbit a mild sedative, but now, as the nerve agent penetrated its respiratory system, it flew into a wild panic, scrabbling at the mesh of the cage in an instinctive desire for survival. But within seconds — 11.56 on Mary's stopwatch — the rabbit's movements were reduced to a mild quiver, and after fifteen seconds it was quite dead.

Mary nodded to the technician to switch on the chamber's extractor fans. It would be safe for human entry in about ten minutes, although protective suits and masks would be worn to make sure. Then Mary would remove the rabbit's carcass and open it up, slicing along the centre of the animal's stomach to reveal its vital organs. Later, she would extract the brain. All these would be tested and examined for the destruction the nerve agent had wrought on them, and Mary would have yet more information and clinical statistics to add to her reports. But first there was lunch — and that tiresome security briefing.

*   *   *

Brennan got the call from Janet three days after his 'audition' for Diatribe Films. He was to wait in the pub directly opposite Salisbury station from eight o'clock that evening. He was to be alone, and provided all conditions were met a filmed interview would take place with members of the Salisbury Animal Militia at a secret location to which he would be transported. Questions could only be asked after a declaration by SAM was recorded first. Brennan was to identify himself in the pub by wearing something green.

'I haven't got anything green,' Brennan spluttered into the phone. 'I'm supposed to be filming an interview, not going morris dancing.'

'Look, I can't call them back about your wardrobe problems, Frank. Have a look through my chest of drawers. There's probably a scarf or a belt in there. Put a pair of green knickers on your head if you have to — wouldn't be the first time, as I recall.'

'Do I get any names?' Brennan snapped.

'No. We've been dealing with a woman called Jenny Forsyth. She fronts the legitimate, non-violent Salisbury animal rights group. She put the word out for us, but doesn't want any other involvement.'

Brennan was still scribbling down notes of his instructions on a pad by the phone.

'OK, anything else I need to know?'

'I don't think so. You'll just have to play it by ear. Bear in mind that they think they're getting some free publicity for their cause, so don't wade into them too soon. Let them make the running before you ask anything specific.'

'Are you coaching me in interview

techniques, Janet?'

'Yes, Frank, I am — this is television. It's totally different from you talking to somebody for a newspaper piece. What *they* say is more important than you mouthing off.'

'I'd hate to work for you on a regular basis. Will you be back before I leave?'

'Don't think so. You driving or going by train?'

'I'd better take the car. Can't exactly guarantee that they'll drop me off where I want.'

'OK — good luck. And don't panic about the camera. It's idiot-proof. Just switch it on and point it, yeah?'

'I think I can handle that. I'll call you as soon as I'm clear. Bye.'

Brennan put down the phone, feeling suddenly and irrationally nervous about his assignment. He was less worried about being threatened with violence than failing to record the interview properly. One of his earliest career blunders had been to interview a politician with a tape recorder fitted with worn-out batteries. The incomprehensibly slurred tape became a standing joke back at the office, with the young Brennan being taunted as the only journalist who'd managed to make a politician sound pissed without buying him a single drink.

So Brennan spent the next hour checking the camera and its power supply, while ensuring that he had a back-up battery available. Once he was satisfied, he searched through Janet's clothes and found a green silk slip. With a bit of creative folding he was able to transform this into what he thought was a rather dashing pocket handkerchief for the sports jacket he planned to wear. By the time he was ready, it had passed six o'clock. There would be rush-hour traffic all the way down the A36 to Salisbury, resulting in an almost certain crawl into the town itself. Brennan grabbed a couple of pens, stuffed a notebook into his jacket pocket and then slung the camera bag over his shoulder. He stopped off at a garage on his way out of Bradford to fill the car with petrol and then set off for Salisbury with a cassette of Oliver Nelson's *Blues and the Abstract Truth* playing loudly for company.

The journey down to Salisbury was less fraught than Brennan had imagined, and by 7.15 he'd parked his car outside the station. To arm himself for the wait he wandered into the station shop and bought a copy of the *Salisbury Gazette*, and there on the front page was a story that Timmy Williams could have written himself. Under the headline 'Troops in Successful Warfare Exercise' was

123

an article giving an utterly approving view of the 'rapid isolation exercise' that had recently been conducted. The bare details of what Brennan had seen were related, but only in the context of a night manoeuvre that had been undertaken with maximum efficiency for the benefit of the public. The newspaper article concluded with high praise for Porton Down and DERA for their welcome openness in revealing the exercise to the people of Salisbury before anyone could get the wrong idea. The writer credited with all this was none other than Luke Barrs.

'Stupid bugger,' Brennan cursed beneath his breath before folding the paper under his arm. He walked out of the station and crossed to the pub, installing himself at the bar with a half of bitter and then carefully rearranging his green 'handkerchief' for maximum display. The pub was a pleasant but nondescript joint, with only half a dozen or so punters dotted around. Most of them had bags at their feet and Brennan guessed that they were rail travellers taking a break between trains. Meanwhile an orchestral version of 'Wonderwall' played on the stereo, and the pub's clock seemed to take an eternity to tick towards eight. Brennan kept one eye on the door as he leafed through the rest of the paper. He had a private bet with himself that Tim Williams had gone straight down to Salisbury the morning after their dinner and had pushed through the idea of 'going public' on the story in order to undermine Brennan's investigation. It was effectively a 'rebuttal' even before Brennan had managed to get into print.

The door to the pub opened and a ginger-haired youth, his features studded with facial piercing, looked around the lounge with a calm gaze. Brennan glanced across.

'Taxi for Brennan,' the youth said, registering the green kerchief, and gestured with his head for Brennan to come outside. Brennan gave a 'thumbs up' gesture and finished the remains of his drink. He made sure he had his camera bag with him and moved outside. There, a rusting car of Japanese make was parked with its nearside wheels on the pavement. The door to the rear seats was already open and Brennan could see that another youth was already in there. The other moved quickly to the driver's side.

'Get in,' he snapped at Brennan, without ceremony. Brennan lowered himself into the back of the car, where a stocky, dark-haired youth held out a hand for the camera bag. The car set off with a jerk as it dropped off the pavement, and then turned away onto the city's ring road. The stocky youth flipped open the camera bag and looked inside.

'Just my camera,' Brennan said. The youth said nothing, and continued his search. Satisfied that there were no tracking devices or even weapons inside, he closed the top flap of the bag. Now he reached into the pocket of his leather jacket and brought out a black hood. He tossed it at, rather than to Brennan.

'Put this on.'

'Look, it's only my second visit to Salisbury, so I've no idea where anything is,' Brennan said, trying to lighten the atmosphere.

The stocky youth tapped the driver on the shoulder and he immediately pulled the car over.

'Put it on, or get out now.'

'Don't you think it will look a bit, well, conspicuous, driving around a cathedral city with a hooded man in the back of a car?'

The youth leant across and opened the door on Brennan's side.

'Fuck off out of it.'

'Sorry, sorry,' Brennan said as he pulled the hood, in fact something more like a magician's velvet bag, over his head. He heard the door slam shut again and the car moved off.

'They'll probably think the Spanish Inquisition's in town,' Brennan said through the

126

hood. Almost immediately, he felt a strong hand on his head, forcing it down onto the seat.

'Stay still and stay quiet,' hissed the stocky youth.

Brennan finally lay quiet and slowly let out a deep breath. He began an attempt at remembering the changes of direction he could feel the car making but gave up after a minute or so. Instead he concentrated on the journey time, counting off the minutes in his head. He also listened, in best espionage style, for any distinctive sounds en route but nothing rose above the general hum of traffic noise. After about ten minutes, he felt the car slow finally, and then the engine was switched off.

'Keep it on,' commanded the stocky youth. Brennan felt the car lift as the youths got out. There were an anxious few moments of silence, when Brennan suddenly wondered if they might have dumped him, but then he felt a hand grabbing his shoulder from the other side, pulling him out of the car. Brennan groped his way out and stood upright. He could tell he was on pavement rather than earth or grass. He felt another hand pushing him forward, and then another gripped his left arm.

'Steps,' said the stocky youth.

Brennan heard his shoes clang on metal steps. And he was going down, not up. He held out a hand, feeling for a rail, but it was pulled back in as the two youths bundled him quickly down the staircase. Then he felt himself pass through into what must have been a basement room and outside noises became distant and muffled. Seconds later, the hood was whipped off his head.

About ten feet in front of him, in a bare cellar, sat a group of about a dozen, all men, he thought instantly, all wearing black clothing and black balaclavas. The group was arranged almost formally, like a football team for a photograph, with six standing in a back row and the rest seated or crouched in the front. Behind them hung a large green banner, across which was stencilled in blood red 'Salisbury Animal Militia'.

The ginger-haired driver and the stocky youth had disappeared. Brennan could see a barred window to his side with the staircase rising upwards. The room was lit by a single central light bulb.

'Evening,' Brennan said, getting no response. He saw the camera bag on the floor, and moved across to get it. Kneeling down, he took out the camera, unfolded its viewing screen and took off the lens cover. Then he set up the camera's tripod and

128

attached the camera to it. As he straightened up, the figure seated in the centre of the front row took out a sheet of paper.

'You film this statement first, then you can ask questions, OK?' the figure said in what Brennan estimated to be a late-teen male voice.

'Right,' Brennan said as he turned the camera onto the group and brought the speaker into the centre of the frame. Brennan switched on the sound and vision and took a step back from the camera, watching the viewing screen.

'Ready when you are, Mr De Mille.'

The spokesman cleared his throat and peered out at the sheet through the eyeholes in the balaclava.

'We, the Salisbury Animal Militia, hereby declare war on all those conducting experiments or vivisection on animals at the Porton Down research centre. All individual scientists and technicians who have anything to do with this senseless cruelty to animals are to be regarded as legitimate targets, and will suffer the consequences. Over 8,000 animals a year are tortured and killed at Porton Down. Those who do this are criminals, and their punishment is at hand. This is not a final warning but a declaration of intent. Anyone trying to protect these criminal sadists will

129

also be regarded as targets. The suffering animals cannot take revenge but we can, and will.'

The spokesman folded his statement away. Brennan leant across and pressed the camera's 'zoom out' button, and then watched until the whole group filled the display screen.

'OK — do you realize that in making this statement you have already committed serious criminal offences yourselves?'

'Anything we say or do cannot be seen as a crime. Our actions are morally justified.'

Smart kid, Brennan thought to himself.

'In that case, why can't the scientists claim moral justification for what *they* are doing?'

'Because they're involved in warfare products from which nobody benefits but the military and industrial corporations who make them.'

'Even when those products are purely defensive?'

'That's the standard line from Porton Down. But it's also a weapons-making institution, not just a chemical and nerve-agent producer. They test bullets by firing them into living pigs. Likewise cluster bombs. They bombed a herd of cattle last year to see how effective those bombs were in killing and wounding. It's a death factory.'

'But you seem to be prepared to kill human beings?'

'Yes, but this won't be for experiments. It's justice.'

'You believe in the death penalty, then?'

Brennan could see the spokesman blink suddenly, as if his train of thought had been interrupted.

'I didn't say that.'

'You said you would kill scientists experimenting on animals in the name of justice. That makes you judge, jury and executioner. Not very noble, is it? Nor, indeed, moral. In fact, it's fascist behaviour.'

'We are *not* fascists! We're freedom fighters, fighting for the freedom of animals to live a natural life.'

Brennan sensed that he had the spokesman rattled, as the pitch of his voice was gradually rising with each sentence.

'Tell me about the weapons *you* have.'

'We can't disclose that.'

'Come on,' Brennan said, in best Jeremy Paxman fashion. 'You decry Porton Down for its manufacture of military weapons, so what are you going to use to do your killings? Slings and pebbles?'

The spokesman stood up and advanced on the camera, putting his gloved hand over the lens in a manner that Brennan knew would

131

delight Mark Beattie. For an instant, Brennan shared that professional pleasure in having reduced an opponent's argument to a gesture of censorship.

'OK, fine.'

Brennan switched off the camera, and detached it from the tripod.

'I thought you were supposed to be a campaigning journalist,' the spokesman said sourly. 'But you're just another shithead working for the political establishment.'

'I don't think they would see me that way, actually.'

'Why aren't you more sympathetic to our cause, then?'

'I'm not unsympathetic. But I won't endorse terrorism. Look, would you like to continue this discussion back at the pub?'

'This briefing is over,' the spokesman said curtly.

'Are you Joe Fletcher, then?' Brennan asked suddenly.

'You don't get any names, mate,' the spokesman said with a laugh. 'Let alone a drink.'

Brennan finished packing the camera back in its bag and slung it over his shoulder. He picked the hood up from the floor.

'Before you do the honours, I'd like to ask two questions. Off the record.'

The spokesman looked around the rest of the group. There was some muttering but no outright objections.

'What do you want to know?'

'A few weeks ago, I was threatened by two men, one with a knife, who claimed to represent your organization. Was it any of you?'

'How could it be? We'd never heard of you till this film company made contact.'

'It was to do with an incident at a farm near Porton Down involving dead cattle, troops in biological-warfare suits. Did you have a hand in that?'

Brennan showed them the front page of the *Salisbury Gazette*. He watched the spokesman's eyes as he read. Brennan thought he detected a look of puzzlement.

'We don't kill animals. Or rescue dead ones. We're concerned with saving those that are alive and in danger.'

He handed the paper back to Brennan.

'Good publicity stunt for you, though?'

'What publicity? Where? You want to get your facts straight. If there was a field with dead cows in it, and troops in C&B suits, only Porton Down could have done the killing.'

The spokesman snatched the hood from Brennan and pulled it unceremoniously over Brennan's head. Brennan felt himself being bundled back towards the staircase.

'How do I get in touch with you again?' Brennan asked through the hood.

'You don't. That's it. And you'll know all about our actions when they take place. The whole world will.'

Brennan was now pushed roughly out of the door, banging his shoulder on the frame.

'Don't you want to know when the film goes out?' Brennan shouted, as two pairs of hands seized him again and pushed him up the staircase. Within seconds he was thrown into the back of the car, whereupon it drove off with a squeal of tyres.

Ten minutes later he was bundled out of the car with his camera bag, with the hood left over his head. By the time he'd pulled it off, the car was already moving away, but Brennan could see that the number plate had been switched from the one he'd noted outside the pub. He wrote down both numbers in his pad before confusion set in, not that he had any expectations of a positive trace. He also wrote three other phrases while he had his book out — 'iron staircase', 'brick-walled cellar' and 'barred window'.

Brennan checked his watch. It had just gone nine o'clock. It was dark, with an autumnal chill already in the air. He looked around. They'd dropped him not at the station but in the middle of a deserted industrial estate, the cheeky bastards. Brennan scanned the skyline. Through the gathering gloom he could make out the spire of Salisbury Cathedral, with its red aircraft-warning lights. For once, he was grateful to the Christian church for giving him some direction.

6

Brennan lay on the bed in a blue funk of depression. He could take being dumped in the middle of nowhere — that had been his emotional starting point to life down here, after all — but the professional failures, both his own and the one that Luke Barrs had accepted, were hard to take. Brennan knew he'd not asked enough questions, or indeed any of the right ones. He'd confronted those posturing masked teenage anarchists with the dubious morality of their declared war, but what he hadn't done was find out who they were, and what they did in their other life. He'd got no leads from them, nothing he could use to provoke disclosure elsewhere in the circle of his investigation. Worst of all, he knew why he'd failed. He'd taken his eye off the ball and stuck it behind the bloody viewfinder of Mark Beattie's bloody camera.

'This is really good, Frank,' Janet said as she sat upright on the bed alongside him, replaying the film on the camera's display screen. Even within the nine square inches of the frame, Janet could see that there were good televisual images. The masks, the banner, the sense of group menace and, best of all as far as she was concerned, Frank's questions: they had really put the militia on the spot.

'It's crap,' Brennan muttered. 'It's a perfect illustration of why print and broadcast journalism don't mix. They were just acting up for the cameras, and I got nothing out of them.'

'I think you've pretty well skewered them, actually.'

'It wasn't a points-scoring exercise, Jan. I needed to find out things. I wanted to get behind the masks and the military paraphernalia. If I'd just been in the room without a camera, I could have teased more out of them. They were exploiting me for their own publicity.'

'All right, but I bet you'll be really surprised when you see this on a big screen, because lots of things register that you think aren't there — their eye movements, the changes in the tone of their voice, their use of language. Details like this will tell you a lot about people — whether they're phoney, serious, deranged, whatever. Why do you think politicians are scared of going on TV? Anyway — this should cheer you up.'

Janet leant across to the bedside cabinet

and took out an envelope, then dangled it in front of Brennan.

'What is it?'

'I think you'll find it's a cheque from Mark. Go on, open it, then.'

'Do you know how much it's for?'

'Nope. He just handed it to me as I was leaving the office.'

Brennan slid his thumbnail under the flap and began to prise open the envelope. Out of it he pulled a Diatribe Films compliments slip that had a cheque paper-clipped to it. Brennan peeked at the cheque, but remained stony-faced.

'How much?' Janet asked eagerly.

'Fifty quid,' Brennan said, deadpan.

'Mark wouldn't be that insulting.'

'Two and a half grand, actually.'

Janet flung her arms round Brennan, knocking him back on the bed.

'See? I told you it would be worthwhile. You'd have to flog a piece to *The New Yorker* to get that kind of dough for a feature. Well done, darling.'

Janet kissed Brennan with a passion to which he, lifted momentarily from his previous depression, instantly responded. Later, as they lay in each other's arms, Brennan resumed his usual pessimistic demeanour.

'I suppose he'll want the money back when he sees the piece of film I shot.'

'Bollocks,' Janet said quietly. 'I wouldn't dare mislead you, darling, but it looks like a really good start. It's got punch. It's topical. And it gives whatever else you film a strong narrative core.'

'That's assuming I know what comes next.'

'Of course. But you must have some ideas?'

'Yeah. I'd like to march into the office of Luke Barrs at the *Salisbury Gazette* tomorrow and ask him why he was happy to print nothing less than a public relations puff for Porton Down.'

Brennan slid out of bed and brought back his copy of the paper, showing Janet the front-page article. Janet began to read it. Brennan watched her for reactions, hoping that she'd feel as outraged as he did. As she finished reading, Janet shrugged.

'Well, it's pretty pathetic — but at least you've forced them to come out with a story, rather than just covering it up.'

'How does that benefit me?' Brennan asked, puzzled.

'Because it gives you something to chip away at. Face it, Frank, this is a little victory. Ninety-nine times out of a hundred, the MoD or the Army will simply deny a story until such time as they're shown to be wrong.

Remember all the lying they did over the use of organophosphate sprays during the Gulf War? Then, two or three years later, they were finally forced to admit that it was true all along. Getting the local rag to print this is a complete reversal of their normal policy of absolute denial. They're *admitting* something happened, but are putting a positive spin on it. When you find out more, they can't now fall back and say that there *was* no incident. Do you see?'

Brennan nodded and smiled, and gave Janet a big peck on the cheek.

★ ★ ★

Timmy Williams strolled up Whitehall with a pronounced spring in his step. How many years he'd trudged the same route to the Ministry of Defence offices expecting to have a hot potato dropped into his lap or some outrageous demand made on his time and energy! But his days as a flunkey were over. The mandarins had to defer to him now, had to seek his advice and act upon it. He flounced in through the main entrance, getting a nod and a smile from the same commissionaire who always used to demand a sight of his pass every day. And, once inside, he was escorted straight up to the Permanent

Secretary's office, where a silver coffee pot was already on the table, along with two china cups, a jug of cream and biscuits on a lace doily. The Permanent Secretary even stood up to shake his hand before pouring out the coffee.

'Well, now — I thought we'd seen the back of our friend Brennan since his 'retirement',' the Permanent Secretary observed as he opened a red folder to consult the notes that Williams's agency had provided for him.

'He's a local pest rather than a national one now,' Williams said wryly. 'And, actually, even that overrates him. He really is a small fish in a very small, stagnant pond. He can't do anything to harm us.'

'Even so, we have to consider the density of our assets in the West Country.'

'I understand that, sir. But, if I may repeat, Brennan's got very little clout now. He doesn't contribute to any of the national papers, except on rare occasions.'

'It's those 'occasions' that I'd prefer to eliminate altogether. This strategy of yours *will* work, won't it?'

'I'd like to think so. Previously the department would concentrate on damage limitation. My approach is designed to prevent damage happening in the first place. Brennan may have his version of recent events, and we certainly have ours. The difference being that our version is now public, so I believe his fox has been well and truly shot.'

'Well, let us hope so,' the Permanent Secretary said, with a smile of approval.

'I'm very confident. Brennan has not got much to go on, and nowhere to go with it anyway. Even if he does manage to break out into print, we've got a few people on the *Telegraph* and *The Times* who are 'on message'. As for the regional papers, they're pretty much inclined not to have much truck with renegades like him. Also, if you look at Brennan's most recent bank statement,' Williams said as he pointed to a yellow marker within the file 'you'll see that he has pretty limited resources for a prolonged investigation.'

'I'll pass your assessment on to the chaps at Curzon Street. I'm sure they wouldn't want Brennan getting in their way on this one. There're one or two who still feel they have a score to settle with him.'

'Have they made any progress with their inquiry yet?' Williams asked eagerly.

'Some, in the sense that they don't seem to have found any terrorist involvement. But it rather means they're poking around in the dark for other rogue elements — freelancers, fringe activists or, worst of all, outright millennial nut cases. And DERA?'

'They're reassessing everyone on-site who has access to that sort of material and re-examining all the pre-employment checks. The internal audit procedures are also being rigorously overhauled. I must say I'd be very surprised if there was any hint of an inside job. The workforce is particularly loyal and dedicated, and has been for decades.'

'Apart from the odd experimental error, I seem to remember.'

'Those days are well and truly behind us now, sir.'

'Anything else I need to know?'

'Perhaps. When I talked to him, Brennan mentioned some animal activists from Salisbury with whom he'd had some contact. They're pretty hostile towards Porton Down, as you can imagine, but we've experienced little or no direct trouble from them in the way of sabotage or stunts. It's possible that they may have raised their game, of course. I believe the local Special Branch is about to look at that possibility.'

'Good. Of course, one minor problem may yet arise. Assuming MPs read regional newspapers, that is. What if questions are raised in Parliament about the 'exercise'?

We'd have to ensure that the Secretary of State was properly briefed.'

'You mean the Parliament that isn't sitting again until October? And the Secretary of State who still has another three weeks left of his holiday in a Tuscan villa?'

The Permanent Secretary smiled. Williams smiled back, feeling better and better about his job for every second that passed. The Permanent Secretary smiled even wider, because he still looked on Williams as an upstart press officer who should know only what the Permanent Secretary thought he needed to know.

*　*　*

Brennan went straight down to his bank in Church Street the following morning and paid in Mark Beattie's cheque. Two and a half grand wasn't exactly a war chest, but it would tide him over while he tried to make a breakthrough. The girls in the bank seemed suitably impressed, but Brennan warned them that unless he backed a few winners on Tote Credit, this cheque would remain a novelty item. He then returned home and gave Janet a lift round to the station. Despite Brennan's reservations, she was taking the footage of the interview with the animal

144

rights militia into the office for Beattie to view.

'Relax, he'll be thrilled,' Janet said reassuringly.

'I'd rather you'd waited until he couldn't stop the cheque,' Brennan muttered.

'First of many,' said Janet, on the verge of giving him a public kiss on the station forecourt before she realized and pulled back.

'Ring me if you hear anything,' Brennan called as Janet walked off into the station's historic Brunel-built booking hall. Brennan put the car, and his mind, onto 'autopilot' and headed for Salisbury once again. He remained impassive throughout the drive, despite the glorious sweep of the Wylye Valley through which the A36 intruded with the violence of a razor slash. Indeed, Brennan would hardly have noticed if Melinda Messenger herself had stepped out to wash his windscreen at the traffic lights, so intensely was he thinking about what he would say to Luke Barrs.

Thanks to his early start, Brennan was able to find a parking space just off the Market Square, a short walk from the offices of the *Salisbury Gazette*. He called Barrs from his mobile phone, giving no clue about his mood, suggesting simply that Barrs might like to join him for an early lunch. Barrs had wavered at first, but once Brennan had mentioned that he'd made some progress on his story, the young editor swiftly agreed to a meeting and suggested a restaurant in the city centre.

With an hour and more to kill, Brennan next sought out the town's animal-welfare shop, the route through which Janet had established her contact with the Salisbury Animal Militia. Brennan found the shop just off Fisherton Street, a pleasingly Bohemian thoroughfare dotted with antique shops, cheap cafés and converted warehouses. The welfare shop, with its hand-painted façade depicting beasts of all endangered species — notably whales, foxes, elephants, pandas and tigers — was essentially an alternative pet food and animal requisites operation. The lettering on the windows included the offer of 'meat-free dog food', without specifying what this contained — vegetable-shaped dog biscuits was Brennan's best guess. One part of the window was also a 'bulletin board', with posters about anti-hunt demonstrations, campaigns and fund-raising events.

Brennan hesitated a moment before going in, as he checked over his lack of animal-welfare credibility — the leather boat-shoes and suede *blouson* probably wouldn't win him too much acclaim. A bell tinkled as he

146

opened the door into the bizarre emporium — part food-store, part novelty shop, all with animals in mind. A blonde woman, with a pinched face and a jewelled nose-stud, emerged from a rear storeroom.

'Morning, can I help you?'

'Good morning — yes, I hope so. My name's Brennan. I'm a journalist. You kindly helped a television company I'm working for make contact with the Salisbury Animal Militia last week. Jenny, isn't it?'

'That's all I did. I'm not doing anything else, mister.'

'Well, I wanted to thank you, anyway. I got my interview . . . '

'Surprised they didn't kill you.'

'What makes you say that?'

'Because that's the way they are: violent. They do our cause terrible damage. I mean, how can you oppose cruelty to animals when you're prepared to hurt human beings?'

'Actually, I asked them that very question.'

'Bet you didn't get much of a reply.'

'Look, I'm trying to contact Joe Fletcher. He's one of them, I believe. He may even have been among them when I spoke to them last night. Do you know where he is?'

'No idea. If you spoke to 'em, shouldn't you know?'

'They made me wear a hood. Took me to a

basement room somewhere in the city. They were all masked.'

'Look, all I did was put the word out, through a few customers. Gave 'em the number of the company in Bristol.'

'Would you mind doing it again — just for this Fletcher kid?'

'Ain't no kid, mister. Thug, he is.'

'Well, here's my card with my phone numbers on. If you can pass it on to someone who might pass it on to him?'

'If he thought I was shopping him, he'd firebomb this place.'

'I'm not a copper. I'm just making a documentary. I didn't get much out of the group other than threats against Porton Down workers.'

'That's all they've got to offer. Much as I hate the place, I'd never threaten people.'

'Do you think they're serious?'

The woman nodded and took Brennan's card, placing it into the breast pocket of her nylon smock.

'I'd do yourself a favour and let the police handle this if I were you.'

'I'm sure they're on the case. Would these militia types be prepared to hurt animals if they thought it would further their cause?'

'They've done that already. Used to spray ammonia into the eyes of the huntsmen's horses when we were out 'sabbing'. That's why we forced them out of our movement. They're hooligans, really, who've just decided that animal rights is the best chance of finding a good punch-up.'

'Right. Thanks for your help.'

'Not going to buy anything, then?'

'I don't have any pets, I'm afraid.'

Brennan caught the look in the woman's eye, and was quick to react.

'But let me make a donation to the group instead . . . '

Brennan took out his wallet and pulled out a £20 note.

'Good luck,' he said as he handed it over. And for once the pinched face broke into a brief smile.

★　★　★

To David Southwell's solicitor, Richard Cochrane, it looked like just another messy burglary, a regular consequence of having a practice in one of Bristol's bad areas. They had used a hacksaw to cut away three of the bars guarding the rear window of his office, and had simply severed the cable to the alarm, probably on the basis that a fast response was unlikely either from the police or the security firm that had supplied the alarms. Fortunately, Cochrane always kept money, cheques and sensitive case files in an old safe that he'd bought in a liquidation sale, and this had remained intact. So the people who'd broken in — he guessed that they were probably teenagers rather than professional thieves — had simply ransacked the place looking for items that they could sell on the streets for drink or drugs money.

But as Cochrane and his secretary restored the offices to some sort of order it looked less and less likely that anything of value had been taken. The phones and answering machines were still there; the secretary's computer and printer were superficially damaged but hadn't been removed from their cabling; and all the minor stationery artefacts were still there.

It was only towards lunchtime that Cochrane's secretary, having restored all the client files to their correct storage cabinets, noticed that the one on David Southwell was missing. She double-checked that her collecting of the scattered papers had not placed Southwell's file inside another, she looked in all the waste bins and she inspected the yard outside the rear window, but no trace of the file was found. She reported the discrepancy to Cochrane, who was more baffled than alarmed. Why should anyone want papers on a man who'd been dead for nearly a month?

'I suppose you're a bit pissed off with me?' Luke Barrs guessed, correctly, as he sipped his first mineral water of the lunch.

'I don't own the paper,' Brennan said curtly. 'The only opinions an editor has to worry about are his proprietor's, not those of his readers. And that's what you took into consideration by running the story. Not that it was a 'story' in the journalistic sense. Press release is the technical term, which I always took to have a hidden meaning in that it 'released' the press from the burden of finding things out for themselves.'

Oration over, Brennan took a long swig from his glass of red wine. He watched as Barrs squirmed on his chair, realigning his bread knife for want of something else to do.

'I was going to call you,' Barrs stammered.

'Before or afterwards?'

'Both. When this chap from DERA turned up . . . '

'Tim Williams?'

'Yes. I was going to call you to tell you what he'd proposed. Going public about the off-site exercise. Reassuring the locals that nothing untoward had happened. He was handing stuff to me on a plate, and I wasn't happy about it. I know you won't believe me, but I wasn't. Then, within ten minutes of his departure, I got the call from the proprietor . . . '

'Who is?'

'Sir Cecil Dee.'

'The retired Tory MP, stood down before the last election?'

'The same. We're only part of a small newspaper group, but it's been in his family for ages.'

'And he calls you regularly, does he?'

'Once every few months. Just to ask how things are going. But this time was different. He already knew about this story. Didn't say how. And obviously he was concerned about what I was going to do with it.'

'In that he didn't want you alarming the local population, or offending the people at DERA. So the simplest thing to do was to print the version that Tim Williams had brought in with him, and tag on a little editorial comment saluting DERA's openness?'

'Well, he didn't come to me with one story and ask me to print another. So I didn't have much choice really, did I?'

'No, I can see that at this stage in your career telling your proprietor to sod off and then refusing to accept DERA's version of events wasn't the best option.'

'So you'd have told me to run with it anyway?' Barrs asked, brightening. 'That's why I was going to phone you, to ask what I should do.'

'But you didn't, and I wouldn't have — approved the story, that is. I can understand the pressure you were under, but *they* must have been under pressure too. Sending in the spin-*meister*, calling up the boss to ask him a favour. You should have strung them along a bit more. Squeezed more information from them. Or made a trade-off. You could even have asked, strictly off the record, of course, what the *real* story was, something they were so anxious to present as a routine event. You'll learn, as your career goes on, that news has no absolute values. It's what people are prepared to project onto it that matters.'

'But, Frank, at a local level it hardly seems to matter.'

'It may seem that way, yes. Where you are, it's all about small-town, middle-of-the-road readerships who don't want nasty shocks or disturbing reality, just reassurance. But if you link that psychology from one local newspaper to the next, and then to the next, and so on, what you end up with is a network of consensus. I mean, it's no accident that the vast majority of regional papers are owned by bigger media businesses in London, or members of a local squirearchy, because they can achieve with the locals what they would love to achieve with the nationals — the control of public opinion.'

'I'm sorry. I lost my bottle, really. I was ashamed to ring you afterwards. Hoped you wouldn't pick up on it.'

'It's OK. I understand. It's basically my fault, anyway. Timmy Williams had been round to try and brief me before he turned up on your doorstep. I should have realized the bastard would do that and warned you. So I'm sorry, too.'

'Well, let's at least enjoy the lunch, then,' Barrs said with a sigh of relief.

'Luke, that depends on whether you're still interested in helping me bring *my* story to fruition. The one that will, I hope, challenge the version you have already printed.'

Barrs went into deep thought as he moved slices of avocado round the strawberry sauce that the restaurant's chef had seen as fit accompaniment.

'But if I assist you, on an informal basis, of course, it could end up with me looking a right prat for publishing that story.'

'That's the downside,' Brennan said with a quick smile. 'The jam-side-up bit is that you'd probably make a big enough name for

154

yourself to get a job on one of the nationals.'

Barrs looked at him.

'You can't guarantee that, though, can you?'

Brennan shook his head.

'So why should I consider it?'

'Because at some stage in your career you have to decide what journalism means to you. If you've settled on a quiet, civilized, treadmill routine in a country town, fine. But if you think it means constantly questioning what the people with power and influence are trying to achieve, then you have to be brave and make an escape one day.'

Brennan tried to fix Barrs with a stare. But the young man instantly looked away.

*   *   *

Brennan insisted on picking up the bill for the lunch with Luke Barrs, not for reasons of grandeur or sympathy, although both of these elements were in play in small measure. The gesture was more to do with the practicalities of their future relationship. Brennan had felt obliged to warn Luke that he would soldier on with his investigation, but that he would neither ask for information nor pass it on to him. This would leave Barrs entirely uncompromised by his contact with Brennan, and so

155

keeping a restaurant receipt away from the eyes of the newspaper's accountant would simply complete the process of disengagement. And any awkward questions that might arise out of Brennan's visit to the *Gazette*'s offices could be put down to the original act of deception on Brennan's part.

After Brennan had shaken hands with Barrs and wished him well, he watched the young man slouch away up one of the narrow lanes that led back to his office. Brennan wondered what Barrs really made of him, leaving aside the shaky nostalgia for that drunken lecture he'd given many years ago. He probably had Brennan down as a paranoid, a loser who saw a conspiracy in everyday life. Thinking about this, Brennan realized that it was almost certainly the truth.

Brennan reclaimed his car just before the expiry time on his pay-and-display ticket was reached. Fuelled by his two glasses of red wine, Brennan found himself fancying another bout of verbal sparring with old farmer Gudgeon. Now that DERA had owned up to using his land for its alleged exercise, Mr Gudgeon could bloody well face the rigours of public scrutiny.

Brennan made his way through Salisbury's thickening afternoon traffic and headed east for Breakheart Lodge. He arrived in the yard to find Gudgeon senior pouring diesel from a jerrycan into the fuel tank of his tractor.

'I thought I told you to bugger off and stay buggered off!'

'But you're a celebrity now, Mr Gudgeon. According to the local paper, you're the man who allowed troops to stage a chemical-warfare exercise on your land. Do you want to tell me about it?'

'Piss off!'

'I can pay you — not as much as DERA did, but it looks like you'll do anything for money. Why did they pick you, Mr Gudgeon, because you've got shit for brains? Or did they pay over the odds for killing your cattle?'

'I'll call the police if you don't piss off now.'

Gudgeon finished filling his tank and carried the empty jerrycan back to a storage shed. He wiped his hands on a rag hanging from his trouser pocket, then reached into the shed and fetched out his shotgun.

'If you threaten me again, Mr Gudgeon, it'll be *me* calling the police, not you.'

Gudgeon promptly fired off two shots, both of them way above Brennan's head, but it was more than enough to make Brennan dive for cover.

'You mad old cunt!' Brennan shouted as he backed away to his car.

Gudgeon cackled with glee and kissed the

stock of the shotgun before tossing it back into the storage shed. Brennan dived into the car and began to reverse. Gudgeon waved at him with an obscene two-fingered victory salute, then mounted his tractor.

As Brennan drove backwards down the farm's drive, there was the sudden crash of an explosion. The tractor and Gudgeon were engulfed in a ball of vivid orange flame that rippled upwards. Tractor parts spiralled through the air, trailing smoke, and then a secondary explosion lifted what was left of the tractor and Mr Gudgeon off the ground, sending the two huge rear tyres in opposite directions.

Brennan stalled the car in shock and scrambled to restart it. His nobler instincts then kicked in and he got out of the car and walked back up towards the yard, taking his mobile phone from his pocket. For the first time that he could remember, Brennan found himself dialling 999.

7

The police questioned Brennan at the farm for just over an hour, while the fire brigade and a forensic team examined the burnt-out tractor. Brennan told them the story straight, although he could see in the police officer's eyes that a professional mistrust had descended once Brennan had mentioned the word 'journalist'. Nor did the circumstances he described — an investigation that had provoked Mr Gudgeon into shooting at him — endear Brennan to his inquisitor. Only when Brennan suggested that there had been two explosions rather than one did the policeman grudgingly accept that this observation might be useful. Brennan left all his personal details with the officer, but took the precaution of getting the policeman's name and telephone number as well before he was allowed to leave the scene.

Brennan cursed himself all the way back to Bradford-on-Avon for indulging in a pointless confrontation with the old man. He didn't blame himself for Gudgeon's death, although there was a nagging suspicion that he might have distracted the farmer from decanting his diesel properly and thereby inadvertently created a flammable spillage of fuel. But Brennan dismissed this because his newsman's instincts were telling him that it had been a bomb that had incinerated Gudgeon. Two spells of duty in Belfast in the 1980s had equipped him with the insider's knowledge of what constituted an act of terrorism.

Brennan could already see the links that the police would forge once they had the evidence that Gudgeon's death was a murder, not an accident. The story in the *Salisbury Gazette* had linked the farm to the Porton Down 'exercise'. Brennan's interview with the Salisbury Animal Militia, once he was obliged to admit it, would give the police a clear line of enquiry, and Brennan would be pitched as a witness into the messy business of an inquest and, quite possibly, a criminal trial. None of this augured well for his own investigation, either as a solo effort or as a freelance job for Mark Beattie's film company. The thought went through his mind that if he kept quiet about his interview with the animal rights militia members he would be less in demand with the authorities. But then this brief ray of optimism was eclipsed by the certainty that if he was found by the police to have withheld what they saw as vital information he would probably end up in the jug himself.

Brennan left the car in the hollow off Conigre Hill that served as a parking area for residents of both Middle Rank and Tory and also as an opportunity for Bradford's teenage thieves to further their apprenticeships. He trudged up the hill and turned off onto Tory, nodding at neighbours who were doing staggeringly ordinary things like watering their hanging baskets. As his key turned in the front door, Janet yanked him into the house with a whoop, with Lester adding his own applause.

'What's up?' Brennan asked irritably.

Janet beckoned him upstairs to the lounge.

'Jan, I'm not in the mood for party games.'

'Don't be a misery, Dad — you're famous again!'

Brennan climbed the stairs, with Lester pushing at his back. Once in the lounge, Janet stood in front of the television, posing like a demonstrator in an electrical shop, and pressed the 'play' button on the remote control. Immediately, images of the interview with the animal rights militia came on the screen. Brennan frowned.

'So you transferred it to videotape, so what?'

The source of the 'celebration' was

revealed when the video cut away after the spokesman's dire threats to a BBC News West presenter turning to a senior uniformed police officer and asking him if the Wiltshire Police took these threats seriously.

Brennan scrunched up his face and spat out an expletive, before rounding accusingly on Janet.

'He couldn't bloody wait, could he! Opportunistic sod!'

'What are you talking about? Mark felt this was real-time news that shouldn't be held back.'

'I'll be *doing* time now this has gone out. Was I mentioned?' Brennan asked anxiously.

'Yes, of course — given full credit. I'll show you.'

'Save it for later. I'm going down to the pub.'

Brennan fled from the room and stomped down the staircase, completing his tantrum by slamming the door as he went out. Lester looked at Janet with complete puzzlement.

'Don't ask, Lester. Even I can't work this one out.'

*   *   *

Brennan bought himself a pint at the bar and then made his way quickly into the Dandy

Lion's low-ceilinged back room, installing himself at the small table in the darkest corner. There weren't usually that many people in at this time of evening, mostly office workers stopping off for one drink on their way home or people who'd booked in early for the pub's always-full upstairs restaurant. Later, the younger crowd would come in, kids who'd been to school in the town but who still lived with their parents despite having jobs or university places in Bath and Bristol. Brennan would be long gone before they arrived. There was nothing more disheartening to the middle-aged man who thought himself still young than seeing what the young *really* looked like these days. On Friday nights, when Brennan drank at the bar while waiting for an Indian takeaway from Saadi round the corner, Brennan would joke to other men of his age that the back room should be christened 'The Crèche', and they would all laugh and nod knowingly.

But tonight Brennan could sit alone, in the corner, and wallow in his mid-life misery. Most of the people he had come to know at the Dandy Lion were daytime customers, the arty set, who popped in for a cappuccino and a chat before lunch, but didn't often come in at night. So there was a good chance that he would be left alone, and an even better one that nobody would come up to him and say 'Just seen your name on the telly, Frank'.

Brennan sipped his pint carefully and tried to loosen and lower his shoulders to make himself relax, but they kept rising up again as a reflex action to the tension he was feeling. Most of that was due to the stress of another busy but apparently fruitless day, which had been crowned by the shock of witnessing, albeit it at a safe distance, old man Gudgeon blown apart. Brennan suddenly wondered if he had mentioned the dead man's son to the police, but resolved that it was their business to find and contact next of kin. Then he tried to anticipate the fallout from a bomb attack. There'd be a shitload of publicity about the animal rights militia and Porton Down, and a whole charabanc of London reporters would probably head west if their editors could sense that the story would be a 'runner'. Christ, what would poor, innocent Luke Barrs do when hardened hacks swarmed in for background? How would Tim Williams put a positive spin on a terrorist campaign against the scientists and technicians of Porton Down? How could Brennan possibly hang on to his story in the midst of this chaos?

'Branching out into telly, I see.'

Brennan looked up from his pint, recognizing the voice just before he saw Robert, his bookselling chum, standing over him.

'Hello, Robert. Sit down.'

Robert placed his own drink on the table and squeezed into the chair opposite Brennan. He made a play of looking around the empty room.

'Are you hiding from your public?'

'I haven't actually seen the segment, Robert. And as I certainly didn't film myself, the public will happily remain ignorant of my face. In any case, it was a one-off. A career cul-de-sac, out of which I am now reversing.'

'I thought it was rather good. Certainly more provocative than the other stuff they had on — a man who's turned his house into a theatre, an auction of stuffed animals: they're not news stories, are they?'

'Not quite, no. Thank you for your kind words. How are things at your end?'

'Stalled, actually. Too many people buying books on the bloody Internet. I hope it's just a novelty, otherwise I'm done for.'

'I'm sure it is just a phase. People need to browse. See the covers, read the blurb. Books are physical, sensual things, not fluff in cyberspace.'

Robert held up his glass in a self-mocking toast.

'There, you've cheered *me* up now. Your health, sir.'

'Cheers.'

They both drank in silence. Robert fidgeted with his glasses.

'My — you are down, aren't you, Frank?'

'Bad day all round, Robert. One step forward, five back.'

'When they introduced your piece on the news they said that the interview was part of a forthcoming documentary. Is that so?'

'I doubt it. I've decided I'm not really comfortable doing telly. The story's taken a bit of an ugly twist, anyway. The animal rights militia may have killed somebody this afternoon.'

'Good God. But that's a story and a half. You must be able to write something about that, surely?'

'Not as much as I want. And once there's a trial, that's it. All the material becomes *sub judice*. So I'm stalled, too.'

'Perhaps you need to stand back from it all for a day or so? I'm going mushroom hunting tomorrow morning. Fancy coming along?'

'Knowing my luck, there'd probably be a fungi rights militia stalking us. What time are you setting off?'

'Seven. It's the other side of Frome, just off the back roads to Wells. My secret place. It's

166

wonderful first thing in the morning when the woods are still silent and damp. We should get a decent haul of chanterelles. We could even have some for breakfast, fried in butter with garlic and parsley, all perched on a slice of thick toast. Delicious.'

'Count me in, Robert,' Brennan said with an eager smile.

'Right. I'll pick you up on Newtown at seven. And bring a basket.'

Brennan went to the bar and bought another two pints. He and Robert talked about how to save the bookshop, with Brennan volunteering to front a campaign in the town on Robert's behalf. By the end of the second pint, Brennan was even expressing a willingness to walk around Bradford wearing a sandwich board.

Brennan walked back to the house in a lighter mood. It was sometimes easy for him to forget when he became embroiled in, and fixated by, an apparently insoluble investigation that a huge swathe of ordinary, undemanding, pleasurable life went on completely independently of his private agony. Meeting up with Robert always reminded him that he could step away at any time and join in with this comfortable normality if he chose.

So the first words on Brennan's lips when

he came back into the house were 'I'm sorry'. Janet's face, however, suggested that Brennan needed to crawl across the floor on all fours in self-abasement to even warrant an acknowledgement.

'Look, it's been a rough day.'

'Obviously. The police in Salisbury have been on the phone for you. They want you to call them back immediately. A Detective Inspector Andrews. Said it was urgent. The number's on the pad,' Janet reported in a deliberately clipped tone.

'I'll tell you later,' Brennan said as he peeled the top sheet off the pad and trudged upstairs to his office. He guessed that the 'urgency' was to do with the forensic unit's findings down on the farm. Brennan dialled and took a deep breath.

'DI Andrews, please — my name is Frank Brennan.'

Brennan waited while the switchboard operator put him through. There was no recorded Vivaldi, no 'Laughing Policeman' to settle his nerves. And then came the stern voice.

'Mr Brennan, DI Andrews — thank you for calling back. I wondered if you could pop down to the station tonight to add to the statement that you gave to my colleague at the farm this afternoon?'

'Well, I've just had two pints actually, and I'm sure you wouldn't want me to drive. Can it wait till tomorrow?'

'It can, but I'll need some words now . . . '

'Of course — it was a bomb, wasn't it?'

'Is that an educated guess, sir?'

'As I said in my statement — I heard two explosions. First the bomb, then the fuel tank.'

'You'll be glad to know that our forensic team agrees with you. They found some wiring remnants and traces of Semtex. So this is a murder case.'

'I appreciate that — how can I help?'

'You were there when it happened. I need to know why.'

'I explained to your colleague. I was on a story. It's all in his notes.'

'Yes, I have them in front of me now. It's just that, obviously, I need to eliminate you as a suspect.'

'You what? Since when did journalists go round bombing interviewees?'

'I have to look at every angle, sir. Start from scratch.'

'Look — here's something to keep you busy until I come in. I did an interview with a group calling themselves the Salisbury Animal Militia the other night. It was somewhere in the city, but I was hooded so I

169

don't know where. They were all masked, but the guy who did the talking issued a direct threat of violence against anyone working at Porton Down. I've got a videotape of the interview, which I'll bring in with me tomorrow. I have no idea how serious this group is, or if they've got access to stuff like Semtex.'

Brennan listened for a response, but all he could hear was the detective scratching down his notes of the conversation.

'Right, I've got that, Mr Brennan. Thank you. Would you have any idea why they might go after an old farmer like Mr Gudgeon?'

'Well — if you look in the current edition of your local paper, you'll see a story about a recent Porton Down exercise involving an evacuation of infected cattle. This was carried out on Mr Gudgeon's land. That might have been enough to provoke somebody — but then I'm sure I don't have to point out to you that evidence will be needed to confirm this connection.'

'Yes, I'm aware of that, sir. You didn't get any names, I suppose?'

'Not directly. But there's one that kept coming up — Joe Fletcher. You should have something on him because he has a conviction. That's all I know.'

'Right. Thank you, Mr Brennan. That's

been most helpful. What time can you make it in here tomorrow?'

'Would ten-thirty be OK?'

'Fine. Goodnight, sir.'

The phone went dead. Brennan hung up and sagged. The delayed shock of the explosion that afternoon, the frustration of failure and the sudden role reversal of becoming a police witness all combined now to drain him of energy as quickly as pulling a plug from an electric socket. He lay his head on the desk and began to doze.

'You OK?' Brennan stirred as he heard Janet's voice.

'Sorry — bit tired.'

'Trouble?'

'I'll tell you later, if you don't mind. Is there anything to eat?'

'A spaghetti with pesto sauce — it's on the table now.'

Brennan dragged himself to his feet and made his way down to the kitchen. He didn't talk all through dinner, and Lester was warned off from asking any questions by a glare from his mother. Brennan ate all his food and then retired upstairs to the lounge. When Janet and Lester heard strains of a lyrically mournful John Coltrane ballad wafting down from above, they both knew that he was using the music as therapy for his state of mind.

''I Wish I Knew',' said Lester suddenly.

'What?' asked Janet.

'No — that's the title of the track he's playing. He always does that — finds a title or a lyric to say for him what he would like to say out loud himself. Neat, eh?'

'It's actually three parts anal retentiveness and two parts emotional constipation, by my reckoning. Still, if it puts him in a better mood, who am I to complain?'

Janet began loading up the dishwasher while Lester wiped the kitchen table down and tied up the black-plastic rubbish bag, estimating that each task would be worth about a pound in pocket money when his domestic contributions were assessed at the end of the week. He looked in on his dad on the way up to bed and was rewarded with a smile of reassurance.

Janet came up into the lounge about ten minutes later, carrying two glasses of Calvados. This was enough to prompt Brennan into telling her what had happened and why he was suddenly embroiled with the police, if not as a suspect, then certainly as a key witness to a violent murder. Janet offered her sympathy, but could find nothing in the way of helpful suggestions. The due process of law was a huge obstacle to freelance investigators.

'I'm not going to dwell on it,' Brennan promised, unconvincingly. 'I'll have a good night's sleep, and then drive calmly down to Salisbury and deal with them. Oh, and I might go mushroom hunting with Robert first thing.'

'Mushroom hunting? How does that help?'

'Robert assures me that it's a wonderful experience, spiritual even. Listen, I need all the help I can get at the moment, Janet.'

'I'll set the alarm, then.'

'Before that, we have to settle this business of the film for Mark. It's not working for me. And, frankly, I found it a betrayal for him to flog the first section straight to BBC News West without telling me.'

'I can understand that, but I think you're wrong to feel that way. He was thrilled with what you'd shot. But the content had a news element that couldn't be ignored.'

'A bunch of deluded wankers in woolly masks sounding off? That's not news. That's access to airtime for nutters. There are supposed to be guidelines against showing that kind of facile propaganda on television.'

'Well, Mark made a judgement. The BBC news desk wanted it as soon as they saw it. Mark got a lot of interest in the finished film.

And, let's face it, it has proved to be highly prophetic.'

'Did they carry a report on Gudgeon's death?'

'No. It must have happened too late to make the six-thirty bulletin.'

'Well, they're going to lap it all up tomorrow, aren't they? Once the police announce the connection.'

'Well, it probably means Mark will want more from you.'

'Oh, sure. I'll take my camera into my interview with the police. They'll love that. Do you realize that if I'd started getting off on making a film, I'd have probably had the camera running when old man Gudgeon got cremated with his tractor. That's a bloody ghoulish thought, isn't it? Even worse is the certainty that Mark would have loved it.'

'He's not that crass, Frank. He's chuffed to bits that you're working for him. Don't write it off after one bad day. Please.'

'I'll think about it. And Mark will have to think about it, too. This is now a murder investigation. I can't get in the way of the police. So I'm a liability as a documentary maker on this particular story.'

'No — you're an asset. You're in pole position, Frank. You must be able to see that? It's what you always wanted to be when you were a reporter — first on the scene.'

'OK — but at face value, there isn't much of a story any more. If Tim Williams is telling the truth, and it's accepted as such, then it looks like a relatively straightforward killing by animal rights activists. I mean, there's no novelty in their use of violence or bombs.'

'But what if it's the start of a campaign, rather than a one-off?'

'That would be different, but it hasn't happened yet. And I wouldn't want it to, just for the sake of a two-bit film. I mean, I get the feeling sometimes that television has an uncontrollable lust for cheap-thrills, disasters or true crimes. And my fear is that Mark would be obliged to see my story this way, too.'

'Well, I'll put your reservations to him tomorrow morning and see what he says.'

Brennan slugged back his drink and thumped his chest theatrically as the spirit burnt its way down his windpipe.

'Time for bed.'

* * *

The moment the alarm started bleeping under his pillow, Brennan regretted agreeing to an early-morning mushroom hunt. His head was still thick with the disappointment and alarm of the previous day, and the alcohol he'd consumed in the hope of a good night's sleep had added to the impression that his brain had been lagged by a plumber while asleep. Brennan stifled the alarm quickly to avoid disturbing Janet and then slung his legs out from under the duvet in a token gesture towards getting up. As he started to drift off back to sleep, the cold draught of air around his feet stirred him back to wakefulness. This time he summoned the energy to swivel his entire body up and out of the bed.

After a shower and a shave — and two cups of black coffee — Brennan could begin to string coherent thoughts together. He even managed a laugh at his own expense when thinking about his diary entry for the day — '7 a.m.: hunt mushrooms; 10.30 a.m.: report to police.' This association then triggered memories of an old investigation of his into corruption in the Metropolitan Police. Halfway through, he'd discovered that the unofficial campaign to obstruct him had been dubbed 'Operation Mushroom' by the cabal of bent Flying Squad detectives, on the basis that they would keep Brennan in the dark and feed him a lot of shit. When Brennan and his team of reporters finally exposed them in an eight-page special, the newsmen drunkenly arranged a delivery of two dozen mushroom pizzas to the station where the officers were being questioned, as an act of petty revenge. It passed into Fleet Street legend. The bitter truth for Brennan was that this anecdote probably lived on today, surviving the air-conditioned, alcohol-free atmosphere of Canary Wharf but now almost certainly preceding the epilogue 'Wonder what happened to that bloke Brennan?'

Brennan wondered what his fellow hacks of that time would make of him now as he emerged from his house in a fleecy windcheater and walking boots, with a shallow wicker basket on his arm.

'You remembered!' Robert exclaimed as Brennan opened the passenger door to the car.

'I may have destroyed several million brain cells last night, but the ones in which our conversation was stored made it through the night.'

Robert eased his old Volvo out onto a deserted Market Street, and then across the stone bridge over the Avon.

'Do you mind if I put BBC Wiltshire Sound on?' Brennan asked.

'Not at all,' Robert said, switching the radio on and pushing tuning buttons until the unmistakable 'parish pump' sound of a local radio station emerged. Brennan listened carefully to the headlines: a heifer had escaped from an abattoir in Chippenham; the AA advised of road works on the High Street in Westbury; and today there would be a cheese competition in a village near Swindon.

'Thanks,' Brennan said as he turned the radio off.

'Perhaps they don't cover stories from Salisbury?' Robert guessed.

'I don't think the police will go public on this one until it looks like they've got a lead. Pointless calling press conferences if they've nothing to say just yet. I've got to go in later this morning for another interview. They'll probably announce something after that.'

'Do you still want to do this?' Robert asked anxiously.

'Yeah. Better than sitting at home fretting.'

Robert took the back routes to north of Frome, until a large forest dominated the road on the left-hand side. He parked the car on the verge and nodded for Brennan to get out. They stepped over a wooden stile and, minutes later, the trees and an eerie morning silence had enshrouded them. Robert led Brennan to the edge of the forest where the trees abutted a high hedgerow.

'Right. Chanterelles are usually clustered

on the forest floor, close to the base of tree trunks. If you go this side, I'll work up this channel here. You know what they look like, I presume?'

'On a plate, yes.'

'Well, they're pretty much the same here. You're a jazz fan, just imagine little brown trumpets lying at your feet.'

They moved on, about ten yards apart from one another, eyes scanning the forest floor.

'Would have been a perfect name for a girl soul group in the 1960s, wouldn't it? The Chanterelles,' Brennan mused absently.

'I remember The Shirelles,' Robert said, from the other side of a large tree.

'A-ha!' he exclaimed before bending low. 'Found some.'

Brennan wandered over to have a look at the handful of fungi that Robert had harvested and was now placing delicately in his basket. Suitably inspired, Brennan returned to his agreed route and, at the next tree, found a cluster of his own. For a full twenty minutes, the two men moved silently through the forest, accumulating a decent-sized haul of freshly sprouted chanterelles. As they reached the farthest edge of the forest, they came together to compare baskets.

'Well done, Frank. That should keep you

going over the weekend.'

'They're lovely, aren't they? I mean, not threatening like your usual mushroom. Some of the other ones look like nuclear warheads exploding.'

'Ceps,' Robert said knowledgeably. 'Right, a slow walk back, then breakfast round at my place.'

They turned and began to walk in the direction they had come. Brennan kicked away a rabbit skull that had momentarily startled him when he'd seen it. In the hedgerow, there was a sudden loud rustling as a badger made its escape from the human presence. And, as the sun began to filter through the foliage, a chorus of wood pigeons started up.

'Can't help feeling the animal rights people have a case at moments like this,' Brennan observed. 'I mean when you contrast a setting like this with something so utterly unnatural as what goes on at Porton Down. The guy I was talking with the other night said they killed over eight thousand animals a year there in experiments.'

'It is a very irrational place when one comes to think about it. Rooted in the warfare of chlorine-gas attacks at Ypres, you know. All stemmed from that. First it was countermeasures — respirator systems, detecting devices — and then building up a stockpile of our own evil stuff, just in case it was needed.'

'You sound as though you've studied this, Robert.'

'Not really. Bear in mind that I'm surrounded by books all day, and that I have a lot of quiet moments in the shop. I know a little about a lot.'

They walked on, with Brennan momentarily envying this glimpse into Robert's gentler, wiser lifestyle.

'You'd think we could have left it all behind by now, though, wouldn't you? Nobody uses horses or bows and arrows in war. There should be a natural obsolescence.'

'In many ways it's become worse these days. Most of the civilized nations may have banned the use of such weapons, but they're a blessing to the tyrants and nutters of the world. Tiny amounts of biological matter or of nerve-agents can wipe out whole cities. That's how Porton Down justifies itself and you can't argue against it, really. Can you imagine the fury if one of our towns or national institutions was chemically attacked, and we had no defence or antidote?'

'Yes, of course. But that makes it all the more baffling that I should get the full bifters of corporate spin thrown at me over what they claim to be nothing more than an exercise. It's a sort of fake openness, like NATO's during the Kosovan war. They let you know that they're doing you a favour by telling you the truth, but then they still lie to you. I don't understand their thinking: it's perverse. Why not just lie outright?'

'Ah, but Frank, isn't the pretence of being open a moral balm to soothe their bad conscience about what they're doing? I think there's an old Chinese proverb . . .'

'There's *always* an old Chinese proverb.'

'And it says something like telling one secret will always allow you to hide two others.'

'I think I've seen that one somewhere — MoD Christmas card the year after the Falklands War,' Brennan said sarcastically.

The two men fell into silence again. As they neared the road, the sounds of traffic began to intrude and by the time they reached the car Brennan's calm had been overtaken by thoughts of his imminent interview with the police. So though he enjoyed the breakfast that Robert prepared for him — and it was every bit as good as he had promised — anxiety stifled their conversation. Robert was used to this, his working life involving brief exchanges with customers and long periods of silence in between. But he wished

Brennan well for the day.

Brennan returned home. Janet had left for work and Lester was enjoying the last days of his summer break by having a marathon lie-in. Brennan changed into casual clothes — an open-necked button-down shirt, cotton sports jacket, jeans — and then set off for Salisbury again with the tape of his interview as companion.

This time he played no music, preferring to hear his own thoughts ricochet around inside his head. He knew that the police investigation would severely restrict his freedom to make further inquiries about the case, but he would still be able to go back and look at the original incident he had witnessed. That was now officially in the public domain, thanks to the efforts of Timmy Williams and Luke Barrs. So, assuming the police didn't arrest him and charge him with murder, Brennan could go back to work. Cheered by this thought, he was even able to smile at the sight of several reporters, including Luke Barrs, gathered outside Salisbury police station as he drove in and parked.

As Detective Inspector Andrews explained to Brennan as they walked towards the interview room, a press conference had been called for 11.15 a.m., in order to announce

183

both the death of Gudgeon and the fact that a device had been used to kill him.

'So you need to have someone in the frame by then?' Brennan remarked cynically.

'That's not the way we work in the shire counties, Mr Brennan. We don't just fit somebody up. We follow clear lines of inquiry and get the public to help us, which they are very willing to do. I just want to make sure of your animal rights militia story before I go public with it.'

DI Andrews held an office door open for Brennan and gestured him in. There was another plain-clothes detective already seated there. He stood up as Brennan moved in.

'This is a colleague, DS Parker.'

'Mr Brennan,' Parker said as he shook hands.

They all sat down and Brennan handed over the videotape.

'This isn't the full version, just the section that appeared on BBC News West last night.'

'I don't remember you saying it had been broadcast already?'

'It wasn't my decision. I assumed somebody here would have seen it.'

'You did this interview two days ago, I understand,' Parker said. Brennan nodded cautiously. 'So can I ask why you didn't contact us immediately, given the nature of the threats made?'

'When you see the whole interview, you will realize that the statement the SAM spokesman made was entirely separate from my questioning. You will also see that they are a militia only in the sense that they wore masks and dark clothes. There were no weapons on display, no explosives.'

'So you didn't take them seriously enough to warn us, thereby enabling us to save Mr Gudgeon's life?' Parker replied, appearing to play the 'hard cop' role.

'As I understand from my inquiries, DS Parker, the SAM have been in action for about a year now, so why weren't they all banged up already if they were that threatening?'

'Gentlemen,' DI Andrews intervened. He gestured for Parker to play the tape. Both policemen took notes on the statement and whispered to each other at various points. When the extract had finished, Parker rewound the tape and then inserted it into an evidence bag and labelled it.

'Shouldn't he ask my permission before he does that?' Brennan said to Andrews.

'We need it, Mr Brennan. Now, is there anything else you can tell me since our conversation last night?'

Brennan shrugged.

'You couldn't identify any of them, for instance?'

'Their faces were masked, and I didn't recognize any voices. The interview took place in a bare basement or cellar, with an iron staircase leading down to it. It didn't look as though it was inhabited, more like they'd just used it for the film. It's approximately ten minutes' drive from the station, but as I was hooded, I can't tell you whether they went one way or another.'

'Did you go to Gudgeon to warn him?' Parker asked.

'Not directly, no. I wanted to talk to him about this 'DERA' exercise on his land.'

'You didn't see fit to tell him his life was in danger, then?'

'If you check his shotgun, which I'm sure you'll get round to eventually, you'll find that both barrels were discharged — over my head, but near enough for me to get out of the cantankerous bastard's way. He wasn't in the mood to receive warnings.'

'OK, that's enough. Thank you for coming in, Mr Brennan. I have to caution you to say nothing about this to the media while our investigation is under way. And, of course, we may have to get back to you as the case progresses.'

'I know the rules. I don't suppose I can

attend the press conference, then?'

'Not a chance,' Parker said firmly.

Andrews stood and escorted Brennan out through the door and back down the corridor towards reception, a repeat of the same etiquette, Brennan noted, that had seen the senior officer rather than the junior one perform the menial tasks. Brennan guessed that it was just down to the fact that Andrews had been his contact. He shook hands with the Detective Inspector and left the building.

As he drove away, the hacks and photographers were being admitted to the conference suite. Brennan imagined the plodding — no pun intended — nature of the affair, with various 'avenues' being looked into 'at this moment in time', and the inevitable 'appeal to the general public to help us stop these dangerous criminals'.

Brennan found his car getting snarled up in mid-morning shopping traffic. He switched on the cassette player and inserted a tape of Wayne Shorter playing 'Footprints'. As the urgent tenor sax filled the car, Brennan found himself staring at the bumper of the car in front and realizing that he'd forgotten all about the two number plates the SAM driver had used to throw him off the scent. He could still remember them. They weren't technically a 'lead', because Brennan knew they'd be false or stolen. But that in turn might provide if not an 'avenue' then possibly a short street to look into.

Brennan dialled the police station number, hoping to catch Andrews before the press conference began. But the switchboard operator confirmed that he'd just gone through.

'What about Detective Sergeant Parker, is he available?' Brennan asked.

'Who?'

'DS Parker.'

'I'm sorry, sir, we have nobody by that name at the station . . . '

8

Brennan had little or no doubt, given his past experiences, that 'Detective Sergeant Parker' was either an MI5 agent or a Special Branch policeman. Given DI Andrews's undue deference to the cropped-haired, much younger man, Brennan was inclined to decide more in terms of 'Five' than 'Branch'. The brusque questions and chippy manner had all the hallmarks of 'one of the chaps' or 'a Big Lad', as they liked being referred to in the shorthand codes of the security services. These were the types who thought of themselves as the absolute dog's bollocks, given that they could swan into any crime situation and take command at a moment's notice, designating senior police officers to more mundane tasks.

Brennan guessed that somebody such as 'Parker' wouldn't have come down from London at such short notice over what was a comparatively 'trivial' murder. A campaign by an animal rights movement against Porton Down would probably have a fairly low priority as far as 'Five' was concerned, given that the MoD had its own police force as well as Special Branch to call upon. Only if that campaign escalated to assume terrorist proportions would the intelligence services be asked to get involved. Bombing an elderly farmer, who had only a chance connection with Porton Down, wouldn't, in Brennan's eyes, necessitate a security-service presence. This suggested to Brennan that 'Parker' had already been in the area on another job and had invited himself in as an observer. The question to ask, then, was, 'What other job?'

For a moment, Brennan thought about going back to the police station to confront DI Andrews. But he knew that this would prove counter-productive. Better to let Andrews think that he'd fooled Brennan. Better to let him think that Brennan was a helpful and cooperative witness. The coppers tended to think in straight lines anyway, so if Brennan went out of his way to make a fuss they'd probably place a restraining order on him, or nick him, even. With the security services, however, you *could* play mental games. It was what they liked and what they were trained for: the warfare of the mind.

With the traffic still crawling ahead of him, Brennan abandoned his plans for a journey straight back to Bradford, deciding instead to find something useful he might do in the Salisbury area. A return visit to the farm was off the agenda, especially as he knew that it was likely still to be sealed off by the police. In any case, his inquiries now lay elsewhere. He pulled off into a side street and checked his OS map. The Porton Down site seemed to sprawl between two A-roads, with at least three villages bordering it. Two of these had pubs marked, which was a good enough start for Brennan.

He turned the car round and headed back for the ring road, finding the exit for the eastbound A30. Soon the city gave way to the countryside, but every half-mile or so it was clear that this land was compromised, marked as it was by signs announcing 'Danger' or 'MoD Property — Keep Out'. Turning off the A30 soon afterwards, Brennan could see some of the site buildings in the distance. The closer he got, the more prevalent the signs became, this time backed up by double rows of closely meshed metal-link fencing, scanned every 500 yards or so by security cameras. Clearly, Porton Down wasn't a place for a casual visit, although he had a bet with himself that someone like Timmy Williams might already have in mind a family-friendly theme park along the lines of the Sellafield Visitors' Centre — perhaps 'The Porton Down Experience: It's a Gas'.

Eventually, the land resumed its rural

identity and Brennan stopped in the next village, having spotted a classically thatched pub with whitewashed walls. On a job such as this there really was no substitute for going back to the basics of investigative journalism and playing the innocent passer-by, eavesdropping on local people gossiping over a drink and engaging 'mine host' in chit-chat. If things went really well, he would be able to buy a round of drinks and do the old number about possibly moving into the area and wanting to know what things were like. Such tactics had often yielded rewards in the shape of expressions of deep resentment towards a local employer, or libellous stories about local 'celebrities'. In fact, Brennan felt that he could probably give a master class in such old-fashioned journalistic techniques.

Brennan parked his car and took a few minutes to let the air dry out the perspiration that the Salisbury traffic jam had formed on his face. It was just past noon so there were only a handful of other cars parked, suggesting that the pub would be less than crowded. Perhaps there'd be some juicy lunchtime trade from workers at DERA, although Brennan suspected that, on such a high-security site, staff would not be encouraged to mingle with the local populace.

Once inside the pub, this suspicion was

readily confirmed by the sight of two elderly couples at one table, tucking in to an early lunch, and a classic local farmer, standing in his worn cord trousers and check shirt at the bar. Brennan smiled at him and wished him 'Good morning' but got no more than a grunt in response. Brennan pulled out a stool and installed himself at the bar. A tubby middle-aged landlord approached, with no great warmth in his demeanour.

'Yes?' he said curtly.

'Morning,' Brennan said, trying to retain his charm. 'I'll have a pint of Henry's IPA, please.'

The landlord went straight to the beer-tap and automatically took out a dimpled jug glass from the shelves below. Producing the jug was a symbolic gesture aimed at visitors' 'outsiderdom', a way of saying that 'We think you're a city type just passing through'. Brennan thought about demanding a straight glass, the choice of the regulars. But the landlord was already filling the jug, so a late intervention wouldn't be welcomed.

'Anything else?' the landlord asked as he plonked the jug on the bar, spilling at least an inch of the beer.

'Yes. Could I see the lunch menu, please?'

The landlord pointed to the blackboard behind the bar and wandered away again.

Ordinarily Brennan might have pointed out the man's complete lack of qualifications for dealing with the public to him, but this wasn't the day or the time. Instead he scanned the board, which was filled with country-pub clichés — Ploughman's Lunch, home-made soup of the day, various omelettes, and steak and chips. The words 'freshly made' appeared as a prefix to the choice of sandwiches, as though this was a favour to the customer rather than a statutory right.

'What's the soup of the day, please?' Brennan asked.

The landlord wandered back towards him and stared at the board.

'I'll have to ask.'

He disappeared into the kitchen with a weary tread. Brennan was grateful that he hadn't arrived in the pub on a busy day. He unfolded his copy of the *Salisbury Gazette* in preparation for the strategic use of the DERA story as a talking point. Not that he expected to get much from this particular landlord. He looked across at the farmer who was swilling down a pint of cider.

'Rum business, this, eh?'

'You what, old mate?' the farmer replied, wiping his mouth.

Brennan showed him the story, and tapped it with his index finger.

'You'd think they had enough space up there without spilling over onto people's land.'

'What's that about?' said the farmer, peering myopically across at the newspaper.

'Porton Down — using a farmer's land for an exercise. Bit cheeky, isn't it?'

'They can have mine for the right money,' the farmer said with a chuckle. He drained his glass, wiped his mouth and headed for the door. Brennan wondered if the police ever went out into the fields and breathalysed farmers driving tractors. The landlord now reappeared.

'Vegetable.'

'OK, I'll have that. And a Ploughman's, please.'

'Stilton or Cheddar?'

'Cheddar, please.'

'White bread or brown?'

'Brown, please. With Flora, not butter — if that's possible?'

The landlord looked suddenly disturbed, as if the foundations of his universe had been called into question.

'It only comes with butter.'

'OK, butter it is, then.'

'Where will you be sitting?'

Brennan looked around the near-empty room with as much patience as he could summon.

'I'll stay here, if that's OK?'

The landlord said nothing and wandered slowly back into the kitchen. He moved at the sort of deliberate pace that Brennan usually observed behind Post Office counters where the staff enjoyed torturing customers with formalized delays. Brennan left the paper on the bar and took a few more mouthfuls of his beer. This was going to be harder work than he'd imagined. Then Brennan heard his mobile phone ringing inside his pocket. He took it out and answered it.

'Hello.'

'Frank — it's Luke Barrs. Can you talk?'

'I'm surprised you can't hear an echo.'

'Where are you?'

'Pub outside Salisbury.'

'Can I join you? It's fairly urgent.'

'I thought we'd decided it was best to go our separate ways . . . '

Out of the corner of his eye, Brennan saw the landlord return and point brusquely at a sign hanging up behind the bar that read: 'No Mobile Phones'.

Brennan held up his hand in acknowledgement, and then gave Barrs the name of the pub and the village. Barrs said he would be there in twenty minutes. Brennan switched his phone off.

'Can't you read?' asked the landlord.

'Yes, I can, actually,' Brennan replied.

'Why did you use your phone, then?'

'Because I didn't see the sign.'

The landlord glowered at Brennan but had no further logic to exploit. He retreated to a stool at the far end of the bar.

'Can I buy you a drink?' Brennan asked.

'No.'

The landlord pulled out a copy of the *Racing Post* from a shelf behind the bar. Brennan glimpsed the possibility of a dialogue that he had all but abandoned, but decided to allow a period of silence before resuming relations. Fortunately a teenage girl appeared from the kitchen with his soup. She smiled at him warmly, so was presumably not related to the landlord.

'Thanks, love.'

'I'll just get you the salt and pepper.'

The girl brought a cruet to Brennan and then offered him a paper napkin.

'Thank you. I'll try not to spill any.'

The girl laughed and went back into the kitchen. Brennan smiled and wondered how she'd got through the pub's recruitment process. He began to eat his soup, which tasted better than it looked, while monitoring the landlord's mood between spoonfuls.

'You a Jumps or a Flat man?' Brennan asked.

The landlord looked up from his paper, his facial expression having changed from sullen indifference to sudden vivacity.

'I love the Flat, me. Too bloody cold to go watching horses in the winter. What about you?'

'I'm a regular masochist at Wincanton. But I like the Flat too, the good races. I've never made it to Salisbury: good there, is it?'

'Lovely, especially on a warm day. You can see some decent horses racing there while they're still on their way up, you know, before they're famous. The trick is to spot them.'

'Didn't Island Sands win there the year before he won the 2,000 Guineas?'

'Yeah, I saw him run! Pity the bloody Arabs got their hands on him, really. Could have been one of ours winning a Classic for a change.'

The landlord slid off his stool and walked back along the bar towards Brennan, animated by this sudden dose of horse-racing camaraderie.

'Well, as we both know, nothing talks louder in racing than money,' Brennan offered as a further encouragement to his blossoming relationship with the landlord. 'If I was an owner and got a good offer from Sheikh Mohammed, I'd bloody well take it.'

'Ah, but would you? If it was something

you loved, and couldn't put a price on?'

'Everyone and everything has a price,' Brennan said sagely, seeing his opportunity to turn the conversation to his benefit. 'I mean, take this bloke here. He owns a farm, got a few dairy cattle, then lets bloody Porton Down trample all over his land for a few bob.'

The landlord looked at the story and shook his head, tapping his nose with his forefinger.

'He's a crafty old sod, that Gudgeon, by all accounts. I bet what's behind that is a compensation job. A lot of the land round here was poisoned by Porton in the 1940s when they let off all sorts of stuff. It got into the soil and everything. Now they have to pay up if you can prove there's anything nasty still there.'

'That's fair enough, I'd have thought.'

'Not if he's poisoned it himself, it ain't,' the landlord whispered.

Brennan returned to his soup, disappointed by this low-level intelligence. He could almost sense a crop-circle story coming, in which cunning farmers laid waste part of their wheat crop in order to attract the Japanese tourists and sci-fi freaks at £5 a head. Brennan couldn't claim to have had an intimate relationship with old man Gudgeon, but he doubted if he was capable of such a scam. The story about poisoned land intrigued Brennan, though. The vet in Bradford had told him how anthrax could develop naturally in soil, but if Porton Down had put it there fifty years ago, that could have generated both an emergency and a subsequent cover-up, despite Timmy Williams's alleged commitment to openness. Brennan finished his soup, bought another pint, and took a seat at a table to wait for Luke Barrs's arrival.

★　★　★

At first, the estate agent had the men down as a couple of queers. He certainly didn't often get two blokes house hunting together as though they were a married couple. They certainly looked the part — close-cropped hair, well-built bodies, designer suits. Still, a sale was still a sale and, frankly, this rather grotty little two-bedroom Victorian semi would take some shifting, so any interest was welcome.

'It's obviously been a little neglected over the years, but this means it has considerable scope for being done up exactly how you'd like it. Very fashionable these days, what with all those television programmes.'

'Who's the vendor?' asked one of the men tersely.

'Ah, well. Between you and me, it's actually being sold as part of his estate.'

'You mean he's dead?' asked the other.

'I'm afraid so. The asking price shouldn't therefore be taken too literally, if you catch my drift. A decent offer for a quick sale is the order of the day.'

'Can we see upstairs?'

'Yes, of course. I'll take you up there.'

'I'll have a look at the garden if I may,' said the other man as the estate agent took his partner upstairs. Once they had disappeared up the staircase, he crossed quickly to where the estate agent had left the front-door key. From his pocket, he took a flat piece of Plasticine and pressed the key into it to give a precise impression. He would have a replica cut within the hour, and later that night he and his companion could come back in their own time and give the late David Southwell's house a complete going-over.

*   *   *

Luke Barrs arrived at the pub looking flustered. Brennan bought him the soft drink of his choice and waited to hear what had alarmed him. Brennan wondered if the police press conference had leaked his name to the hack-pack in a clear breach of protocol. If

201

they had, Brennan would have DI Andrews on toast.

'What's the flap, Luke?' Brennan asked pointedly. 'Feeling guilty about running Timmy Williams's story because it led, indirectly, to Gudgeon's death?'

'The police aren't making that connection. I know it exists, and I feel very sorry about it. But I was just doing my job.'

'Let's not get into that again, shall we? Now look — if there's any blame to be attached it should go straight onto Williams and DERA. They concocted their little press release. They put Gudgeon into the firing line for the animal rights militia to shoot down.'

'You were there at the time, I understand. So how do *you* feel?'

'Who told you that?'

'That's what I wanted to tell you. After the press conference, the detective . . . '

'Andrews?'

'That's the one. He took me back to his office and introduced me to this other chap.'

'Short hair, mid-thirties, stroppy attitude?'

Barrs nodded.

'He went by the name of Detective Sergeant Parker when I met him this morning.'

'He's not a policeman, Frank.'

'I know that. The switchboard had never heard of him.'

'So you know he's MI5?'

'I guessed it, but I'm grateful for the confirmation. What did he want from you?'

'Anything I picked up, but *especially* what your interest in the case was. He knew that you'd been to see me, Frank.'

'The day I visited you, my car was broken into and searched. That's what they do — at a very basic level, of course.'

'He's worried that you've got something damaging on DERA.'

'Did he actually say that?'

'Not in so many words. But that was his drift. Frank, he offered me £500 a month for providing information on anyone sniffing around. I don't know what to do. I mean, this is heavy stuff for a provincial editor.'

'Luke. Don't panic. It is pretty much standard procedure for 'Five' to have journalists and editors on their payroll.'

'Really?'

'Of course. It saves them a lot of legwork. I was approached several times by various faces.'

'What did you do, tell them to piss off?'

'That's one approach. But the snag is that they can be helpful, too. If you sign up with them and prove useful, you're deemed to be on-side. One of the chaps. They'll feed you interesting snippets when it suits them to rubbish some politician or local bigwig. They pick up the scandal, but you get to publish it. Some journalists have made a complete living from it.'

'You didn't answer my question. Did you sign up?'

'No, of course not. I played them off. There were times when I had something I couldn't print that was useful to them, usually about somebody I didn't like. But I never betrayed anyone I respected, and the older I got, the less cooperative I became. That's the danger. That you become so dependent on the security services for information, or a favour, you end up as a cripple without them. In the end, they'll always drop you — nicely if you've been a good boy, unpleasantly if you've crossed them. When I was put on trial for offences against the Official Secrets Act, 'Five' made sure the prosecution had all the information they needed to put me away.'

'What should I do, then?'

'That's entirely up to you, Luke. It's up to your conscience, if you want to make it a moral choice. I mean, six grand a year doesn't seem enough to throw away your integrity, if you ask me.'

'What if I say no to them?'

'They'll probably just leave you alone. Depends what's going on in your area. I'd have thought that, with so many defence-related sites on your patch, they'd go for someone else if they couldn't get you. And then you'll find yourself out of the loop. Not getting the right stories, not being invited to all the right parties. If you can live with that, fine. But you must realize that you've already made a gesture of defiance by coming to tell me.'

Barrs looked at Brennan, grateful for this moment of approval.

'I think it was more a sign of panic than of personal courage, actually. I think I'll sleep on it. The bloke gave me a week to think about it.'

'Did you get his real name?'

'No, I'm afraid not. I don't think he mentioned one. He just showed me this fancy warrant card. I was a bit scared, to be honest. It's not every day that you get secret agents turning up in your office.'

'Don't feel bad about it. That's how the bastards work, by way of emotional blackmail and references to patriotism.'

'Thanks for your help, Frank.'

'Look, I have to ask this — you're not setting me up, are you? Following his orders to come and tell me?'

Barrs's young face was suddenly a picture of consternation.

'No. I can see that you aren't. I'm sorry,' Brennan said.

Barrs nodded his thanks, and a pale smile returned to his face.

'Where do we go from here, then?' he asked, with a sigh.

'Well, I'm now a key witness in a murder trial, so I'm not allowed to talk to people like you. In any case, you're going to have your hands full dealing with the hunt for Gudgeon's killers. I presume the police are going to try and round up animal rights militia members?'

'They didn't specify, other than that they were following a highly promising lead.'

'That just means they don't want to look stupid by arresting people they mention at a press conference who then turn out to be innocent. What they'll do is pull some of the tame animal rights activists in and get names. Then they'll try and find the militia's leader . . .'

'Joe Fletcher?'

'If he's the one. It all depends how the militia is organized. From my brief sighting, they looked to be fairly amateurish. And I shouldn't think that there are many hiding places in a city like Salisbury. Once they've got him, the interview I filmed and whatever forensic evidence they've found should be enough for a charge, whether he did it or not.'

'Do you mean they'll fit him up?'

'I didn't say that. What I meant was that it will be terribly convenient to lots of people and reassuring in general if this murder, or manslaughter, can be ascribed to a fringe protest group, or one deranged individual. Much though police say they are keeping 'an open mind', my experience tells me they don't.'

'So you'll be out there, looking for other suspects,' Barrs said with an admiring smile.

'I'm off *this* case, by dint of the law, but I'm still not convinced that we're getting the truth from Porton about its so-called exercise. I know it's the kind of place that automatically generates rumours and stories because of what goes on there. But that doesn't stop me wanting to find out.'

'It's more rational and ordinary than you think. But then, I was given special access, so my view is tainted.'

'I won't be coming to you for help, then — which should please your new friend.'

Barrs took a long drink of his orange juice and soda water and swirled the icy debris around the bottom of his empty glass. He checked his watch nervously.

'I'd better get back to the office. Look, I want to help you, Frank. I don't want to play their game. I want to be a proper journalist, not a glove puppet.'

'Good. We'll see how it goes. You should be aware, though, that every journalist starts out with the most noble of intentions and then finds that his career consists almost entirely of abandoning them. I know, because I've done it myself. Right, now the sermon's over, tell me if you think this man who came to see you is just visiting or is down here permanently.'

'He asked me to recommend him a good French restaurant, so I presume he's a recent arrival.'

'That's what I thought he might be. Take care of yourself, Luke.'

Barrs shook hands with Brennan as he stood up, then placed his business card on the table in front of him.

'All my numbers are on that — work, home, mobile. But if you're on the Internet, maybe my e-mail address is the safest way of communicating. Good luck, Frank.'

'You too.'

Barrs nodded to the landlord and left. Running into the spooks for the first time was always an unnerving experience for a young journalist, because it was always heavily hinted that careers could be made or ruined by falling into line or not. In Brennan's day, there was an editor or a board of directors to whom you could report the approach. But it seemed to Brennan that Luke Barrs had nobody he could really turn to if the anxieties grew too strong, and nobody to watch over him when life turned ugly. As Brennan knew it would.

*　*　*

Mary Ashton was not told about her 'annual interview'. Her divisional supervisor simply arrived and requested her immediate presence in the office of the Director of Human Resources. She was escorted all the way there, being given no time to change out of her lab coat or to go for a pee or even to refresh her make-up. These security checks, disguised as 'personnel file updating' or some other jargon, were usually conducted on a random basis but with at least a day's notice and a great deal more civility. The abrupt nature of this summons had Mary on edge, even though she knew that she had done nothing wrong.

Sitting next to the Director of Human Resources was a late-middle-aged man with thick-lens glasses and the sort of halitosis that could strike from ten feet. Mary hadn't seen him before but that hardly mattered. She held all psychoanalysts in contempt for not being pure scientists.

'Sorry to drag you away from your work so abruptly, Mary, but Dr Liebmann has a busy schedule.'

Liebmann peered over his glasses at Mary, then lifted his clip-folder off the desk and onto his knee.

'This won't take too long, Miss Ashton.'

'It's Dr Ashton. I have a PhD, just like you, Dr Liebmann.'

'My apologies. Let me run briefly through the details — you are thirty-eight years of age, divorced, and you have nearly eight years' work experience here, yes?'

'One always thinks one's life adds up to more, but that's basically it.'

'Are you happy?'

'In what sense? Professionally or personally?'

'Tell me about both.'

'I enjoy my work. I hope it's up to standard. I like my colleagues. I'm also happy with my life outside the site.'

'You have not remarried?'

'No. Once was enough.'

'Do you want children?'

'I think that's an impertinent question,

whatever the justification. You wouldn't ask a male scientist the same question.'

'I'm sorry.'

Mary glimpsed a brief wink of reassurance from the Director of Human Resources.

'Now, Dr Ashton,' Liebmann resumed. 'Have you developed any moral qualms about your work?'

'Why should I? I knew what was involved when I applied for the job.'

'People change. They come to question their life. They get depressed, or angry. Working with animals that you must kill can arouse hidden sensitivity, no matter the level of professionalism. You also work on antidotes to highly toxic nerve and chemical agents, knowing that a foreign power may use such weapons against your country. You know the effects they can have. Things such as this can disturb even the soundest equilibrium.'

'If you'd like to show me pictures of ink blots, that may be of more help to you, Dr Liebmann. My life feels stable and purposeful. I don't have nightmares about biological warfare, or screaming rabbits in their death throes. I do my job to the best of my ability.'

Mary looked at her watch impatiently. It was approaching one o'clock. She was hungry, and could sense the level of her blood sugars dropping. This bastard Liebmann had probably chosen precisely this period to drag her in, calculating that more might be revealed in weakness than in strength.

'Dr Ashton — I will let you go after one more question. Your answer will be regarded with the strictest confidence.'

'As all of them should be.'

'Do you mistrust any of your colleagues? Does any aspect of their behaviour concern you?'

'No.'

The Director looked at Liebmann with a pained smile.

'Very well. Thank you, Dr Ashton. You may go.'

'Thanks, Mary,' the Director said with a hint of apology in his voice. Mary refused to look at Liebmann as she left the room.

'Tense and defensive,' Liebmann said quickly in judgement.

'I thought she just disliked some of your questions, Doctor.'

'That's what I'm paid for,' Liebmann said as he finished his notes.

★ ★ ★

Brennan couldn't resist the temptation to drive past Breakheart Lodge on the way back to Bradford. He could see from some distance away that there was still a police presence around the scene of the explosion, in the form of two white forensic-unit vehicles. A structure of blue plastic sheets had been erected around and over the immediate site, instantly reminding Brennan of the night he had seen the dead cattle lying in the field with the blue plastic bags tied over their heads. As Brennan drew closer, he could see that a uniformed officer was pacing up and down at the entrance to the farm's private track. Brennan pushed the car through a little quicker in order to avoid provoking the constable into taking his registration number.

Brennan also knew that he would have to increase the speed of his investigation. The police would be in a rush to get hold of a 'prime suspect' to parade before the cameras. It was quite likely that some if not all of the members of the Salisbury Animal Militia would be easily rounded up and charged. The long pre-trial hiatus would see life around Salisbury return to its normal sedate pace. People would go about their usual business, relieved that a bombing campaign had been aborted. And just as their anxieties faded, so too would their memory of this violent episode. Equally, Timmy Williams would no doubt make sure that Porton Down would maintain a gentle profile, systematically erasing any connection it had with the events at Breakheart Farm.

Brennan attempted to construct a new strategy as he continued his drive home, this time using the B-roads that skirted the great expanse of Salisbury Plain. He would need to go to London to confront Williams again, this time with the certain knowledge that MI5 was crawling all over the events surrounding what had been passed off as a planned exercise. This would also give Brennan the chance to recruit his old pal Tommy Preston for a few days of legwork down in Wiltshire. If Brennan himself couldn't investigate Gudgeon's murder directly, Tommy would be able to do it for him by proxy. It would, in any case, be fun to see Tommy again and catch up with the 'ducking and diving' that he had turned into an art form.

Brennan found himself parking his car in the hollow on Conigre Hill in an unexpectedly cheery mood. He was confident that this would be enough to protect him against whatever Janet was going to unload on him that night about his abortive career as a documentary film-maker. He even felt strong enough to think about paying back most of Mark Beattie's two-and-a-half-grand advance. This irrational euphoria was even able to anaesthetize Brennan's initial shock at seeing a well-built man emerge from the bushes in front of him and point a handgun at his head. Brennan raised his arms by reflex, but his legs weren't responding to any escape response. The man stepped closer and spun Brennan round, holding the gun to his neck. The gunman's mouth nuzzled Brennan's ear, projecting hot breath and spittle onto his neck.

9

Brennan sat at the kitchen table, praying that neither Janet nor Lester would come home just yet. He rationalized that it would be at least seven o'clock before Janet got back from the office, but Lester was a worry. His last few days before the school holidays ended usually found him following a pattern of brief 'refuelling' stops at home for food, money and a change of clothes before venturing out with his pals again. Brennan felt confident that he could bargain his way out of trouble with the gunman if the two of them were left alone. But if Lester turned up, the gunman could demand anything he wanted: Brennan knew he'd have to give in to save his son.

'Do you want a drink of any sort?' Brennan asked as his assailant surveyed the kitchen.

'No,' the man said, continuing to prowl.

'You can sit down if you want to.'

'No, thanks.'

'You're making me nervous, you know. You've got the gun and yet you're the twitchy one,' Brennan observed drily. 'Why don't you sit down, tell me what you want me to do, and then we can sort our way out of this?'

'Way out?' the young man asked, frowning.

'Well — I don't want to be over-confident, but if you were going to kill me, you'd have done it back there in the car park. But you want to talk. You want help. Is it the coppers on your back, Joe? Is that it?'

'Who said I was called Joe?'

'Well, I know that you're the bloke I interviewed as the spokesman for the Salisbury Animal Militia. I recognize the voice, and the eyes. And I also know that Joe Fletcher is probably the group's leader, and therefore the police's first target in their murder enquiry.'

'We didn't kill that old bloke. This is all a big fit-up.'

'Excuse me, but you said on the film that violence against Porton Down's people was legitimate. You've made threats at other times, too. You, personally, have a history of violence against people who you think have been cruel to animals. You obviously have no qualms about carrying a gun. That isn't a fit-up — it's an obvious line of inquiry.'

'But we didn't do it!' Fletcher screamed at Brennan.

'Hang on — I didn't say that you had. Now, calm down and tell me how I can help you.'

'You could have helped us by not showing

that film on telly. Or by not handing it over to the police.'

'The decision to show part of it on the news was out of my hands. And the police had the legal right to seize it as possible evidence of motive.'

'What motive? We don't actually go round killing people, let alone innocent old men.'

'Ah, but the police might say that he wasn't 'innocent' in your eyes. If you'd read the article in the newspaper, you might have interpreted him helping Porton Down to conduct an exercise on his land as a provocative act. By cooperating with them, Gudgeon turned himself into a legitimate target. That's what the police will say.'

'But that was all a bluff. Yes, we *threatened* violence, but we've never committed any. I got a conviction for chinning a hunt supporter, but I was defending myself at the time because he had a bloody baseball bat. Once he lied in court I was a goner. They just love convicting sabs.'

'Why are you carrying a gun, then?'

Fletcher slid the gun across the table to Brennan.

'It's an air pistol. Not even loaded. I've got it with me because I think the cops will try to kill me. They're swarming all over Salisbury.'

'They'll certainly kill you if you wave this at

them. Do yourself a favour and get rid of it.'

Fletcher made no move to recover the gun. Brennan picked it up and dumped it into the kitchen's swing-bin.

'Right, that's one step in the right direction. So you're on the run, I presume?'

'I guess so.'

'What about the rest of the militia?'

'I dunno. Some will have left Salisbury. Some can't. Those who've got jobs or families to worry about.'

'But not you, obviously?'

'I've got nothing.'

'How do you live?'

'I move around various squats. Sometimes sleep rough. I don't sign on or anything, if that's what you're thinking. We get a few donations from supporters. You know, people who back our campaign but who don't want to put themselves into the front line.'

'Do you have any idea what you're going to do next?' Brennan asked.

Fletcher shrugged.

'Can I suggest that you get yourself a sympathetic lawyer and then turn yourself over to the police?'

'You must be joking.'

'The longer you stay on the run, the more guilty you'll look. If you've got a defence, ideally an alibi, then talk it through with a lawyer. Let him present your case to the police.'

'How do I prove that I didn't do it, though?'

'Basically, you'll have to break down the police case against you. They've got motive and intent. But they'll need to prove that you were at the crime scene, and that you had access to bomb-making equipment. You'll need to show that you weren't and that you didn't.'

Fletcher stood up and paced the kitchen with his head bowed. It didn't look as though Brennan's advice had inspired much confidence.

'Problem?' asked Brennan.

'In the past week we've sent out fake bombs to a couple of the scientific staff at Porton Down.'

'*Fake*? In what way?'

'A shoebox, with a timing device, batteries, wiring — but no explosive. And a warning that it would be real next time.'

'Christ — you *are* in the shit, then. From what I know, Semtex was used in the device that killed farmer Gudgeon. So all the police would have to do would be to suggest that you and your militia could have gained access to some, from a quarry or somewhere like that. Then you'd be looking at a life sentence.'

'I'd better forget about bloody lawyers, then, hadn't I? I'll have to smuggle myself out of the country. Or top myself.'

Fletcher slumped down on a chair and laid his head on the kitchen table.

'How did you send these 'bombs'?'

'Over the past three months, we've been trailing workers home from Porton Down, finding out where they live. Then finding out their names from the voters' register. We targeted a few who had 'Dr' in front of their names, because they were obviously scientists who probably experiment on animals. Last week, I left a box on the doorstep of one of them. Other members of the militia planted two more at separate addresses. Same stuff, same message.'

'Do you know if these were reported to the police?'

'Not sure. I suppose they might have been.'

'So in the same week that your group deliver three fake devices at the homes of Porton Down scientists, somebody places a real one under Gudgeon's tractor.'

'Looks bad for us, then, doesn't it?'

'No, hang on a minute. If your three devices were all unarmed, and left outside houses, the one that killed Gudgeon doesn't fit into that pattern at all. Could any of your people have made a real bomb, and planted it on their own initiative?'

'No, no way. We'd all agreed on a campaign of intimidation, but there's nobody who could actually make a bomb.'

'You can get designs off the Internet now, if you know where to look.'

'Maybe so, but none of our lot would do it. We discussed our tactics at secret meetings. We were prepared to threaten, and to defend ourselves if we were threatened. But, like you said in the interview, it wouldn't have been right to kill humans when you're trying to save the lives of animals. I was just putting it on for your benefit, trying to frighten our opponents into thinking we were serious.'

'Well, I believe you, but I doubt if a court will. Now look, was your group pretty secure, tight-knit?'

'We all knew each other. Some of us go back three or four years. And we took precautions, as you know.'

'The driver of the car that picked me up, and his pal, didn't go in for much disguise, apart from switching around the car's number plates. Who were they, *junior* militia?'

'No, just mates of mine from the squat. It was my idea to use different registration numbers. Throw you off the scent.'

'And you trusted them?'

'Sure. We look after each other at the

arsehole end of society, you know. Bloody got to. What are you getting at? That one of them was a traitor?'

'Not necessarily. But you *do* realize that your group either was, or was about to be, under the scrutiny of Special Branch? Or, quite possibly, the security services.'

Fletcher looked genuinely shocked by this suggestion.

'Us? A little activist group in Salisbury, watched by agents?'

'This is a heavily militarized area. Rightly or wrongly, you would have been regarded as a threat. At the very least they would have put you under surveillance. They may even have tried to infiltrate your group.'

'Bloody hell. I thought it was just us against the plods.'

'Did you know anything about this so-called exercise that the army and Porton Down carried out on Gudgeon's land? Any whispers or rumours?'

'First I heard was when one of our lads told us what was in the paper.'

'Well, I witnessed it. Dead cattle, with blue bags over their heads. A helicopter lifting them away. Soldiers in biological-defence suits. Only I don't think it was an exercise. I think there was an accident, an incident of some sort involving a nerve or biological agent. All quickly followed by a cover-up. Killing Gudgeon may just have been part of that cover-up.'

'You mean there's a chance you can prove somebody else did for him?'

'A small one. But my movements are restricted by the fact that I'm a material witness to Gudgeon's death.'

'Hang on: you saw this incident *and* you saw Gudgeon getting blasted? If I was the police, I'd be thinking you might have done it.'

'I'm sure they'll get round to that in due course. If not you, me. If not now, then later. Which is why you can't stay here, or we may both go down for this.'

'Fair enough. But what do I do?'

'I'll get you some money to live off. When my wife comes home, she'll put us in touch with a solicitor who can represent you. He or she may advise you to turn yourself in, I don't know. But as long as you're not lying to me, and I don't think you are, I'll do what I can to help.'

'I promise I'm not. On my old mum's grave.'

'OK. What I need from you next is the name and address of the scientist whose home you planted the shoebox in.'

'It was outside, actually, next to a geranium

pot. Dr Mary Ashton. Got a little cottage in the Ebble valley, near Bishopstone.'

'Show me,' said Brennan firmly, as he fetched one of his maps out of a kitchen drawer.

* * *

The two men returned at just after eight o'clock to the house where David Southwell had lived, confident that not many people would be viewing houses in a ratty area such as this when the light was fading. They knew from what Southwell had told them that he had been on his uppers, a consequence of the crummy MoD pay and his self-inflicted habit of backing slow horses with what money he had left to spare each month. Southwell had also been a bit of a boozer, on his own admission, with a bottle of Scotch a night being his minimum consumption. So they weren't expecting to find cash or valuables in the house as they began to make their way through it. Nor were they interested in his clothes, which had already been bagged up in black-plastic rubbish sacks in his bedroom, prior to being unloaded at the nearest charity shop. What they wanted was just a name or a number or an address that was significant enough to be concealed or encoded or otherwise rendered special.

The file they'd stolen from the solicitor's office had yielded only the bureaucratic debris of Southwell's life — bank-account statements, social security numbers, driving licence, mortgage deeds and so on. Somewhere in the house was his own private address book, perhaps, or a diary, or some letters of a personal nature that would yield the ultimate clue to the man with whom he had been proposing to do his deal.

They first searched the obvious places — his reproduction antique desk in the front room, then the drawers, wardrobe and cupboards of his bedroom — but found nothing of obvious significance. Then they sliced open the bin bags and searched the pockets and linings of all his suits and jackets. Again, they found nothing.

'I bet you the bastard kept all his best stuff in his computer at Abbey Wood,' one of the men said in frustration, kicking the clothes all over the room.

'I don't think so,' the other said confidently. 'They'll have some spooks sweeping through all the computers overnight. They'd have recorded all his phone calls, too. Even a lush like Dave would have been careful.'

'Telephone directory!' the other man

exclaimed suddenly, and they dashed down-stairs with an urgency born of conviction. There was a small side table in the hall on which the phone stood. On a rack underneath there was an edition of *Yellow Pages* and a directory for the Bristol area. Southwell had written several numbers on an inside page, but they were annotated with terms such as 'plumber', 'tiler' and 'electrician'. The men decided to take this with them, just in case. And then, in the tiny drawer of the side table, they found Southwell's last phone bill, with several pages of itemized calls. They began to scan these eagerly.

'What was the date we made contact?'

'The eighteenth.'

'Look, here. Four calls on the nineteenth, all to the same number.'

'You know where the 01722 code is for, don't you? Bloody Salisbury!'

The other man took out his mobile phone and quickly dialled the number. He waited while the ringing tone was established, then held the phone off his ear so that his colleague could listen in. The ringing tone seemed to go on for ever.

'No answer. Must be a work number,' one of the men mused quietly.

Then the tone was a broken by a recorded message, with a detached female voice announcing 'You have reached the main number for the Defence Evaluation and Research Agency at Porton Down. There is nobody here to answer your call. Please try again tomorrow'.

'Not much bleedin' help,' cursed one of the men.

'No, but now we know where, all we have to find out is who,' said the other, folding his phone and putting it away.

★ ★ ★

Brennan walked Joe Fletcher down into Bradford and gave him the £200 that he withdrew from the cash-point machine on Church Street, Brennan's account still being in credit thanks to Mark Beattie's cheque. Then they crossed the road to the Swan Hotel and, while Fletcher booked himself in under an assumed name, Brennan waited in the bar. Janet had arrived home after Brennan had smuggled the air pistol out of the swing-bin and upstairs to his room. So, without having to go through the whole story in detail, she was happy to accept Brennan's guarantee that Fletcher was an innocent man on the run who had come to Brennan for refuge and support. Janet had even bought Brennan's proposal that she take Fletcher in to meet Mark the following morning so that a sympathetic lawyer could be found for him. He was part of their unfinished documentary after all.

Fletcher joined Brennan in the bar after checking in, and they took their drinks to a quiet corner.

'Can't thank you enough for your help, Mr Brennan,' Fletcher said suddenly, in the tone of a helpless teenager rather than that of the fearless activist.

'Well, I hope it works out for you. I'll tell my wife the key points of your defence and she can pass them on to whoever represents you. The police have strong circumstantial evidence against you, especially if this Dr Ashton has handed over the fake bomb to the authorities. But that's all it is, circumstantial. If you can find a reliable witness to say what you were doing the day that Gudgeon was killed, they won't actually be able to prove anything. So a good barrister should be able to take their case apart if it ever comes to court.'

'You should have been one yourself, Mr Brennan.'

'Well, I certainly spent enough time in court to qualify,' Brennan said with a smile.

'What are you going to do next, Mr Brennan?'

'I'm going to see Dr Ashton, your intended victim.'

Fletcher looked slightly alarmed at this prospect.

'That's going to drop me in it even more, isn't it?'

'Not if she's kept the box — it will prove that you intended no actual harm. If the police have already got their hands on it, I wouldn't put it past them to slip a little wedge of Semtex in there, so they can have a nice open-and-shut case. It *has* been known to happen.'

Brennan finished his drink and stood, gesturing for Fletcher to stay where he was.

'Relax, have a few drinks. If you want something to eat, the Dandy Lion has got a decent little restaurant upstairs.'

'I'd better just have a few sandwiches in my room.'

'Good luck tomorrow. Janet will be down about nine-fifteen to pick you up.'

'Thanks again, Mr Brennan.'

'One last thing,' Brennan said, turning back. 'Was it you and your mates who ambushed me in an alley up there and put a knife in my face?'

'Absolutely not, Mr Brennan. Promise,' Fletcher said, putting his right hand over his heart.

Brennan left quickly. Bradford was a small enough town for the arrival of a stranger to be noticed, especially if his face or description was likely to pop up on a 'Crimestoppers' feature at any moment. Although Brennan was happy to help Fletcher, he would have to keep him at arm's length or he would risk a charge of perverting the course of justice. Brennan could just imagine the look of glee on Tim Williams's face if that came about, not to mention the ensuing campaign of character assassination.

Janet had already gone some way to envisaging the same scenario.

'You should never have let him across the doorstep, Frank. Taking the side of the underdog is one thing, but pissing off the police in a big way is another. Let Mark handle it.'

'I intend to. Did you ring him?'

'Yes.'

'And?'

'He loves the idea of a documentary company coming to the aid of one of its subjects. He wants to film another interview with Fletcher tomorrow morning, with the solicitor present, of course.'

'Christ, he's risking more trouble than me by doing that.'

'The biggest risk Mark's taken is unloading

two and a half thousand quid on you, Frank. You're going to have come up with more ideas and set-ups for the film, you know?'

'I know, I know — I'm working on it right now,' Brennan said as he went to the cupboard and pulled out the bottle of Calvados. 'I have to tread carefully, though. There's just a chance that this Fletcher kid is lying through his teeth and is simply using me as his best line of defence.'

'If you think that, why have you set him up with help from Mark and me?'

'Because I want a second opinion. Your instincts are good, Jan. Especially when it comes to lying men.'

'Lot of practice,' Janet said with a grim smile. 'I'll warn Mark before we get in too deep.'

★ ★ ★

Janet phoned Brennan as soon as she got to the office the following morning to confirm that she had successfully picked up Joe Fletcher. Mark's lawyer was due in at eleven o'clock and, after the interview, they would follow his advice on how to proceed. Brennan was already planning an afternoon visit to Salisbury Police HQ to confront Detective Inspector Andrews about allowing an MI5 agent to sit in on his interview without telling him. He was, he told Janet, already rehearsing a speech about his civil liberties being infringed. They agreed to touch base in the afternoon, after Brennan had been updated about the police enquiry. Nothing would be decided about what to do with Fletcher until then.

Brennan set off for the Dandy Lion and his morning cappuccino with a spring in his step. He was ahead of the police, and felt morally justified in continuing his own investigation despite being a key witness in their case. In fact, the more he thought about it, the more convinced he was that he now had a licence to be a thoroughgoing pest. Brennan joined in with the Dandy Lion's writers' set for half an hour's chat about 'all the crap that gets made for TV these days', an ongoing theme as far as this particular bunch was concerned. Brennan modestly let slip his own minor entanglement with television by way of a documentary and was immediately welcomed as a spiritual brother whose future pain and suffering at the hands of treacherous producers would entitle him to full membership of their jokily self-pitying group.

'If you think you know when you've been

lied to as a journalist, Frank, it's ten times as hard to detect it from a television producer,' one of the writers warned him with a mocking laugh.

'The other early lesson to learn is that you mustn't expect the transmitted programme to bear any resemblance to the one you think you've been making. No matter how late you deliver it, the producer will always make changes behind your back.'

'You're not giving me much encouragement here, boys,' Brennan joked. 'But actually, at the moment, I seem to have been given a completely free hand.'

The three writers all looked at each other, pulling faces like the witches in *Macbeth* and shaking their heads in doubt.

'Noooo-ooh!' they wailed at Brennan in admonishment.

'Are you trying to say that I'm being naive?' Brennan asked, archly.

'Naive would be good, Frank,' said one. '*You're* still at the stages of trust and innocence.'

'But I classify myself as a quick learner,' Brennan said with a smile as he stood up. 'Anyone for another cappuccino, or do you have to get back to your PC screens?'

The writers all looked into their empty cups, debating for a nanosecond whether they should return to work. But then each of them, almost by instinct, looked up at Frank with grateful faces and said 'Yes, please'.

★ ★ ★

Mark Beattie conducted the introductions with well-practised charm as he closed the door to his office.

'Richard, this is my assistant producer and head researcher, Janet . . . '

'Pleased to meet you,' Janet said, shaking hands firmly and making good eye contact.

'And this is Joe, who may or may not be in a bit of trouble, partly of his own making, but also partly because he gave us an interview for a documentary we're filming.'

'Hi, Joe,' Richard said with a kind, reassuring smile.

'Just to say that Richard and I go back a very long way, junior school to be exact,' Mark confirmed. 'We grew up in the same rather rough neighbourhood, but while I've become a member of the trendy media classes, Richard has remained faithful to his roots and serves the local community with great diligence. All of which leaves me riddled with guilt, but that doesn't mean I defer to Richard. We understand each other well but will happily disagree with each other. All of

235

which, I hope, goes to assure you, Joe, that this is not a stitch-up. Richard will advise on what's best for you, rather than what's best for the company, OK?'

'Thanks, Mr Beattie,' Joe said shyly, intimidated by both the designer offices and the fact that a group of smart, articulate people seemed to have taken up his cause.

'OK, I'll order us all some coffee and then I suggest we show Richard the film of the interview so he can see what we're up against,' Mark said, before sticking his head out of the office and calling one of his young assistants to get the coffees in.

'Who did the interview?' Richard asked.

'My husband, Frank Brennan,' Janet said. 'It was meant to be part of a documentary on a possible incident at Porton Down. Then events took a turn for the worse with a farmer being killed by a small bomb that someone had fitted to his tractor. Joe is technically a prime suspect, but obviously denies he did it. Frank believes that the death may have been part of a wider conspiracy.'

'To do what?' Richard asked with a frown.

'To cover up what really happened, I guess.'

'Is Frank coming to this meeting?'

'No, he thought he'd be better out of it. Besides, he has a few questions to put to the police at Salisbury.'

'And he's going to see the lady I sent a package to,' Joe added in an attempt to be helpful.

'Package?' Richard asked, with a worried look.

'Joe?' Janet prompted.

'It was part of our campaign to frighten Porton scientists by sending them imitation bombs. No explosives or nothing. Just a few batteries and wires, with a warning note.'

'Saying what?' asked Richard curtly.

'Something along the lines of 'Stop what you're doing to animals, or the next one will be real'.'

Richard scratched the back of his head and grimaced, making a note on a yellow legal pad with his free hand.

'You realize that this lays you open to a minimum charge of threatening behaviour?'

'I didn't mean it.'

'I'm afraid that won't matter to the police. Even if they don't charge you with murder, they'll certainly have a go at nailing you for this,' Richard said before sighing deeply.

'OK, let's roll the film,' Mark said, inserting a cassette into the video player in his office.

★   ★   ★

'What's it about, Mr Brennan?' the sergeant on the reception desk asked warily.

'It's a confidential matter between myself and Detective Inspector Andrews,' Brennan said, with a confident smile.

'Does it relate to an ongoing inquiry?'

'Very much so.'

'Right, I'll see if I can track him down. He's a very busy man, you know?'

'I would hope so — that's what he's paid for,' Brennan retorted before retreating to a chair in the reception area. Brennan settled down for what he expected would be a long wait. He watched the sergeant go to his desk and pick up the phone, then turn his back on Brennan while he spoke into it. Brennan picked up a copy of a police magazine and began to browse idly through it. Seconds later, out of the corner of his eye, he saw the sergeant put down the phone and return to the reception desk.

'He'll be right down,' the sergeant said gruffly, disappointed by the visitor's little victory.

'Thank you very much, sergeant,' Brennan said with forced gratitude. He stood up and strolled around the reception area, scanning the various 'Have You Seen This Man?' posters. None of them included Joe Fletcher, masked or otherwise. Brennan switched on his mobile phone to see if there were any messages, but no tell-tale symbol appeared on the display screen. Brennan switched the phone off again and replaced it inside his jacket. The entrance door to the main body of the police station clicked open, and the head of DI Andrews appeared round it.

'Come through, Mr Brennan,' Andrews said brusquely, as though Brennan had interrupted his lunch or a key frame of snooker in the recreation room. Brennan followed him down a corridor and into an anonymous office. There was no glimpse to be had of the incident room for the Gudgeon murder case.

'What do you want, Mr Brennan? I'm very tied up with work at the moment,' Andrews said, looking at his watch for emphasis.

'Maybe I can help?'

'I'd rather you stayed out of it until summoned to the trial, actually.'

'Well, as a working journalist I have an interest in the case now.'

'I can arrange for a magistrate to make the point to you more forcefully, if you wish?'

'I'm sure he'd be very interested in you passing off an MI5 intelligence officer as a serving policeman.'

Andrews stiffened instantly.

'What the hell are you talking about, Brennan?'

'Shouldn't that be *Mr* Brennan?'

'Not if you're an interfering journalist. If you have a complaint, take it the PCA.'

'I'll take it to your Chief Constable. Or does he allow MI5 instant access to witnesses too? Or is 'Detective Sergeant Parker' just a Masonic chum of yours?'

'There are security implications in this case, Brennan. I can call in whoever I want.'

'I don't think you called anybody in. I think 'Parker' — first name 'Nosey', no doubt — invited himself onto this case because he has something to hide.'

'I'm not prepared to get into a discussion about operational matters with a fucking journalist, Brennan.'

'Falling back on the usual defence, eh?'

'You can go now.'

'Ah, but I have important information about the Gudgeon case.'

'You couldn't find a fart in a curry house, Brennan,' Andrews spat out, as he stood up and opened the door.

'I know where Joe Fletcher is, which is more than can be said for any of your men, including the dickhead from Five,' Brennan said, staying in his chair.

'Are you winding me up, Brennan? Because if you are, I'll have you up on a charge of wilfully obstructing justice.'

Brennan took out his mobile phone and switched it on, waiting for a signal to appear before dialling.

'Fletcher is with a solicitor at the office of the company for whom I'm making the documentary. He is willing to help you with your inquiries, not least to stop you from barking up the wrong tree,' Brennan said, before breaking off as his call was answered. 'Janet? It's me. I'm with Andrews at Salisbury nick — what did the brief decide? OK. Can you put him on to me?'

Andrews glowered at Brennan as this bizarre negotiation was discussed on police premises.

'Hi, yes, this is Brennan. I have DI Andrews here so I think you should speak directly to him about your client's position,' Brennan said, before handing the phone over to the detective. 'The brief's name is Richard Cochrane,' Brennan said helpfully.

'Andrews. Yes, Mr Cochrane, I would like very much to interview your client,' the detective said through gritted teeth. 'How soon can you get him down here? Right, four o'clock it will have to be, then. I look forward to seeing you both.'

Andrews passed the phone back to Brennan, who switched it off before returning it to his pocket.

'I'm waiting for a thank-you,' Brennan said sarcastically.

'You're lucky I don't nick you on the spot, Brennan. The moment you knew where Fletcher was, it was your duty as a citizen to call the police so that we could effect an arrest. Not to fix up the prime suspect in a murder case with a brief.'

'I'll remember next time. I expect you'll call another press conference now, won't you? You know, to announce how quickly you've tracked Fletcher down.'

'Listen to me, Brennan,' Andrews snarled, bringing his face right up to Brennan's. 'You are already a convicted criminal . . . '

'Ah, information you got from your mystery guest, no doubt?'

'If you get in my way on this case again, I'm sure it can be arranged for you to be put back inside.'

'Was that a threat, Detective Inspector?'

'Statement of the obvious, Brennan.'

Andrews pulled the door open, and nodded for Brennan to leave. As he passed, Andrews hissed deliberately into Brennan's ear.

'Take care of yourself. There are people out there who wouldn't mind you *dead*, Brennan.'

'Evenin' all,' Brennan said in retaliation, mockingly saluting the detective before walking away down the corridor.

10

Once Brennan had got clear of the police station, and the undoubted consternation he had left behind, he made a point of telephoning Luke Barrs to fill him in on the developments. Barrs was suitably grateful, but Brennan asked only a small favour in return — that DI Andrews should not be allowed to get away with any official 'show-boating at the press conference'.

'You know what I mean by that, Luke, don't you? It's when a senior policeman comes on television or into a briefing and announces that his men have made a significant breakthrough. But what he *really* means is that some Joe Public or other has done their work for them because they've been too dim or too lazy to see it through themselves.'

'I get the picture,' Barrs said down the phone. 'I'll give him a hard time, don't you worry.'

'Has your friend from the security services been back in touch?'

'No. Nor have I made any attempt to contact him.'

'Well, you'd better expect some activity now. Once the police have arrested Fletcher, the guy from Five will want more 'bodies' on the charge sheet to make him look good, too. And I've got a feeling he'll be after me next.'

'What are you going to do then, Frank?'

'If I tell you that, you'll only have to lie to him when he turns up in your office. Let's just say that I think *I'm* close to a breakthrough. You'll be the first to hear.'

'Good luck, Frank.'

Brennan switched his phone off and made his way back to his car. He looked around for parked cars or anonymous white vans with drivers 'innocently' reading a newspaper, but he couldn't see anybody as he scanned the immediate area. Brennan took the threat that Andrews had made against him seriously. He might not have had much respect for the police's methods or their general intelligence, but he knew that if they wanted to play it dirty they could suddenly become very competent. Most of the coppers of his professional acquaintance had, at some time, spouted the line about being able to clean out criminals and undesirables if only the law could be laid to one side. The very institution that they were obliged to uphold was an encumbrance as far as many of them were concerned. How much better life would be if they could just lock up those who they knew to be guilty rather than having to prove them to be so in a court of law!

For the security services, however, proof and legality were hardly a burden at all, with both concepts being readily disposable in the constant task of defending the realm. Now that Brennan had crossed both the police and the Big Boys, he had to assume that either — or both — could do their worst to him at any time. This meant him being on constant alert, not just in a physical sense, for 'tails' or other kinds of surveillance, but also mentally for any lapses by himself into smugness or over-confidence.

So, with due solemnity, Brennan completed two circuits around the police station and the surrounding streets before he could convince himself that none of the vehicles that appeared in his rear-view mirror was actually following him. Once out of Salisbury itself, he made one stop in a lay-by to monitor traffic movements both behind and ahead of him before resuming his journey with a fair certainty of being completely alone.

He found Dr Ashton's cottage with reasonable ease, not least because it was the only dwelling in a long stretch of the Ebble Valley, a lush hollow in a great sweep of the Wiltshire downs. Brennan parked his car further down the road, close to the gated entrance of a public footpath, to make it look like a walker had penetrated this secluded spot. He left his half-open map on the dashboard to enhance the impression. Brennan then walked back up the road towards the cottage, studying it as he went. It was of classic brick-and-flint construction, with a stone porch and small windows that were adorned with Mediterranean-style flower boxes. Brennan could see the geranium pots flanking the porch, corroborating Joe Fletcher's account of where he had placed his fake bomb. The neatly cropped lawn and immaculate flower-filled borders completed the image of rural perfection.

Although Brennan could see no car parked on the gravel arc to the side of the cottage, he approached the front porch in any case. Dr Ashton might have a husband or lover waiting at home with whom Brennan could establish a rapport before the scientist returned from work. Brennan found a brass bell-pull to the right of the half-panelled door. As he pulled, hearing the muffled brassy tinkle inside the house, he took the opportunity to peer through one of the glass panels.

To the left was a large living-room area, with an open fireplace set in the far wall. To the right, a smart, limed-oak fitted kitchen with a waxed pine table at the centre. There was no sign of another person in the house. Indeed, Brennan guessed from the needle-point cushions on the sofa and the pastel colours of the décor that this was definitely a lone woman's home.

Brennan retreated from the porch. There was nobody around, no neighbours and no passers-by. For a moment he had an irrational urge to break into the cottage to find what secrets it held, but then laughed at the thought of resorting to such low-rent methods. Instead, he moved around the front garden and down the side of the cottage where a stone patio, decked out with a table and four chairs, edged out into a neat lawn, with a small orchard beyond. To one side was a small, windowless stone barn that Brennan presumed to be a bespoke garden shed, given the amount of work that must have gone into keeping the cottage grounds so manicured and precise.

Brennan checked his watch. It had just gone 6.15 p.m., and he wondered if they worked overtime at Porton Down. He was just thinking about adjourning to a local pub when he heard the drone of a car's engine in the near distance. Brennan quickly returned to the road, as trespassing on Dr Ashton's property was probably not the ideal way to secure an interview with her. A smart Volvo estate appeared further up the road and then slowed before turning in to the cottage's parking area. Behind the wheel was a handsome blonde woman in her late thirties, not the mousey, bespectacled spinster that Brennan had imagined.

Brennan stayed behind the cottage's boundary wall, keeping his distance, knowing that the last thing a single woman wants to see when she returns home is a complete stranger hanging around her property. Dr Ashton opened the door to her car, and climbed half out of it, leaving herself the option of getting back in quickly.

'Can I help you?' she asked Brennan in that English way which suggests the sub-text 'Who the hell are you?'

'I'm terribly sorry to disturb you, Dr Ashton. My name is Frank Brennan. I'm a journalist and I need to ask you a couple of questions,' Brennan said, holding up his yellow laminated press card as reassurance. Brennan made no move towards her, nor did Dr Ashton leave the sanctuary of the car.

'What about?' she called.

'I'm investigating an animal rights group. One of its members claims that he left a fake bomb in your porch last week. I just wanted to confirm this with you.'

'It's a police matter, don't you think?'

'Yes, of course, but I don't believe they know anything about it yet. Did you report it to them?'

'That's my business, I'm afraid.'

Dr Ashton finally removed herself from the car and locked the door. She walked around the Volvo and began to cross the garden towards her front door. Brennan stayed where he was.

'Can I buy you a drink, Dr Ashton?'

'No, thank you,' she said with a first hint of a smile. 'But you can come in for a G&T if you want.'

Ashton opened her front door and went in, leaving the door open behind her. Brennan opened the garden gate and walked up the path to the cottage. He stepped slowly inside the cottage, carefully wiping his feet on the coconut matting inside the step. He peered around into the kitchen. Dr Ashton had taken her jacket off and was placing bottles of gin and tonic and two glasses on the table.

'Are you sure this is OK, Dr Ashton?'

'In what sense, Mr Brennan? You *are* old enough to drink, aren't you?'

'I meant about my coming into your home.'

'I invited you,' Dr Ashton said with a welcoming smile. Brennan noticed that despite — perhaps *because* of — the absence of make-up, she had really fine features, matched by dazzlingly green eyes.

'Ice and a slice?' she asked as she reached into the fridge.

'Perfect. This is a very pretty cottage, if you don't mind me saying so.'

'Thank you.'

Ashton placed three cubes of ice into each glass, poured a generous measure of gin over them and added a slice of lime to each glass before pouring in the tonic. She stirred the mixture with a teaspoon, then held out a glass for Brennan. He stepped forward to take it from her.

'Thank you. Very civilized.'

'Well, helps mark the divide between work and pleasure, I find.'

'Not a distinction that journalists of my age are used to making.'

'What paper do you work for, Mr Brennan?'

'I'm freelance. I used to be in what was called Fleet Street, but I work from home now. Moved down here about four years ago.'

'Here?'

'Bradford-on-Avon, to be precise.'

'Very pretty town. But I prefer my isolation. Which raises the question of how you found out about me?'

'It's a longish story. But basically I interviewed a young lad for a documentary I'm making. Somewhere in this process he confessed to placing a shoebox outside your home, filled with bomb-like equipment but without explosive.'

Dr Ashton put her drink down on the table and crossed to a cupboard. She opened the door and took out the box that Fletcher had left by her geranium pots. She walked across and handed it to Brennan.

'I'm normally more careful, but I opened this one. Lucky me, eh?'

Brennan lifted the lid and saw the tangle of batteries, timer and wires, together with the threatening note.

'Why didn't you report it?'

'Who said I didn't?'

'The police don't seem to know about it.'

'People like me have to report such things to a higher authority. You know where I work, presumably?'

Brennan nodded.

'So did you tell them?'

'Too much bother, Mr Brennan. We're all security risks there, so it seemed rather selfish to make a fuss about one incident. Besides, I'd have had MoD police protecting me night and day. Not what I want at all.'

'I'm afraid the police will get round to you eventually.'

'That's a drag. May I ask why?'

'Did you hear about the farmer who was killed last week?'

'I don't keep up with news too well. I switch off from everything as soon as I get home. A consequence of the work I do, I suppose.'

'Well, the man was killed by a bomb on his tractor.'

'My goodness. Not by the same chap who left this for me?'

'That would be the neat solution as far as the police are concerned, but I don't think it would be right. So I'm collecting evidence on his behalf. May I take this with me?'

Brennan pointed to the shoebox bomb.

'Won't the police object? I mean, I'd like to help, but I don't want to get into trouble. It could affect my job.'

Brennan paced around the table, sipping his drink.

'Unfortunately, I can't see any way that the police will leave you out of their inquiry. The animal rights chap is in custody now, being questioned. So at some stage they will turn up to interview you.'

'And they'll be pissed off that I didn't report this incident to them?'

'Yes, I'm sure they will. But, if you let me take the box to them, they can be pissed off with *me* instead. It may seem perverse, but the fact that the lad planted this harmless device may help his defence.'

'OK. Take it with you, then. I'll blame your powers of persuasion. Another drink?'

Brennan paused. He hadn't expected this to be easy, let alone sociable. But now it was all a breeze, which made him uncomfortable.

'I have to drive.'

'A small one, then.'

Dr Ashton poured two more measures of gin, splashes this time rather than slugs. Brennan watched her, wondering what an attractive woman like this did for the rest of the evening apart from knock back the gin.

'May I ask what you do at Porton Down?'

'I'm a microbiologist. Cheers.' Ashton clinked her glass against Brennan's.

'What does that involve?'

'Can't tell you,' Ashton said with a grin. 'I've signed the Official Secrets Act.'

'Bane of my life, in more ways than one,' Brennan said ruefully. 'I went to prison once for breaking it.'

'How exciting,' Ashton gushed.

'Six months in Erlestoke isn't exciting.'

'I'm sorry. I meant exciting in terms of your job. Isn't that what all journalists dream of, taking on the State?'

'Not so many these days.'

Brennan drained his drink.

'I ought to go.'

'Would you like supper?' Ashton asked suddenly, and Brennan sensed emptiness in her life. It didn't sound like she was propositioning him, though it was a flattering thought. She seemed more as though she needed some company to fill her perfect little cottage in its beautiful isolation.

'That's kind of you, but I must get this to the boy's lawyer tonight.'

Ashton nodded bravely.

'Some other time, perhaps?' she suggested.

'Sure. But on condition that I take you out to dinner.'

'I accept your condition, Mr Brennan.'

'Frank.'

'Mary,' Ashton said, extending her hand. Brennan shook it gently. Then he picked up the shoebox and made his way to the door.

'I don't suppose you know anything about a biological-warfare exercise last month? It took place on the land belonging to the farmer who was killed.'

'And you're investigating that too, I suppose?'

'There's no link yet, as far as I can see, but there may be one.'

'I'm sorry. I'm strictly a civilian employee. And even if I did know something, I wouldn't be able to tell you.'

'Of course. Sorry for asking. But thank you very much for your help. I'll be in touch.'

'I look forward to it,' Dr Ashton said as she closed the door behind him.

Brennan turned his car round on the road and headed back past the cottage on his way to Salisbury. Mary Ashton was out in her front garden, watering her plants, with her glass of gin and tonic in her hand. She waved cheerily to Brennan as he passed, as though he'd been a long-lost friend paying her a visit. Ashton was plainly a bright and attractive woman, with a high-powered job, but it seemed to Brennan, perhaps presumptuously, that she was making a premature bid for dotty spinsterdom. Brennan wondered what unhappiness in her life had brought her to such a state of brittle isolation.

Before he rejoined the wider road up to Wilton, Brennan parked the car, took a long pee in the hedgerow and then found a packet of mints in the glove compartment, filling his mouth with three of them at the same time. He couldn't take the risk of turning up at the police station either looking or smelling pissed. With the evening rush-hour traffic having melted away, Brennan reached the police HQ much faster than he thought. However, an obstructive woman constable at the reception desk, who wouldn't acknowledge that Cochrane and Fletcher were at the station, stymied his hopes of a quick getaway.

'Look, I know you're only doing your job, constable,' Brennan pleaded 'but I have important information and evidence to pass on to Mr Cochrane on behalf of his client, Joe Fletcher.'

'I cannot confirm or deny the presence of these men,' the WPC repeated robotically.

'Can I see Detective Inspector Andrews, then?'

'Not without an appointment.'

'Can I make one for, say, five minutes' time?'

'I cannot confirm or deny his presence, Mr Brennan.'

'I'll just sit down and wait in that case,' Brennan said petulantly as he retreated to a chair in the reception area with his shoebox. He knew that he probably looked a bit of a madman but, even allowing for that, Brennan was convinced that Andrews had put out an 'all-points bulletin' in an attempt to freeze him out of the inquiry. Brennan imagined there might be one of those computer-generated images of himself behind the desk, instructing the entire force to 'cock him a deaf 'un', as the Cockney criminal parlance had it.

Brennan took out his mobile phone and began to dial his home number.

'Sorry, can you make that call outside, please?' the WPC said firmly.

'Why? I've got nothing to hide.'

'It might interfere with our radio traffic. So outside or not at all.'

Brennan stood up and took his phone and the shoebox outside with him. He redialled the number and was hugely relieved to hear Janet's voice.

'Jan, it's me. Have you got a mobile number for Cochrane?'

'Not to hand. I'll have to ring Mark to get it. What's up?'

'Don't ask. They did go to Salisbury police station this afternoon, didn't they?'

'Yes, set off about three-thirty. Are they not there?'

'There's a WPC who's refusing to tell me.'

'Right. I'll call you back in a moment.'

Brennan paced along the steps outside the police station, muttering to himself. He calculated the journey time from Bristol to Salisbury, how long it would take for Andrews to interview Fletcher and then organize one of his inevitable press conferences. They *had* to be still in the building

. . . unless MI-fucking-5 had stepped in to claim *droit de seigneur* on the case. That would explain Brennan being blanked, and even the WPC's stolid ignorance. They'd be able to hold Fletcher for seven days under the anti-terrorist laws and kill any publicity about the case for the same length of time. His phone rang to interrupt his *sotto voce* rant. Janet gave him Cochrane's number, but when Brennan dialled there was only the lawyer's message service on the line. Brennan left his own number and a request for information. Now he had to decide whether to wait there in Salisbury for a few hours or to return home. Then he remembered Luke Barrs — he would know where Andrews was.

He fumbled for the editor's business card, but eventually found it in the deepest recesses of his wallet. Brennan tried the office first, but there was only an answering machine. Then he tried the mobile, but a female voice told him it was switched off. Finally he tried Luke's home number where there was neither a response nor an answering machine. Brennan felt like chucking his mobile phone under a bus. For every possibility it created for communication, the frustrations increased exponentially. It seemed that people became harder to track down because they knew that they could hide behind an indirect system of pagers, faxes, answering machines and e-mails.

'Bollocks,' Brennan said out loud, as a constable returning from foot patrol passed him on the steps.

'Sorry, officer,' Brennan apologized. Then his phone rang to spare him further embarrassment. It was Cochrane.

'Where are you?' Brennan asked urgently.

'Still in Salisbury nick with Fletcher. They're taking a break from questioning. He's been arrested but not charged.'

'I'm right outside. I've got the fake bomb with me. Only the WPC on the desk won't admit you're there.'

'I'll come out. See you in a moment.'

Brennan switched his phone off and went back inside the police station. The WPC eyed him malevolently, as though he was a drunk reporting a sighting of a flying saucer.

'Mr Cochrane is coming out to see me,' Brennan said tartly. Moments later, Cochrane appeared at the security door and was allowed out by a uniformed officer. He crossed to where Brennan was standing.

'How's it going?' Brennan asked.

'It's tough. They think they've got him but he's holding up well under the pressure.'

'Good. Here's the, uh . . . evidence. Dr Ashton had kept it. She can provide a statement when you need it,' Brennan said as he handed over the shoebox 'bomb'.

'Thanks. I hope it helps. Better get back in. I'll phone you later.'

'Fine. Good luck.'

Cochrane headed back towards the door.

'By the way, I've asked your wife to pass on details of a few weird things that have been happening to me. Perhaps you could help me out if you have time?'

'Sure. Happy to oblige,' Brennan said with a brave face. Inside, his heart was sinking. He could feel a 'favour' coming on, whereby someone who was being paid to do his job expected Brennan to do something for nothing in return. Brennan made his way out without a backward look at the WPC and walked quickly to his car. This time he didn't even check if anybody was following him. He simply wanted to get home.

* * *

Mary Ashton was just settling down to her grilled chicken breast with tarragon sauce when the phone rang. The opera she was listening to on Radio 3 was reaching its climax too, so she felt inclined to let the bloody phone ring without answering. She sipped some more red wine and took a mouthful of the chicken. Even though she'd cooked it herself, it tasted fine. Still the phone rang. She guessed that it might be this Brennan chap who had suddenly walked into her quiet life and disturbed it. Then she thought it might be the police, calling to complain to her for not reporting a serious incident. Leaning back in her chair, she picked up the receiver.

'Yes?'

'Hello. I'm a friend of the late David Southwell's,' said a male voice that she didn't recognize at all. 'I found this number on his phone bill and wondered if you knew that he'd died?'

'I'm sorry, but I think you must have the wrong number. I don't know anybody named David Southwell,' Ashton said calmly.

'But he rang you three times on the night of the eighteenth of July . . . '

'He may well have done but he must have been dialling incorrectly.'

'Oh. OK. May I ask your name then?'

'No, certainly not. Go away.'

Ashton slammed the phone down, then switched the answering machine on. Realizing that her name was on the recorded message, she switched it off and took the phone off the hook. She returned to her plate of food but found that her appetite had gone. She took another slug of red wine and turned up the volume of the opera on the radio to maximum, grateful that there were no neighbours to complain about the noise.

★　★　★

Brennan trudged into the house hallucinating about a bowl of seafood pasta and a bottle of Barolo, so exhausted and famished was he by the events and strain of the day. Janet had anticipated this, having noted the tetchy tone in his phone call a few hours earlier. While the red wine, Chilean as it happened, was open and ready on the table, Janet had taken the precaution of making a slow-cooking pork casserole, knowing from past experience that Brennan's estimates of his arrival time at home were often way out. Indeed, deep in Janet's memory still lurked a vivid cameo from a decade ago when Brennan had failed to turn up at a dinner party in his own home, having gone off on the piss with colleagues from the paper. Janet had waited up in the kitchen until he came home at close to 2.30 a.m. and staggered into the kitchen. Seeing Janet sitting at the table on which rested his uneaten portion of the supper, Brennan had charitably announced that he wasn't hungry, whereupon Janet had chucked the plate at him like a discus, just missing his head.

Tonight, though, Brennan fell into her arms in gratitude.

'Bless you. I thought about phoning through with an order but I thought you might go off your hostess trolley.'

'Go and have a shower, and I'll serve this up in five minutes.'

Brennan nodded, poured himself a glass of wine to take upstairs and toasted Janet with it as he left the room. In the shower the torrent of hot water stopped his head spinning. Dr Ashton's gin and tonics had certainly contributed to this, but it had been the sheer volume of new information that had sent Brennan's brain into overload. By the time he came down to the table, wearing just his dressing gown, Brennan had sifted the data into a coherent order — the threatening tantrum from DI Andrews, the bizarre encounter with Dr Ashton, the validation of Joe Fletcher's bomb-planting story and finally Richard Cochrane's angling for help. Brennan admitted that it had almost been too much for him.

'I think you'll find that Cochrane is on our side, actually. He's charging Mark the bare minimum for this case. It was also very good of him to take Fletcher on at short notice. He doesn't seem like a taker or a self-promoter, either.'

'Sorry, I misjudged him. I was tired. And you know what it's like when someone you've just met looks as though they want something out of you? I mean, it's a bit like being a doctor. Every time you go to a party, somebody will come up to you and say 'I've got this pain in my shoulder, any idea what it might be?' That's how it is for me, sometimes.'

'You didn't think much of his story, then?'

'He didn't tell me about it. Just said that you had all the details.'

'Well, I think he's being a little paranoid. He was appointed to finalize the estate of this guy who killed himself. But since he took on the work, his office has been broken into, with the file on the client being stolen. And then the dead guy's house was apparently ransacked. It has to be said, though, that both Cochrane's office and the house are not in one of Bristol's nicer areas.'

Brennan sat forward, with some puzzlement on his face.

'If burglary is a common occurrence, what's he getting so worked up about?'

'Well, the fact that whoever it was took only this client's file. And that two well-dressed men posing as buyers to an estate agent are thought to be involved in the break-in at the house.'

'What did the dead guy do for a living?'

'Apparently he was a pen-pusher at Abbey Wood.'

'What, the MoD building?'

'Yes. He was found hanging on the station platform outside. It seems as though he'd been deeply worried about redundancy.'

Janet got off her chair and crossed the kitchen to the dresser where her shoulder bag had been dumped. She began searching inside it.

'I went back through the Bristol papers and found a mention of the inquest.'

Janet returned to the table with a cutting no longer than two inches.

'David Southwell,' she said as she handed Brennan the fragment of newsprint. Brennan scanned while he ate. Then paused to look across at Janet.

'His body was found in the early hours of the nineteenth of July,' Brennan said meaningfully.

'So?'

'The night I saw the soldiers and the dead cattle was the eighteenth.'

'Sorry, I don't see the significance. Abbey Wood's sixty or seventy miles from where we were.'

'I know, I know. Just seems an odd sort of coincidence — Porton Down and Abbey Wood are both MoD establishments.'

'Of a widely different nature, employing several thousand people between them. Don't complicate matters for yourself, Frank.'

'I may not have the time,' Brennan said with an innocent shrug.

'Well, let *me* ask around about it. I'm working in Bristol anyway.'

'I don't see that much that you can do, Jan. The inquest's done and dusted. The police are hardly likely to be interested in the theft of a legal file on a dead person. People blagging their way into an empty house is nothing to get excited about. You'd have to find out what was so interesting about this Southwell chap. But you won't get anywhere with the MoD, even though he's dead.'

'You're trying to get onto this yourself, aren't you, Frank?'

'How can I be carpet-bagging? You're the one telling me that we should help Cochrane out. He asked me to do him a favour.'

'Don't bullshit me, Frank. I know your ways. You're interested in this because, in your warped, conspiratorial view of the world, you think it connects with your other investigation. And you're such a control freak that you won't let me anywhere near it.'

266

Brennan stuffed a forkful of food into his mouth.

'And now you're buying time by eating, you slippery sod,' Janet said with a knowing smile.

Brennan *ummed* his innocence through his mouthful of food, and Janet knew that was as far as she was going to get with him that night.

★　★　★

The following morning, Brennan slipped out of bed while Janet was still asleep. He dressed downstairs and let himself out of the house without making the slightest noise. He caught the 8.08 train from Bradford as he had planned, watching shop girls and office workers clamber blearily on board as the train stopped at Avoncliff, Freshford, Bath, and then Oldfield Park. The smell of scent, aftershave and freshly shampooed hair wafted through the carriage. Brennan watched the to-ing and fro-ing of people with regular jobs with a detached bewilderment. How could they cope with such routine? Were they all having sex in the office as a way of sustaining their self-belief? But now, with most of the commuters decanted at either Bath or Bristol, a dozen or so remained on the train.

Sober-suited gentlemen with leather brief-cases, from whom Brennan, in his jeans and polo shirt, stood out like the village scruff.

At Filton Abbey Wood, the station specifically built for the MoD complex, the suited men got off. Brennan followed them down the platform, up over the footbridge, and then onto the path that led to the pedestrian entrance to the huge spread of buildings. Brennan watched as the men in grey flashed their security passes to the MoD police at the gate. Brennan retreated to the platform where David Southwell had ended his life. He studied the design of the shelter in which Southwell had somehow managed to suspend his body. And then, as he moved around the shelter, he saw the MoD security cameras high above the station that would have recorded the last moments of South-well's life.

11

When Janet arrived at her office just after ten, she was both surprised and irritated to find Brennan already there, sipping coffee and chatting with Mark Beattie. Brennan's furtive early-morning departures always suggested to her that he was up to something dangerous or irresponsible and was trying to avoid her disapproval. But it looked as though this particular excursion had been planned to outflank her on her own territory.

'Thanks for the note,' Janet said with leaden irony as Brennan stood up to kiss her.

'I just woke up early and thought I'd get on.'

'With?'

'I'll get you a coffee, Janet,' Mark said, tactfully removing himself from the conflict. 'Frank's come up with some interesting new evidence.'

Janet looked fiercely at Brennan once they were alone.

'So — partners but not partners?'

'Janet, I had an idea that I wanted to follow up after last night.'

'And this just happens to involve you seeing my boss before I can get to him.'

'What are you talking about? I didn't come here first. I've been up to the railway station where this Southwell guy killed himself. Then I contacted Cochrane and arranged to meet him here. This wasn't an attempt to keep you out of the loop, because there is no loop. Not yet, anyway.'

'What's new, then?'

Behind Janet, Brennan could see a weary-looking Cochrane arriving, pausing at the coffee machine to talk to Mark Beattie.

'Cochrane's here. I'd best wait until we're all together.'

'OK, but just tell me what made you decide to go to Abbey Wood — apart from sheer bloody-mindedness, that is?'

'I needed to get an idea of the place before I started erecting any new theories, I suppose. I mean, I've been past the complex dozens of times without really taking it in.'

Mark escorted Cochrane into the office, a comforting arm round his shoulder.

'They charged Joe Fletcher with murder at one o'clock this morning,' Beattie reported. 'Richard didn't get to bed until three.'

'I'm afraid the shoebox bomb was viewed as damning evidence at this stage,' Cochrane said, with a beady look at Brennan.

'How did Joe take it?' Brennan asked in return.

'He was a bit shocked by the formal procedure of being charged, but he thinks he'll cope with being on remand all right. He's scheduled to appear before a Salisbury court this afternoon. I'm on my way down there shortly.'

'I didn't mean to burden you even more, but when Janet told me about the Southwell case . . .'

'Sure, sure — anything you can do to shed some light would be welcome, Frank. Although, obviously, Fletcher takes priority over a dead man now.'

'Well, maybe one can help the other,' Brennan said with a deliberate hint of *misterioso*.

'I'm afraid that Frank thinks there may be a connection,' Janet cautioned the others before Brennan could lure them any closer to his line of thinking.

Beattie looked excitedly at Brennan, sensing further opportunities to make an impact on television.

'Give it to us, Frank!'

'There may not be that much. But I have three pieces to play with. In the first instance, Southwell appears to have died roughly six to eight hours after I witnessed this chemical-warfare exercise at Breakheart Lodge.'

'Wow,' Mark purred.

'Hang on — at the moment they are two unrelated facts, a coincidence. As Janet has told me several times, I can have a fevered imagination. But there is at least a vague MoD connection, which is probably nothing but *might* be worth exploring.'

'Southwell was in the army before he became a suit with Defence Procurement,' Cochrane added. Mark made a note on his ever-present yellow pad.

'The second element I want to mention is that I now have fairly convincing proof that MI5 are onto me and the Fletcher case. They may well have been involved with Southwell too, for reasons we don't yet know.'

'This is a bit of a hop, step and jump, isn't it, Frank?' Janet said sceptically.

'Look, I know that two men threatened me with a knife early on in this case. They made out they were from the animal rights militia but I'm not so sure. There was a bogus policeman sitting in on my talk to Andrews. Almost certainly the Branch or Five. From what Richard has reported, a burglary in his office and two guys ransacking Southwell's house, I'd lay odds on the same people being involved.'

'Frank, you're trying rather desperately to yoke two separate incidents together. And given what happened in Salisbury, and at

Abbey Wood, why *shouldn't* the security services be involved?'

'Salisbury, certainly. Why Southwell, though? A boozer and a nobody, about to get the sack, who decides to top himself outside the office as a last 'fuck-you' to his employers? A bloke like that wouldn't be worth this level of fuss. And remember, all this is taking place *after* his death. Unless they've got a ouija board, what can he tell them? So they must be after something he left behind.'

'Even so, it would be pretty difficult to open up another line of inquiry in one half-hour documentary, Frank.'

'I know that, but to be honest, Mark, I don't care. This is what we talked about at the outset — keeping an open mind rather than travelling down a single track. We have to be prepared to take other routes — because that's the way I work. If you don't like that or it's too expensive, you can drop me out.'

'Stop being pompous, Frank,' Janet said with a scowl.

'We can discuss this matter after Richard's gone,' Mark said, assuming the role of chairman. 'Now, is there anything else you want to pass on, Frank?'

'Maybe. I need to know about the inquest — who appeared before the coroner, what evidence was submitted and so on.'

'Well, briefly,' Cochrane said, with a sigh, 'it was open and shut within a morning. The pathologist's evidence stood up well. There was the Human Resources Manager for Abbey Wood who spoke about Southwell's likely redundancy. There was the rail driver who first saw the body and called in, and four MoD policemen who attended the scene.'

'What did they say?' Brennan asked eagerly.

'I don't recall in detail. Just how they found Southwell.'

'How did they know he was there?'

'I'm sorry?'

'If the train driver was the first to report a sighting, who told them? Him, the regular police, who? More importantly, why did they *have* to be told when there are two security cameras scanning the platform and the footpaths? If they were doing their jobs properly, they should at least have seen the body, perhaps even the poor bastard actually stringing himself up.'

Cochrane looked distinctly troubled by what Brennan had said.

'I'm sorry, but nothing like this was discussed at the inquest. Nobody mentioned cameras. Everyone assumed it was straight-forward.'

'Did you not think to ask about the precise sequence of events?' Brennan asked.

'Look, I was landed with this case. I didn't know Southwell at all. Never met him. I was just appointed by the coroner. I get a lot of low-rent work like that, rough sleepers found dead in doorways, jumpers from Clifton Bridge whose families are long gone. Somebody has to clean up the legal mess these people leave behind.'

'What was the coroner's name?'

'Mr Charles Morrison.'

'And if I went to him with these questions, what kind of reception would I get?'

'I don't know. Legally, if there's new evidence, he has the power to call a second inquest.'

'Would you object if I went to see him?'

'Well, it might have more clout coming from me — as a lawyer, that is.'

'But you've got your hands full with Joe Fletcher.'

Cochrane nodded and shifted uneasily on his chair.

'You'd better be on your way, Richard,' Mark said. Cochrane gratefully seized the chance to make his exit. Brennan allowed a silence to settle while Cochrane left the building. Janet glared at Brennan for his roasting of Cochrane.

'Interesting stuff, Frank,' Mark said.

'Perhaps. I know Richard's your friend, Mark, but do you think he's up to defending Joe Fletcher?'

'A barrister will do that in due course,' Janet said pointedly.

'You know what I mean. He's up against heavy-duty people down there who will do their worst to put Fletcher away for life.'

'At this moment, I'm paying his fees as part of the company's commitment to defending Fletcher,' Mark said. 'Until such time as I'm unhappy, he stays on the case.'

Beattie raised himself from his chair, folded his yellow pad closed and stood at the door.

'Perhaps you could let Janet know a few of your ideas for further filming, Frank. At the moment we have one sequence which we will almost certainly be unable to use while Fletcher's trial is pending.'

Mark closed the door shut behind him.

'You prick, Frank,' Janet hissed.

'I don't think so, my love. Save your scorn for your boss's mate. But for his professional ineptitude, we might have had the MoD by the short-and-curlies, which might in turn have helped me put some pressure on Tim Williams.'

'Frank, you're becoming a serial fantasist. There's no connection between this and what you're investigating, and even that is beginning to look decidedly cut and dried. Mark's paid you good money. I suggest you get out there and start earning it.'

Brennan stood up and headed for the door, plainly intent on not speaking to Janet as he left.

'The camera's still at the house if you care to use it,' she added as he left. She watched him stalk his way through the outer office, resolving at that moment to pay Mark back the money herself if Brennan didn't shape up over the next few days. She was also determined to stand her ground on this issue. Her husband's arrogance was fine when it fuelled a genuine sense of purpose, but almost unbearable when he refused to accept that he had lost the plot.

★ ★ ★

DI Andrews had just managed to catch Mary Ashton as she was leaving for work, his car very nearly running into hers as it pulled out of the parking area next to her cottage. Though she was irritated by the unannounced appearance, Mary knew that it was better to have the police turning up here than at Porton Down. One set of questions was more than enough to answer. At first she had feigned anger at his driving, and then mystification at a police presence so early in the morning. But then Andrews had produced the shoebox bomb, now sealed in a plastic bag. At this point, Andrews had let loose a barely controlled tirade about her withholding vital evidence from the police and then releasing said evidence to a scumbag freelance journo like Brennan.

'Perhaps that was because Mr Brennan had the wit to find me, Inspector,' she had snapped back, prompting another volley of abuse that was topped off with a warning that she might well have to face police charges of obstruction in due course. He had then asked her to confirm her identification of the 'bomb' and the date of its discovery and, rather grudgingly, she had obliged. Andrews had then told her to report to Salisbury police station at six that night to make a formal statement, warning Ashton that if she didn't turn up he would 'throw the book at her'. Mary had resisted the temptation to ask what book he had in mind and had closed her car window and driven off with a surge of acceleration that was designed to show her anger at his overbearing manner.

★   ★   ★

Brennan returned home on a train from Bristol, knowing that a change of clothes would be essential if he was to fluke a quick appointment with the coroner for the same day. He knocked up a mushroom omelette for lunch in the kitchen and switched on the television as he ate. The local BBC news led with the appearance in court of Joe Fletcher, who had been charged with the murder of Edgar Gudgeon. The reporter stood outside the Salisbury Crown Court giving the bare details of the case. The report showed the traditional arrival of the police van containing Fletcher and its subsequent departure after he had been charged and remanded, both events taking place against the background of noisy demonstrations by animal rights supporters who waved placards proclaiming Fletcher's innocence. Brennan smiled in support of their defiance. Fletcher would feel less alone when he heard their chants, while the police would realize that they had a high-profile case on their hands, one that they couldn't just shuffle quietly to the bottom of the pile. Brennan caught a glimpse of Richard Cochrane leaving the court with DI Andrews and two colleagues behind him. Then there was a shot of Breakheart Lodge, filmed on the day of the explosion, with police tape sealing off the track. The report ended and

Brennan switched the television off with the remote control.

As he ate, Brennan considered just how much detail would eventually come out in court when the case came to trial, and indeed what else he might uncover before that even happened. He even enjoyed a short-lived fantasy of being alongside Joe Fletcher as he walked free before the case came to court, after dramatic evidence that Brennan had uncovered forced the police to drop all charges. It was good to dream occasionally. Brennan's thoughts were disturbed by a noise from upstairs. At first it was just a scuffling noise, but then it became the distinct sound of footsteps.

Brennan edged across to the stairwell and looked up. The noise stopped. Then he saw Lester's face, topped with tousled hair, staring down at him.

'Afternoon, Lester. What time did you check in?'

'About ten this morning, dad. Went to an all-night party. There was nobody around when I got back.'

'Well, your mother and I have to work in order to support your lifestyle.'

'What time is it now?' asked Lester blearily.

'Just gone half-one. Do you want some lunch?'

'No, thanks. Well, maybe, actually.'

'Perhaps I should call it breakfast to fit in with your body clock.'

Lester fell silent suddenly.

'You promise you won't get angry?'

'I have to know what I'm not supposed to get angry about first.'

'Jasmine's with me. You remember?'

'I do. So, she's in the spare bed, right?'

'Not exactly.'

'Ah, so I'm not to get angry about you shagging during the day, is that it?'

Lester nodded.

'Look, take a shower, get changed, then you can both come down and I'll cook you some lunch.'

'Actually, would you mind going out, Dad? She's a bit embarrassed to come down while you're here. I told her you wouldn't throw a wobbler or anything, but you know.'

'Yes, I know,' Brennan said patiently. 'Can I get changed before I go out?'

'Sure, sure. No problem.' Lester said, cheering up.

'And you'll tidy up before mum gets back, won't you?'

'You're safe,' Lester said with a nod.

'Right. You'd better get back into your love nest then.'

'Thanks, dad. You're a top man.'

Lester scuttled back upstairs to his room, leaving Brennan on his own again. He couldn't find it in himself to get angry with Lester, although he was aware that there were reactionary thoughts rushing around inside his head, their effect only quelled by Brennan's desire to be seen as a liberal parent. While he was grateful for this, he was at the same time aware that he just didn't know how Janet would react, or even if he should tell her. Maybe she should just find out for herself at some stage — but then, if Janet discovered that he had known all along, it would be a nightmare. Brennan banished the confusion from his mind as he moved quickly upstairs to get changed. After putting on a shirt and tie, and the one suit in his possession, he raced back downstairs and found the number for the Bristol coroner's office in the directory, then loaded it into the memory of his mobile phone.

Brennan left the house and felt a surge of relief wash over him. What the *Guardian* would term his 'parenting skills' had never come up to scratch, although the settled relationship he'd enjoyed with Janet since the move to Bradford had certainly helped Lester during his adolescent years. But now that Brennan's son was suddenly a young man with an active sex life, the realization began to sink in that Lester would be gone in a few years, out of the house, leading a life of his own. Brennan felt a spasm of guilt and panic — guilt that he hadn't been a good enough father, panic because the chance of achieving that goal was now receding by the day.

Brennan paused by his car and phoned the number for the coroner's office in Bristol. The coroner himself was not available, but one of his officers was. Brennan explained to the rather starchy-voiced lady that he had urgent information, perhaps even new evidence, that might affect the verdict in a recent case, but her façade of officialdom was impenetrable. No, he couldn't leave a message for the coroner, nor come in today and talk to one of his officers. The correct procedure would be a letter, detailing his points.

'How do you feel about a fax?' Brennan asked tersely, aware of the smutty innuendo he was ladling onto the question. The secretary didn't pick up on it in any case. A fax would be acceptable, provided that Brennan declared his status and any interest he had in the case, or any connection he had to the deceased. He would also have to give his phone number and address on the understanding that he was not to pester the coroner but to let him get in touch in due course.

'I appreciate your caution about not allowing any old nutter access to your boss,' Brennan said with unrestrained sarcasm, 'but if my reading of the situation is correct I will be able to spare him considerable embarrassment, and quite possibly save his job from going down the toilet.'

There was a profound silence at the other end of the phone.

'Now — do you want the number of my mobile phone or don't you?'

★ ★ ★

The MI5 man arrived without an appointment to see Luke Barrs, giving 'Parker' as his name. Barrs broke away from his desk and stalked out of his office and down the staircase to reception, forcing a smile onto his face.

'Sorry to bother you, Luke,' 'Parker' said as he stretched out his hand to shake Barrs's.

'That's OK,' Barrs said politely.

'Can I just have a couple of minutes?'

'We go to press this afternoon, actually, so I'm a bit up against it.'

'It will only take a few seconds, and it may save you some bother,' 'Parker' said with a thin smile, nodding for Barrs to follow him as he moved to the quietest corner of the reception area. Barrs followed dutifully, hoping that the receptionist wasn't watching too closely.

'Look, I haven't had time to think about your offer yet,' Barrs said, trying to pre-empt any pressure from 'Parker'.

'No rush, Luke. In a few weeks, when all this fuss has blown over, we'll have a lunch and see how you feel then.'

Barrs nodded.

'In the meantime, I just want you to finesse a few details in your reporting of the Fletcher case.'

'In what way?' Barrs asked firmly.

'Well, we're aware that Mr Brennan has been putting around various bits and pieces about his involvement in the case. Interviewing Fletcher and so on.'

'But that's already appeared on television. It's in the public domain.'

'We'd rather it wasn't, so we'd be grateful if you could drop that out of the story. In fact, we don't want any mention of Brennan in it at all. Not the fact that he was a witness to Gudgeon getting barbecued, nor anything about his former career. And keep Porton Down out of it if you can. Leave it all for the court case. And then, when Fletcher goes down, we'll make sure you get the inside line on what happened. Look on it as a trade-off.

A little bit less for your paper now in exchange for a lot more later.'

'People will have seen Brennan's interview with Fletcher on the news. They will have heard Fletcher make threats against Porton Down staff. How can I possibly lose stuff like that?'

'Those that know can know. But those that don't, needn't — if you see what I mean. There is a lot of potential aggravation for the whole area if this case gets too lurid. And we can't have DERA Porton Down in the front line. It's bad for business, the local economy, everything.'

Barrs checked his watch, anxious about his production deadlines.

'Look, I need something from you now that tells me you won't stiff me on this,' Barrs said with sudden boldness. 'Parker' looked pained that a young kid could start bargaining with him.

'Such as?'

'Such as something you know now that hasn't come out yet but may do later. Look on it as a trade-off,' Barrs said, somewhat cheekily.

'OK. This probably won't come out in court so you won't be able to use it anyway, but we think that old man Gudgeon was probably not the real target,' whispered

'Parker'. 'His son, Nathaniel, works in the animal husbandry section of Porton Down. You know, rearing animals for experimentation. But, like I said, we'd prefer things to be quiet on that front.'

'OK, thanks. I must go,' Barrs said, shaking hands again as he turned and headed back up the stairs, taking them two at a time.

'Cheeky little sod,' mouthed 'Parker' as he left the newspaper reception area without a backward glance.

* * *

Brennan kept his mobile phone switched on, leaving it lying in anticipation on the passenger seat next to him as he drove down to Salisbury. But nobody called, least of all the Bristol coroner. By way of killing time, Brennan took a route that would pass Breakheart Lodge, on the off chance of getting a civilized word from Gudgeon junior. But, as he approached the entrance to the farm, he could see an estate agent's large sign announcing the sale of the property and its land. Brennan parked on the drive and made a note of the agency number. His initial surprise at seeing the sign soon gave way to a more sympathetic logic. Gudgeon junior had seemed a bright if introverted chap, and it couldn't have been much fun for him living and working under his father's foul-mouthed rule. Equally, the place would probably hold few pleasant memories, given the violent circumstances of the old man's death. Brennan drove on up the lane to the farmhouse itself, hoping to pass on his sympathies.

As he drove, he noticed that the cows had disappeared from the field to his left, presumably to market — unless, of course, the army had sent a Chinook helicopter to collect them for another 'exercise'. Brennan arrived in the main yard of the farm, and although much of the major equipment was still on view, the milking shed and other outbuildings were padlocked shut. Brennan got out of his car and walked across to the house itself. There was no sign of life. No car, no farmyard pets running around and, as he listened at the door, no sounds of movement inside the house. It looked as though Brennan would have to make an appointment with the estate agent to get to talk to the surviving Gudgeon. Dutifully, Brennan shot a few minutes' footage of the deserted farm with his digital camera, improvising a voice-over about 'mysterious events' while trying not to sound like Edward Woodward.

Brennan was walking back to his car when

he heard his phone ringing. He broke into a run and pressed the answer button.

'Hello. Brennan here,' he said, panting slightly at the sudden exertion.

'This is the coroner's office in Bristol,' said the starched female voice. 'The coroner will see you in his office at 2.30 p.m. tomorrow.'

'Fine,' Brennan said, and the phone was hung up without further ceremony. 'No lunch on offer, then,' Brennan mumbled to himself as he got back in the car and set off for Salisbury. Half an hour later he was at the reception desk of the *Salisbury Gazette*, only to be told that Luke Barrs had gone to the printer's to watch this week's edition rolling off the presses. The receptionist didn't use those words exactly, but they were the ones conjured up in Brennan's mind and were still capable of producing potent memories of the nights when he'd been allowed down onto the printing floor to watch one of his front-page stories appearing, still smelling pungently of ink. Brennan left a message, requesting that Barrs contact him, recalling that e-mail was probably the safest form of communication between them while MI5 were still sniffing around.

Brennan wandered around Salisbury for half an hour before phoning Mary Ashton. It was just past five o'clock, so he hardly expected her to be at home. Instead, he got a terse message on her answering machine, asking for the caller's name and number to be left without giving out her own. Brennan managed to mumble a message about hoping she was OK, wondering if the police had been in touch with her and, as an apparently innocent afterthought, whether she wanted to have dinner with him that night.

Brennan switched off his phone, hardly daring to acknowledge what had prompted him to get back in touch with Mary Ashton so soon. Yes, she could well be a vital witness for the defence at the trial of Joe Fletcher. Yes, there was the possibility he had glimpsed that she might loosen up and talk about what went on, and had gone on, at Porton Down. But there was another element at work, one that Brennan pushed to the margins of his mind, and that was a raw sexual attraction for Mary Ashton that he felt compelled to pursue.

Brennan drove out to her cottage, hoping to share a few more G&Ts in the ravishing quiet of the valley's early evening. But when he arrived her car wasn't there. He parked in her space and took a walk around the house, filming it for more than documentary purposes. He also filmed the windowless stone outhouse with its padlocked door. He fancied that its original usage had been as a larder or perhaps even an icehouse, with the thick walls of hewn stone denying the attempts of external heat to penetrate inside. He walked to the very end of the garden, where the trees of the small orchard were still laden with pears and apples, many of which had fallen and decayed in the long grass. Brennan decided that this was an idyllic place, truly isolated, where a personal solitude could be readily achieved. His own bolt-hole in Bradford, despite the historical associations of the Middle Rank terrace, provided only 'keg' solitude, a city dweller's idea of peace, with all modern amenities no more than a short walk away. But here, in Mary Ashton's garden and cottage, Brennan imagined that a higher plane of contemplative life could be reached.

Brennan stopped filming, eventually feeling that it was intrusive and sly. He returned to the car and locked the camera in the glove compartment. He then made two calls, one to his home, leaving a message for Janet on the answerphone, saying that he was doing an interview and would be back late. The second was to the hotel where he and Janet had dined on the night when all this fuss had started, making a reservation for dinner for two. He then scribbled a note for Mary Ashton, requesting her presence at Howard's

House at 8.30 p.m. that night, if she was free and still ready to be wined and dined by a scumbag journalist. Brennan drove off in the direction of the hotel, leaving to fate rather than his own will any further intimate contact with Mary Ashton — a very Catholic compromise, he thought.

★   ★   ★

DI Andrews thought that he had given Ashton a hard time, rebuking her for her downright stupidity in failing to report a bomb threat to the police. He told her that if it turned out that her neglect had compromised the successful prosecution of Fletcher, he would bring charges against her and seek her dismissal from DERA Porton Down. Andrews insisted that they were all in the security business together, keeping the country safe from the constant threat of a variety of lunatic groups, both domestic and foreign. It was therefore vital that Dr Ashton should perform her duty under the Official Secrets Act and inform the security forces and police of any contact, however slight, with such a group. She looked pretty impassive, despite his verbal assault. But once the opportunity for her to speak came along, her face became alive with indignation.

'Mr Andrews, death threats are a feature of my working life. If I came to you every time I received a letter, or found a note on my windscreen, or received a strange phone call, you'd soon get very pissed off with me. I have to use my discretion over what I report because, if I kept doing it, it would drive me round the bend. I'd have no time for a social life or anything — it would just be work and police interviews. You're only angry with me because Mr Brennan found out about the evidence before you and your men did. And I resent being talked to like this because of your inefficiency. Now, unless you have anything sensible to say, I'm going home this minute.'

Ashton stood up and marched to the door of the interview room. Andrews held his hand across it momentarily, before turning the handle and opening the door.

'I'd be grateful if you didn't talk to Mr Brennan again, Dr Ashton,' he said as she passed.

'I've no intention of doing so, Inspector. Goodbye.'

Andrews gathered up Dr Ashton's formal statement about receiving the fake bomb, pausing only to guess what the smell was that was lingering in the room. It wasn't perfume.

It was less pleasant than that. Something scientific, he guessed, sniffing — what was the stuff all the pathologists used, formaldehyde? That was what she smelt of, the stroppy cow.

★ ★ ★

Brennan decided that the evening was still warm enough to sit at one of the tables outside. He'd warned the head waiter that his guest might be delayed, or that she might not be able to turn up at all, but the waiter had responded with charming cooperation. He brought Brennan the wine list to study and then a plate of designer titbits hot from the kitchen. He left the night's menu on the edge of the table, suggesting that orders could be taken at any time up to nine-thirty.

'I'll give her until half-past eight and then I'm eating,' Brennan said with a show of male jocosity, getting a knowing smile back from the waiter. Brennan went through the wine list, determined to try something different from his last visit when he'd over-indulged in the heavy-duty Côte Rotie. Recalling how pissed he'd got that night with Janet, Brennan began to look at the half-bottles. If Mary Ashton didn't turn up, and it was looking increasingly unlikely that she would, he didn't want the challenge of finishing off a whole bottle by himself and then driving home. How happy D.I. Andrews would be to find Brennan's name on a charge sheet the following morning.

At about eight-fifteen, Brennan checked his phone for messages but there were none. He called Ashton's number, but found only the same answering-machine message and hung up before the tone. He signalled the waiter, muttered something in general about the unreliability of women, and ordered his first two courses and a half-bottle of a Californian cabernet sauvignon. There were no other diners in the garden, so Brennan didn't feel too self-conscious. Besides, he'd eaten alone hundreds of times when he'd been out working for the paper and had mastered the art of making it look as though this state was intended, rather than being the result of a broken date. Tonight, however, Brennan felt uneasy.

It was out of character for him to mouth off about a female guest in blokeish fashion as though he was trying to disguise the fact that he was an unloved bachelor. Belatedly, Brennan realized that his change in behaviour was simply down to the onset of advanced guilt from anticipating the seduction of Mary Ashton. If a Catholic priest had walked into the garden now, Brennan would probably have fallen at his feet and begged for absolution.

Instead, it was Mary Ashton who appeared, wearing a chic black dress and jacket and being escorted to Brennan's table by the waiter, who already had a lubricious look in his eye. Brennan stood to welcome her and she offered her cheek for him to kiss.

'What a wonderful surprise,' Ashton said as she sat down. 'Especially after being lightly grilled by Detective Inspector Andrews.'

'He didn't waste much time, then,' Brennan said as he offered her his menu to read.

'I'll just have the same as Mr Brennan,' she said, turning to the waiter who nodded and left them alone.

'Don't you want to know what I ordered?' Brennan asked.

'This is such a treat for me, I don't care. Besides, it adds to the surprise.'

Brennan poured her a glass of wine, smelling an enticing waft of spicy perfume and herbal shampoo as he leant close.

'Did he give you a really hard time, then?' Brennan asked.

'He probably thought so. But the regular interviews we have inside Porton Down are far more testing. Cheers.'

They clinked their glasses together.

'These are — what? — psychological tests or something?'

'In a way, yes. A kind of personality screening to make sure that none of the workers is about to do anything alarming. I had one only a month or so ago, in fact.'

'May I ask why?'

Ashton gave him a patient smile.

'Look, I need to know who I'm having dinner with, whether I should keep the cutlery away from her and so on,' Brennan persisted, deadpan.

'You'll be glad to know that I passed with flying colours,' Ashton conceded. 'More than that I can't say because it would only get me into more trouble than I'm in already.'

'You shouldn't tease an investigative journalist like that,' Brennan said, narrowing his eyes in pantomime fashion. 'I don't give up, you know?'

'Neither do I, Mr Brennan. So, tell me how you ended up in Wiltshire.'

'She said, changing the subject.'

At that point their first courses arrived, and Brennan meandered through his curriculum vitae while they ate: the scuffling journalistic career that had finally found some definition during the oppressive years of Thatcherism; the diabolic pacts with drink and gambling; the fall from grace;

and, finally, redemption and reconciliation with wife and son.

'You make it sound bleak when it can't possibly be,' Ashton observed.

'Do I? I suppose it's the ghosts of the past, or something like that. You know — Catholicism, not enough sex in early life, finally seeing your true place in the world when you thought you were the dog's bollocks. I *do* like jazz and horse racing, though. And Cuban cigars.'

'I'm opera, long steamy baths and G&Ts in the garden on a summer's evening.'

'Do you not have children?' Brennan asked clumsily, and instantly saw a flicker of pain in her defensive smile.

'I'm afraid not. Inherited plumbing problems. The main reason why my marriage broke up.'

'I'm sorry.' Brennan fidgeted with his fork, trying not to catch her eye. Fortunately the waiter arrived with their main courses to break the silence, and Brennan ordered more wine, a full bottle this time, in the hope that the drink would lift the gloom that had fallen on their table.

'So what did you want to ask me about DERA Porton Down?' Ashton said, looking at Brennan with a firm gaze. 'You didn't invite me out for my company.'

'I did, you know. I feel rotten about getting you involved in this.'

'I was already involved before you came along.'

'Yes, but it might have passed you by if I hadn't started stirring things up.'

'You think this Fletcher boy is innocent?'

'Possibly. But I think there's more to this case than animal rights doing a bit of sabotage.'

'They *are* quite determined people, you know. It only needs one to go to extreme measures. And people like me are top of their hate list, killing animals for science.'

'But he didn't — kill you, that is. So why should he take it out on this old farmer? It doesn't make sense . . . *except* . . . '

'Except for what?'

'What could kill a dozen or so cows, swell their bodies, force troops in biological-warfare suits to put blue plastic bags on the heads of each? That's what happened at the farm the night I stumbled across it.'

'You want me to guess, is that it?'

'You're more likely to know than I am.'

'OK, Frank, but promise me that you won't let on that I told you this.'

Brennan put his right hand across his heart.

'When they were clearing up Kuwait

after the Gulf War, a lot of dead animals were flown back to Boscombe Down airbase and sent over to us for examination. They were all blue-bagged, a warning by the recovery teams that they thought they'd probably been killed by a chemical or nerve agent.'

'And had they?'

'Yes. It's not the official line, as you well know, but there's no doubt that Saddam Hussein *had* deployed these weapons at certain times in his campaign. We found traces of sarin, anthrax and bubonic plague in these animal corpses. Which is why people like me have spent the best part of the last decade working on antidotes, for military *and* civilian purposes.'

'Because you can't take the chance that it won't happen here?'

'Exactly. Now, all I can I guess about what you saw is that it was an exercise . . . '

'The official line again,' Brennan said laying on the irony.

'Or, that the cattle were affected by anthrax and needed to be isolated. It occurs naturally in the soil . . . '

'I know, I asked a vet,' Brennan said with a knowing wink.

'Well, there's your story, then. The farmer reports his cattle are sick. His vet diagnoses anthrax, so DERA and the army are informed and told to effect a clean-up.'

'Or a cover-up. The following morning I went back to the scene and new cattle were grazing in the same field. If it was a polluted area, why would they let them in there?'

Ashton shrugged and took a sip of wine.

'I can't answer that.'

'What about a leak from Porton Down?'

'Impossible. The storage of pathogens and nerve agents is given maximum security.'

'Could it have come from a chemical or biological weapon, then, something fired on Salisbury Plain?'

'The British army doesn't use them — there's a worldwide treaty which over 140 countries have signed. Only rogue govern-ments or terrorists would contemplate such weapons. Sorry, not much help, am I?'

'On the contrary. You're only saying what any newspaper editor to whom I put up the story would say. But if I put together your information, what I saw, and the fact that you were questioned by DERA executives, then I might have something.'

'I wasn't the only one. It was a general security check.'

'So maybe this incident doesn't have as innocent an explanation as you would like to think.'

'Is that how you work?' Ashton asked with a smile. 'Assembling pieces of disparate data and stitching them all together?'

'Unless the answer's obvious, yes.'

'Well, it sounds pretty unscientific to me — but good luck.'

Brennan poured Mary some more wine and resumed eating. They chatted about the food, agreeing that it was high-class. Brennan had cheese instead of a dessert, while Mary insisted on trying the bread-and-butter pudding with Calvados. She offered Brennan a sample on his unused spoon, feeding him like a toddler. When the waiter returned to offer them coffee, Mary quickly insisted that Brennan should come back to her cottage for this.

'I think I should be getting home,' Brennan said limply.

'It's not eleven yet. We can have mugs of Irish coffee in the garden and watch the stars. Have you ever looked at the skies round here? You can see whole constellations on nights like this.'

'OK, how can I refuse?'

Brennan paid the bill and then followed Mary Ashton's car down twisting, darkened lanes, passing no other cars on the way. It felt, to Brennan, like a headlong tilt towards an assignation. Once inside the cottage, Ashton lit a dozen or so candles that were dotted around the room and began to play an opera, Brennan had no idea which one, on her CD player. She almost danced from there to the stove where she began to prepare a pot of coffee. Brennan guessed that she was more than a little tiddly by now and, while her physical attractiveness remained potent, the eccentric aspects of her lifestyle were an effective bromide against further temptation.

Ashton came away from the stove and gave Brennan an impromptu kiss on the cheek.

'Thank you for a very pleasant evening,' she said, putting a hand on Brennan's shoulder. She stepped in a little closer. Brennan saw the lights of the candles reflected in her eyes.

'Shall we go to bed?' Ashton whispered.

'I think it would complicate matters,' Brennan said, giving her a gentle kiss on the forehead. Ashton put her other hand on his shoulder and pressed her body against his.

'It would just *equalize* matters, actually. I've given you my secrets, time to share some of yours,' Ashton said before kissing Brennan lingeringly on the mouth. She tightened her hold on his shoulders, and Brennan could feel his resistance weakening. She pulled him back towards the kitchen table, and Brennan's hands came down to lift her up onto it. But as Ashton lay back, momentarily breaking the embrace, Brennan glimpsed a half-lit face at one of the windows and broke away with a start.

'Jesus, there's somebody out there watching . . . '

The face disappeared into the night's shadows as Brennan moved across to the door. But Ashton had locked it.

'Where's the key, where's the key?'

'Over there, by the stove,' Ashton said, sitting up. 'Are you sure there was somebody there?'

'Definitely.'

'Not just your Catholic guilt, then?'

'If I were you, I'd be more worried about safety. Have you got a torch?'

'I'll get it,' Ashton said as she slid off the table. She returned with the flashlight to find Brennan hovering at the open door, looking out into the garden.

'Don't go out, Frank. It was probably just one of the kids from the village.'

'How do you mean?'

'I sometimes get the odd peeping Tom up here. I'm a sitting duck, really.'

'You mean this has happened before?'

'Not quite in the same circumstances. Just lads who want to watch a woman undress, that sort of stuff. I'm sure you've scared him off.'

Brennan played the beam of the torch all along the front garden, up to where their cars were parked, but saw nobody. He came back into the house and locked the door.

'Do you want me to call the police?' Brennan asked.

'Well, they're hardly the right people at the moment, Frank!'

'Sorry. Look, let's have a coffee, then I must go.'

'We can go upstairs . . . ' Ashton offered.

'Oh, yeah, and then we'll find ourselves being watched by the local morris-men standing on each other's shoulders. I'm sorry, Mary — I'm flattered that you wanted me, but it isn't right. For either of us.'

'Do you know, I think you might be a moral prig, Frank.'

'You're almost certainly right, Mary. But I bet you that tomorrow morning you'll be glad you didn't sleep with me.'

'I'm already glad,' Ashton said quickly. Brennan laughed, and she joined in. They shared a chaste kiss, and then drank some coffee — with Irish whiskey — before Brennan took the flashlight and did a quick tour of the garden to check that the voyeur had gone for the night. He said goodbye to

Ashton at the door, waiting until she had locked and bolted it before leaving. As he reached his car, he looked back at the cottage and saw her going round the room, blowing out the candles.

Brennan stuffed a couple of mints into his mouth and then set off down the road, his car's headlights on full beam in case any flashers or village perverts were still out on the prowl. As he made a turn towards the A36, he found a dark Mercedes saloon parked carelessly on the verge, leaving too narrow a gap for him to get through. Brennan looked around. A half-moon hung in the clear night sky, and by its light Brennan could see that there were no cottages or farms nearby. Somebody had run out of petrol, or got pissed and decided to walk home. He got out of the car and moved towards the Mercedes, hoping to find a sleeping driver. But the car was empty. Brennan swore under his breath and walked back to his car. But then two men climbed over the drystone wall to his left. Brennan broke into a run and dragged open his car door, but they were too quick for him. While one held him, the other pulled a large blue laundry bag over his head. As Brennan shouted and kicked out, he felt a fist drive hard into his stomach, doubling him up in an instant. As he fell, his arms were grabbed and then his hands were taped together. The men lifted him off the road and carried him bodily, despite his struggles. Although the bag muffled their noise Brennan could still hear their panting breath and muttered oaths. Then his legs hit something hard, and seconds later he was tipped over into the boot of a car, hearing the lid slam down with a firm clunk. As he struggled to free himself, the car lurched into motion, spinning Brennan against the walls of the boot, and his face smacked into something angular and metallic. Giddy and aching, Brennan tried not to think of a naked Mary Ashton and the night of passion that would have saved him from whatever danger threatened him now.

12

Brennan gave up trying to free himself after less than two minutes. The effort and the tension combined with the stifling effect of the plastic bag to produce something akin to an asthma attack. Brennan could also feel his face running with what he hoped was sweat rather than blood. So he tried to lie as still as he could and recover his breath. Stretched out on his back, Brennan began to think less of escape than of simple survival. He told himself that if these men had wanted to kill him, they could have done so easily back in the lanes around Mary Ashton's cottage. So he concluded that they wanted him alive — for now, at least — because they must need something from him.

Brennan also tried to guess who he was dealing with. Although MI5 would have been pleased to have got Joe Fletcher charged, they would probably also have wanted Brennan himself banged up or publicly discredited, so further intimidation on their part couldn't be ruled out. There was also the possibility that the two men looking into David Southwell's background had cut across Brennan's path.

But 'how' and 'why' remained unclear, as did the men's identities. The thought then occurred to Brennan that the men were covering exactly the same territory as he was because, as he had speculated, there was a hidden connection between Southwell's death and the events around Porton Down. The use of the blue plastic laundry bag was either a pure coincidence or a direct connection back to the first incident. Maybe these two were taking the piss out of him, as well as trying to terrify him.

Brennan felt the car slow, then go through a turning manoeuvre. It began to bump a lot more now, despite the sophisticated suspension. Brennan guessed they were on a country track: he tried to imagine the world outside his double layer of incarceration. The car turned again, and the ride became even bumpier. Then it paused for a moment, engine still running, and Brennan heard one of the doors open and felt the vehicle lift a little on its springs as one of the men got out. The car edged forward a short way and then paused again as the man on the passenger side got back in, closing his door with a muffled thud. Brennan pictured the car passing through a gate to a field, or an entrance to a warehouse or factory, a place of isolation.

The car travelled on for a few minutes more and then stopped. Brennan heard the engine cut out. He felt the car lift again, and heard both doors open and close. He tensed his body, waiting for the lid of the boot to open. He felt the rush of cool air almost as soon as he heard the lid rise. Then two pairs of hands grabbed him and lifted him unceremoniously from the boot. Brennan wobbled as he tried to stand straight but then felt hands on his upper arms, propelling him forwards. The ground wasn't concrete or tarmac but the rough grass of a field. Brennan could feel its random undulations as he was frogmarched onwards in silence.

'You know, I think I'm lost,' Brennan said loudly through the bag, hoping for a response. But there was none. In that instant it seemed to Brennan that these were professionals, not the usual cowboys that MI5 employed to do their dirty work on a deniable basis. The low-life operatives liked a bit of backchat and verbals because it helped them feel on top of their target, and they were full-time lippy in any case. But the pros, usually from police or military sources, stuck to their own rules of engagement and held their silence as a means of exerting mental control over their victims. They worked on presence, not personality.

Brennan stumbled on, nearly falling on several occasions. Then he felt the terrain change. It was suddenly gravel, then concrete and now he heard the unmistakable sounds of footsteps rattling on a wooden floor. They were indoors at last. A house, it seemed, rather than an office. Brennan was man-handled around and then pushed down onto a chair, a wobbly wooden one that gave instant discomfort. Then he felt a hand fumble under the laundry bag and push inside his jacket, lifting out his wallet. Another hand returned in what seemed like an attempt to frisk the rest of his upper torso. Brennan then felt his socks and lower legs being searched. Brennan realized that if the two men needed to look at his wallet to check his identity and also thought that he might be carrying weapons, then they must have had no idea about who they were picking up. Brennan had either been grabbed at random or, more likely, because he had passed through the orbit of Mary Ashton.

'You a real journalist?' a voice asked. Through the almost opaque blue plastic that shrouded his head, Brennan could make out a dark outline, looming over him.

'Look, if this is the NUJ membership committee, I promise I'll pay my overdue subs, OK?' Brennan said, trying to test their humour. He thought he glimpsed the dark shape move: an instant later, a heavy punch landed on the left side of his face and knocked him off the chair. Brennan told himself that this was probably no time for jocosity. A pair of hands dragged him back onto his feet and two shapes swirled around in the pale blue haze in front of him.

'Don't fuck us about. Tell us what we ask or we'll hurt you,' the other voice said, very close to Brennan's face. Brennan was tossed back onto the seat.

'Now, let's try again — are you a real journalist?'

'Yes.'

'Who do you work for?'

'Anyone who's interested. Apart from Rupert Murdoch, Conrad Black, the Rothermere mob, the *Mirror* and the *Express*.'

Brennan took another, lesser blow to the other side of his head but, as he'd been expecting it, he'd been able to brace himself to avoid the indignity of hitting the floor again.

'You didn't let me finish — I'm a freelancer, OK? It gives me better cover.'

'For what?'

'Same sort of thing as you, I guess.'

'Which is?'

'You tell me.'

Brennan braced himself again, but no punch came.

'Where is it, then?' the first voice asked.

'Where's what?'

'We asked your lady friend where it was and she said she'd given it to you. So you must have it.'

'Oh, right, so that was you watching at the window, getting your pervy kicks, was it?'

'Where. Is. It?' said the voice with leaden weight.

'Oh, *that*. Well, it's not with me, obviously, nor in the car. You wouldn't carry it around, would you?'

'Where is it?' the voice said again, with a tone of strained patience.

'You don't expect me to tell you that. If you want to know, you have to offer me a deal,' Brennan said confidently.

'The deal is you stay alive,' the voice said, and for the first time Brennan felt the unmistakable pressure of a handgun's muzzle pressed against his temple.

'But if I don't tell you and you kill me, you won't find what you want,' Brennan said, trying to point out the obvious. 'So that's no deal. I have it — but I'm not telling you where it is unless you offer me something in return.'

'You mean a percentage?'

The pressure of the gun barrel lifted from Brennan's head. His pulse began to race. As well as being spared, he was beginning to tease small mistakes and fragments of information from them. The mention of a percentage meant that something was up for sale, not just for recovery.

'Yeah, a percentage, a finder's fee — something like that. Then we can do business.'

There was a silence and then some muttering between the men. Brennan strained to hear what they were saying but couldn't make it out since they were walking around the room. Then the footsteps became louder as they came closer.

'OK — we can sort something out for you and your girlfriend. But it has to be very quick. Like two days or less.'

'You may not be the only buyer, have you thought of that?' Brennan said boldly, and waited for a reaction.

'Listen, we offered a good price last time. It still stands. If you try and cut us out, the same thing will happen to you as — '

The voice broke off suddenly, as if caution had suddenly set in or the speaker had been restrained. Brennan guessed that the name that had been withheld was that of David Southwell.

'How do I get in contact with you?' Brennan asked cheekily. 'You going to leave me a business card?'

He heard some ironic laughter from the men.

'You'll get a call from us, Mr Brennan. We know where you live now.'

'Yeah, but how will I know it's you — I get calls from all kinds of nutters asking me if I want double glazing, a conservatory, a timeshare in Tenerife . . . '

'We're in logistics, Brennan,' a voice said, close to his right ear.

'That's one of those new buzzwords for moving things about, isn't it? Freight, as was.'

'Logistics. Remember that, Brennan, OK?'

Brennan heard footsteps again, retreating this time.

'Leaving me here isn't very conducive to a good partnership,' Brennan called out.

'Maybe not,' a voice shouted, echoing. 'But it shows that we're serious. Oh, and don't go out for a few hours, Brennan.'

Brennan listened as the footsteps ebbed away. He tried to peer through the plastic but couldn't see shape or movement. He waited, wondering if they were trying to bluff him. But after five minutes, Brennan guessed that the two men were neither hanging around nor coming back. Brennan stood up and then edged around the chair until his bound hands could get a grip on its frame. He then tugged the chair over, letting it fall to the floor, and bent down. As he knelt, Brennan felt his left knee jar against a small, hard object that pressed painfully against the bone. He lifted his knee and lay down. Rolling over, he was able to make contact with the chair again, feeling his way down it. With a rough idea of the length of the chair's legs, Brennan began to try and hook his plastic hood onto one of them so that he could pull it off his head. Images of duck-apple night as a child swam into his mind as he strained his neck in pursuit of the prize of freedom. After more than a dozen attempts, Brennan finally felt the pull of the chair leg on the bag and slowly began to wriggle himself out of it, like a snake shedding its unwanted skin.

He sat up as the bag finally released its grip, and took in several deep breaths of the cold night air before looking around. The room he was in was large, but even in the dim light he could see that all of the window frames and some of the wooden floorboards had been stripped out. As his eyes adjusted, Brennan could make out a broken cornice in the ceiling and a gaping hole, like the gap left by a rotten tooth, where a large fireplace had been torn out. He was in a big house, but one that had been looted of anything resembling fodder for the growing reclamation industry. With this evidence of theft in front of him, he was surprised to see that his captors had done him the courtesy of leaving his wallet behind on one of the window ledges. Brennan tried to stand but, with his hands tethered behind his back, he couldn't get a sufficient push off the floor to lift himself up. His flabby midriff didn't help matters.

Instead, Brennan slid along the floor like a rower, stretching out his legs and then dragging his backside along as he bent his knees until he was able to position himself against a wall. Tucking his legs and feet right in, he pressed back hard and pushed upwards — but the effort was too much for him to sustain and he slid back down onto the floor again. He waited a few minutes to recover his breath and then counted down to a renewed effort.

'Three . . . two . . . one . . . LIFT-OFF!' he shouted as he pushed upwards again on his haunches like an Olympic weightlifter. His back slid up the wall. Brennan pulled his feet closer in and pushed again, straightening his legs, and this time the force was enough to propel him upwards and onto his feet. Brennan's guts heaved with the effort, and he sensed the imminent reappearance of his expensive dinner. But a slow walk around the room eventually settled his stomach. As he walked, he trod on a sharp object. Brennan scuffed it out from under his shoe and looked down to see a bullet casing. He scanned the floor and saw dozens more, discarded all over the room, and a clammy sense of fear began to take hold. What had one of the men said to him — something about staying put for a few hours? Brennan instantly thought of booby traps or worse and stood stock-still while he tried to collect his bearings. He hadn't been able to time his journey precisely, but he guessed that he'd been in the boot of the car for fifteen to twenty minutes, while the forced march had taken up at least another twenty. This would have put him between ten and fifteen miles from Mary Ashton's cottage, so he was well within range of all those military establishments he had once circled so eagerly on his Ordnance Survey map. Brennan looked out of one of the windows but the clear sky and half-moon of earlier in the evening had now given way to an intense darkness that obscured the landscape. There didn't seem much point in stumbling out into it with no sense of direction. Brennan instinctively went to look at his watch, forgetting for a moment that his hands were tied. Obliged to guess the time, he figured it

318

to be somewhere between midnight and one o'clock, although the events of the night had almost certainly distorted his perceptions.

As his head cleared, Brennan began to establish a sequence of priorities. He should try to free his hands first, and then he could call for help on his mobile phone. But then, if he didn't know where he was, phoning Janet would be pointless, while contacting the police would plainly provoke more trouble than support. He also realized that, what with the booby-trap risk and the threat implicit in his kidnappers' last shouted instruction to stay put for a few hours, he would almost certainly have to wait until dawn before leaving the confines of the dilapidated house. Brennan began to walk carefully around the room, as much for the warmth of the exercise as for the delights of exploration. He reached a doorway that led out into a wide hall, and he could make out a wide staircase, albeit one stripped of its banister, that rose up to another floor of the house. Brennan saw a light switch on the wall to one side and managed to flick it down with his nose, but no lights came on.

Brennan shuffled back into the main room and went across to a window on the other side. The view from here was no clearer — he could just about make out a patch of almost bare gravel, dotted with weeds, but not much else. Suddenly, from nowhere, came a rapid, eerie wail like the noise of a jet streaking overhead and seconds later a huge ball of flame erupted in the near distance. The blast wave from the explosion hit Brennan even as he stumbled for cover as it burst through the open window and slammed through the room. Within thirty seconds there was another screech in the sky and another explosion, closer than the first, that now rocked the house itself. Brennan flattened himself against a wall, well away from the window. His heart rate accelerated. He now recognized the connection between the distant thuds and rushes of air that he'd observed at night in Bradford and the explosive impacts outside the house. He was on, or close to, one of the artillery ranges on Salisbury Plain, with a night-time live-fire exercise under way. But for the fact that he knew he wouldn't be able to get up again, Brennan would have curled up in a ball in a corner of the room. Instead, he jammed himself upright into one, standing with his face as far into the junction of the two walls as he could get it for fear of being hit by shrapnel — or by debris from the house if it took a direct hit. As the bombardment intensified, so too did the screaming of the shells in the sky above. But Brennan couldn't even put his fingers in his ears to deaden the deafening noise.

★ ★ ★

Janet phoned Brennan's mobile at half-hourly intervals, but it was switched off and so she simply kept updating the time of her message rather than its content — which was a simple 'Frank, where the hell are you?' She lay in bed, watching the phone, willing it to ring, but as two o'clock passed she became resigned to the fact that Brennan was not going to respond. Her worst fear was that he'd had a road accident, or been beaten up. But there was also a subliminal anxiety about the possibility that he'd started an affair with another woman. For this reason, she held back from phoning the police, in case such a call would bring their ridicule down on her. She was mindful, too, of her professional duty as a reporter's partner not to panic or involve the police unnecessarily in Brennan's investigation. So, like a wife with a husband away in some distant war, she would have to wait for the call — from him, from the police or perhaps even from a hospital.

Janet switched off her bedside light and settled down for sleep. But, as always happened when she was on edge, there was an additional small disturbance to occupy her mind. The bedroom faced south and, as the night wore on, the windows were frequently rattled by waves of disturbed air from artillery fire on Salisbury Plain. And tonight of all nights the exercise seemed particularly prolonged.

* * *

Brennan waited fully five minutes after the last explosion before emerging from his corner sanctuary. A layer of dust had settled on the floor of the room, shaken loose from the crumbling ceiling by the scores of blasts from the live-fire exercise. Brennan approached the nearest window cautiously and peered out. The first lightening of the sky was evident and he could make out the shapes of houses in the near distance, with the Plain spreading out behind them. Brennan turned around, lowered himself on bent knees and managed to pick up his wallet from the window ledge. He then stepped out through the window and walked slowly away from the house before turning.

Although it was now a bit of a wreck, he could see from the remaining red-brick structure that at one time it must have been an impressive and handsome building. He guessed that when the military had taken possession of Salisbury Plain the house's fate had been sealed. Now, as the darkness lifted, he could see close by a collection of squat, flat-roofed breeze-block buildings, oddly shaped and layered over two or three storeys. They looked like flats or houses but were plainly uninhabited. Brennan wandered in amongst them and, seeing the walls pock-marked with bullet-holes, realized that this must be Imber, the village that had been taken over by the army in the 1940s, later to be developed as a facsimile Eastern European town in order that troops could practise their Cold War street-fighting techniques. Such was the devotion to realism that the street signs and notices had been rendered in the Cyrillic alphabet. There was even an Eastern European-designed phone box on a street corner to complete this surreal vision. Brennan crossed to it and nudged the receiver off its bracket with his nose, then bent down to see if the phone had a dialling tone. But the army's quest for verisimilitude had not stretched as far as connecting the phone to a network. He walked away, leaving the receiver dangling.

Brennan now took his bearings from the first meniscus of the rising sun, and headed due north towards the ridge that overlooked Westbury. He passed the abandoned village's ancient church, which was now surrounded by barbed-wire fencing, and then, further on, the remains of what must have been Imber's only pub. On a faded, peeling sign dangling from the eaves of this building, Brennan could make out a design and lettering for 'The Bell'. He fantasized briefly about it being open again, serving fry-up breakfasts and strong ale to the hungry traveller: him. But the pub was dead, the whole village an empty tomb. The unchallenged power of the military had swept the people from it, and now their sons and daughters and grandchildren would never be allowed to go back, peace dividend or not.

Once he was clear of Imber, Brennan came across a rough rock-and-gravel road that headed north-west. He could see that scores of tracked vehicles, probably armoured personnel carriers, had left their marks — although, as he strode out, the rolling downs around him were completely silent apart from the first tentative choruses of birdsong. The longer he walked across the chalk-flecked hollows and hummocks, the more Brennan began to feel a perverse pleasure at this, the ultimate morning stroll in the largest unpopulated area in southern

England. Occasionally he stumbled on the rutted track, unable to balance with outstretched arms, but the sweet morning air and the almost overwhelming sense of freedom made for a pleasant consolation for the claustrophobic experiences he'd been through during the night.

As a twist in the track unfolded, however, Brennan could see the outside world looming into view once again. He stopped for a moment, peering at buildings that were probably no more than a mile away but that nevertheless seemed light years away from the wild nature around him. The track snaked away towards the largest cluster, over which a large Union Jack flew. Brennan guessed that they must be barracks or storage depots for military vehicles. Walking off Salisbury Plain at the crack of dawn with his hands tied behind his back wouldn't look too innocent to any soldiers who saw him. Lengthy questioning and serious complications would undoubtedly be on the agenda.

So Brennan veered off the track and angled his walk away from the barracks, down towards a farm nestled on the fringe of the military area. The sun was fully risen now behind him, a great splash of terracotta colour in the sea of grey, dawn sky. Brennan even imagined he could feel its heat on his back, but it was simply the exertion of his walk that had warmed him. As he reached the edge of the vast Plain and ducked under a wire fence onto arable land, Brennan paused to look back at the huge, bleak sweep of land that had been sealed off for close to a century. Brennan felt that, in a bizarre way, the military had acted as unwitting conservationists, saving the land from the rapacious agri-businesses and their quest for the fastest buck, genetically modified or otherwise. He looked at the tamed, exploited fields that now beckoned him and almost pitied them for the wildness that they had lost.

Brennan marched on, careful to stick to the edge of the fields so that no charges of criminal trespass could be levied against him if he was stopped. As he approached the farm buildings, he could already hear the early-morning rustle of traffic on the A36 and a sense of relief superseded his recent empathy with the natural world.

'Oi! What you after?' a male voice shouted suddenly.

Brennan turned his head. A middle-aged farmer stood staring at him, wiping his hands on a rag.

'Sorry!' Brennan called back, smiling. 'It was my stag-night last night and I'm afraid my mates pulled a bit of a stunt on me.'

He turned round to show his tethered hands. Brennan turned back and saw the farmer walking towards him.

'They dumped me on the Plain. Been walking for hours.'

'You in the mob, then?' the farmer asked as he reached Brennan.

'Used to be,' Brennan bluffed. 'My old stamping ground over there, Imber and such. I guess that's why they must have done it.'

'Takin' a bit of a risk, weren't they? They was firin' out there last night.'

'Well, keeps you sharp, on your toes, I suppose. You couldn't cut this tape for me, could you?'

'Aye, all right. Follow me. What 'appened to your face, by the way?'

Brennan had forgotten about the blows that his inquisitors had landed on him.

'Oh, that. Fell over in the dark. Looks bad, does it?'

'When you getting married?'

'Tomorrow.'

'You'll 'ave some explainin' to do even then, I reckons.'

The farmer disappeared into a shed and came out with a blade. Brennan turned around, hoping that the man wouldn't see the wedding ring on Brennan's left hand. He felt the tape that bound his hands loosen and then part and he instantly stretched out his arms in relief.

'God, that feels better. Thank you very much indeed.'

Brennan rubbed his wrists and flexed his fingers to restore full circulation. He put his wallet away and then reached into his other inside pocket and pulled out his phone.

'I'd better organize myself a lift back,' Brennan said as the farmer watched him.

'Want a cup of tea?'

'Fantastic,' Brennan said as he began to listen to Janet's messages stored in the phone's memory.

★ ★ ★

It was obvious within a few minutes of telling his story that Janet didn't believe Brennan. It seemed too fanciful, too far-fetched even for his complicated life.

'Who did you have dinner with, then?' she asked brusquely.

'This doctor from Porton Down. The one who received a Joe Fletcher bomb.'

'So it's a woman, then?'

'Did I say that?'

'No, you didn't, which is why I know that it was.'

'Yeah, all right. Mary Ashton. She's a

DERA scientist. Gave me a lot of good stuff last night. And by that I mean information.'

Janet said nothing further as she drove on, with exaggerated care because she'd had to borrow Robert the bookseller's car. With all the local taxi offices closed at that hour, Janet had turned to Robert because she knew that his routine of meditation, fasting and yoga began at first light. So he had been entirely placid and unperturbed when she had knocked on his door. Now she was following Brennan's directions to where he hoped their car was still parked. Her alarm at receiving a phone call at five past six in the morning had barely receded, despite the relief that hearing Brennan's voice had brought. Nor had the shock and suspicion raised first by Brennan's dishevelled and bruised appearance and then by his garbled account of the night's events.

'These guys must have tracked her down somehow, and then tried to pressurize her . . . which was why she put them onto me, I suppose.'

'Did you fuck her, then?'

'Janet, come on. I don't do that sort of thing. You know that.'

'She must feel fairly close to you to pass on her problems with those men.'

'She hasn't got anybody. She lives alone. These guys are not Five or Special Branch.

They're heavy-duty but, unless I read it wrong, they're not part of any firm. They're professionals but I think they're chancers, with some connection to the military. They knew how to get onto the Plain. They knew there was a live-fire exercise. They were armed. No wonder Ashton panicked.'

'So what are they after?' Janet asked, suddenly more interested in the story than in the possibility that Brennan had strayed.

'I don't know. I'm fairly certain they were connected to Southwell. Either working with him or getting him to do something for them. They knew about his death, that's for sure. So that suggests arms, weaponry, perhaps even something to do with the stuff at Porton Down. They think that Ashton had something that she told them she'd passed to me.'

'And you haven't got it?'

'No — but I convinced them that I had.'

'Jesus, Frank — why didn't you just say no? They'll be threatening you, me and Lester next.'

'I've got a couple of days to set something up. Plan my defence. They think I'm some kind of middleman. So I will be.'

'You terrible bullshitter, Frank.'

Janet shook her head in exasperation. Brennan pointed through the windscreen. His car was at the roadside, exactly where he'd left it the night before even though it had remained unlocked with the ignition keys still inside. Brennan got out and walked across, checked that all was present and correct, and gave Janet a thumbs-up gesture before getting behind the wheel. Janet wondered how she could ever have doubted that Brennan would be faithful to her, when it was so obvious that he would always put his journalism before casual sex.

★   ★   ★

Brennan showered and shaved as soon as he got home, then smeared antiseptic ointment onto the bruises and cuts on his face. He came down to the kitchen in his bathrobe and slugged back a coffee that he stiffened with a brandy.

'You need sleep, not booze, Frank,' Janet said as she cooked scrambled eggs.

'I haven't got time.'

Brennan crossed to the wall phone and dialled Ashton's number, checking the time on his watch — seven-thirty. It was too early for her to have gone to work, but late enough to put in a call. But all he heard was her answerphone message.

'Mary, it's Frank Brennan. It's seven-thirty in the morning, and I hope you're all right. I

331

met up with your 'friends' last night, but I'm OK. I need to speak to you. Please call me on my mobile today. If you get scared, don't be afraid to go to the police. Bye.'

Brennan hung up the phone and sat down at the table. Janet brought the scrambled eggs and toast to him.

'What does she do, this Ashton woman?' Janet asked.

'She's a microbiologist. Works on antidotes to germ and chemical warfare agents — although that's a secret.'

'Must be a clever woman.'

'Clever but a bit brittle, I'd say. The police gave her a hard time yesterday, about not reporting the bomb. So I need to look after her, if you see what I mean.'

'You feel obliged?' Janet said with a knowing smile. Brennan nodded as he ate.

'What will you do today, then?'

'I've got an appointment with the coroner in Bristol. And I need to talk to Cochrane again first. I'll take him with me if he's available. I've also got some more film to show to Mark Beattie. It's nothing special. Just to show him that I'm still on the case.'

Janet leant across and kissed his forehead. After breakfast, Brennan dressed, putting on a jacket and tie again in order to impress the coroner. He'd put his phone on recharge in his office as soon as he'd come in so now, as he collected it, he checked on his computer for e-mail and found one message.

Frank — I thought it best not to call. Just had the MI5 man back in again. They're still after you. He also let slip that Gudgeon's son, Nathaniel, is in charge of animal husbandry at the farm at Porton Down. I presume this means he rears the animals for experimentation. Thought you should know. Take care. Luke B.

Brennan switched off the computer, rushed downstairs and told Janet about the message in a breathless tone.

'Is this good or bad news?' Janet asked.

'It's bad all round, Jan. It beefs up the police's case against Joe Fletcher because the son would have been a prime target for the Salisbury Animal Militia. The prosecution will almost certainly claim that Fletcher planted the bomb and got the wrong man. It's a clear motive. And they'll love that.'

'I see what you mean. Better tell Cochrane a.s.a.p., then.'

'And you know what's worse? Mary Ashton *didn't* let on to me that Gudgeon worked there. She must know him or about him. She must have known about his father getting killed, but she didn't say anything about it. Didn't acknowledge the connection.'

'Which means she must have something to hide,' Janet suggested.

'Come on,' urged Brennan. 'Let's get into the office.'

13

Brennan and Janet took the 9.10 train from Bradford to Bristol, with Brennan taking the opportunity of their having a quiet half-hour together to tell Janet about Lester's love life. Breaking the news on the train would also limit Janet's capacity for a tantrum: he certainly expected she'd have one, not so much about Lester as about Brennan's holding back the news.

'Why did you choose this moment to tell me?' Janet hissed.

'Because it's the first time we've been able to have a proper talk. I'm sorry.'

The apology went some way to dousing Janet's fire, but she still wanted all the details so that she could share this rite of passage with Lester herself later.

'How did you feel about it?' Janet asked Brennan after he'd revealed the circumstances.

'Fine. Surprisingly unshocked. Although I will admit to a twinge of jealousy.'

'About the girl?'

'Not exactly. It was more the thought that Lester has now got more sex to look forward to than I have. All fathers probably think like that. Don't they?'

Janet gave him a pitying look.

'Well, don't mothers get jealous that their little boy has found someone else to love?' Brennan offered as his defence.

'Eventually. When they leave home, get married. Right now, it's just concern. That the sex Lester and this girl are having is both safe and pleasurable. First time is usually a nightmare for boys *and* girls. Was for me, anyway.'

Brennan sensed that several of their fellow commuters had begun to tune in to the conversation and so stifled his response, allowing the normal silence of early-morning train journeys to settle over the carriage. Janet took the hint and began reading her copy of *The Independent*, leaving Brennan to think about what he had to get through that day.

The first target was achieved quite readily. Brennan reawakened Mark Beattie's interest in the documentary investigation, first with the account of his kidnapping and then by showing Beattie the footage he had shot the previous day. Although it looked relatively innocent, Brennan's improvised voice-over and the rapidly thickening plot had Beattie rubbing his hands with anticipation. The one problem they all had, though, was proving

Joe Fletcher's innocence. When Richard Cochrane joined them later in the morning, his assessment of the new information about Nathaniel Gudgeon's work was that it made things look very difficult for Fletcher.

'They would have had to disclose this before the trial, of course, but at least we know the bad news now rather than later,' Cochrane said, trying to see a glimmer of silver lining in the dark cloud. 'So now we have to plan a defence that not only proves Fletcher didn't do it, but also didn't have a motive for doing it. And that will be tough. Very tough.'

'Nathaniel would have had to stay quiet about his work at Porton Down. All the people there have to, both because of official secrecy and also in self-defence,' Brennan said, trying to be helpful.

'Unfortunately, Fletcher's admitted to finding out where Mary Ashton lived so the prosecution will simply insist that he did the same for Gudgeon. Followed him home one night, logged the address, put him on a list of targets and then planted the bomb. In fact, I think we should be prepared to lose this one.'

'It isn't over yet,' Brennan said, bristling at the first hint of failure. 'I think there's a lot more to come out.'

'OK. But can I ask you not to close your

mind to the possibility that Fletcher might be guilty. Have you thought about the implications of that for your investigation?'

Cochrane looked first at Brennan and then at Beattie to emphasize the point he was making. Brennan sensed a man wanting out.

'Look, if you're unsure about this case, you should drop it now, because we don't want to go too far down the road and then find you're not interested. Or not up to it,' Brennan said in retaliation.

Beattie sat forward in his chair and held out his hands in a gesture of mediation.

'Richard, I asked you to come in on this because you're a mate. If you *do* have professional doubts you've got to tell me. If we continue with this investigation, the company is going out on a fairly long limb.'

'Well, I'd advise a fairly swift retreat, in all honesty. I know this type of case inside out, and all the time one's instinct is for the underdog against the police or whatever. But with Fletcher I'm beginning to think that he did it. I can't back Mr Brennan's hunches, I'm afraid.'

'Well, you should leave immediately,' Brennan snapped. 'I've got a meeting with the coroner this afternoon and I won't have it compromised by your indifference.'

'Frank, please,' Janet chided. But Cochrane

had already got to his feet and was now heading for the door.

'I'll invoice you for my work so far, Mark,' he said. Then he just left, without a look or a nod to either Brennan or Janet. An unpleasant silence fell while Beattie, Janet and Brennan absorbed the implications of Cochrane's dismissal.

'If you're waiting for an apology, I'm sorry, but there won't be one,' Brennan said.

'It's OK, Frank. It was my mistake to bring a friend in. Should have known better.'

'I'd like to say that I think Cochrane did some good work at short notice,' Janet announced, glaring at Brennan whom she plainly blamed for this disruption.

'If he'd done his job properly, we wouldn't have this mess to sort out this afternoon, Janet. And now he's walked out I've got to face the coroner as Joe Public, without a member of the legal profession to back me up.'

'I'm sure you'll manage,' Janet said witheringly.

'More importantly,' Brennan continued, concentrating his gaze on Beattie, 'we have to find a lawyer to look after Fletcher's case. I think we — meaning the three of us making this investigation — have a moral obligation to see that he's represented. And I'm

339

perfectly willing to give what remains of my fee towards his costs.'

'Janet and I need to talk,' Beattie said ominously.

'Fine, you should. If you're serious about this story, you will have to commit more resources to it. If you're not, then I will need to look elsewhere for support. Whatever you decide, let me know as soon as possible.'

Brennan stood, shook hands with Mark Beattie and gave Janet a brief kiss on the cheek before making his exit. Even before he'd reached the ground floor, Brennan knew in his bones that Beattie was going to pull the plug on his investigation — and leave Fletcher stranded.

* * *

Mary Ashton took time off during her lunch break to enjoy a quiet stroll away from the concentrated cluster of buildings at the heart of Porton Down towards the animal-husbandry department. Though serviced by the same small-scale road network that linked all the other sections, 'The Farm', as it was known, at least looked as though it belonged in the Wiltshire landscape. Though the animals that Mary experimented upon were usually shipped down already caged to her on

340

an electric buggy, she often liked to go and 'meet' them beforehand. To some outsiders, a last act of comfort to an animal that she was about to vivisect would seem both mawkish and hypocritical. But she liked to think that her patting and talking were expressions of professional kindness, a small communication from one species to another just to say that a creature's imminent death at human hands was not personal, just business. She applied this courtesy to all the animals, even the pigs and cattle, but she was especially concerned for the rabbits because their fear was always the most violent. The screeches they made as the cold steel of the laboratory knife descended upon them were truly heart-rending, the stuff of several nightmares. While pigs squealed quite loudly, they seemed genetically disposed to giving up their lives, going out with a stoic defiance. Cows didn't really know what hit them. But the rabbits — they were almost childlike in their terror of death.

'Hello, Dr Ashton,' Nathaniel Gudgeon said as he emerged from the main storage barn. 'Long time since you paid us a visit.'

'I thought I should leave you alone to do your grieving, Nat. Sorry. How are you feeling?'

'Not too bad now. I miss the old bugger,

but mainly in the way that you miss an old dog that's been round the house a long time.'

Mary gave him a little smile.

'I'm sure your feelings go deeper than that, Nat?'

'Aye, I suppose so. Still, farm's on the market now. Already had a few looking around. Mostly city types wanting to get out of the rat race — as though farming isn't.'

'What will you do with the money?' Ashton asked suddenly. Gudgeon fell silent and looked down at his boots.

'I think you know what I'd like to do.'

'But you've got your own life all ahead of you now,' Ashton said in kindly fashion. 'You can get out of here. Fulfil your dreams.'

'Can't do that without you, though, can I?'

'You'll find someone your own age, Nat. Start a family. Be free.'

'Not what I want, though.'

'It was you at the window last night, wasn't it?'

Gudgeon looked away, his face colouring with embarrassment.

'I just needed to see you, Mary.'

'Well, watching me with another man hardly counts, I think. It's got to stop, Nat. For your own good.'

'You didn't say that when I was helping you out. I thought you really liked me then.'

'I did. I still do. Look, I'm sorry, Nat. I've had a pretty depressing time, too. I'm thinking of getting out of here.'

'With the bloke you were with last night?'

'Don't be silly. He's not even a friend. Nothing happened between us.'

Gudgeon made a sulky noise.

'You're the only man I can trust,' Ashton said, reaching out and touching his arm. 'The only one, Nat. Maybe I should see some sense and build on that trust. Recognize what you have to offer me.'

'That's up to you, Mary. You know I'll do anything for you. Anything.'

Ashton moved closer and nuzzled her lips against Gudgeon's ear.

★　★　★

Brennan excused himself to the lavatory as soon as he'd confirmed his arrival at the coroner's office. The Georgian offices boasted a cool, stone-built toilet with marble urinals, but it was the framed mirror that Brennan sought out most eagerly. Some of the bruising from the night before had gone down, but the discolouration and several scratches remained. Brennan ran a tap and splashed his face with cold water in a futile attempt to make himself look more presentable. Presenting a controversial argument to an officer of the law while looking like a navvy who'd been in a pub fight wouldn't be easy. Brennan dried his face, then patted down his hair with his wet hands. He checked in the mirror again. The look was train-spotter meets bar-room lush, he thought. But it would have to do.

Brennan re-emerged into the reception area and took a seat, giving the secretary with the gruff voice an ingratiating smile. This was greeted with an even more withering stare than he'd received when he first arrived.

'It's gone two-thirty,' Brennan said, tapping his watch urgently. The secretary ignored him.

'Only I'm a busy man, see. Lots of other people to catch.'

The secretary turned away to her computer keyboard and began to type. Brennan stood and strolled around the high-ceilinged room that was lined with 'paint-by-numbers' portraits of previous coroners, with the dates of their years of office. Brennan wondered if it would have been an appropriate touch to have their causes of death listed underneath as well.

The phone on the secretary's desk rang, and after a brief starchy burst of 'Yes, he is' and 'Yes, of course, sir', she hung up and called across to Brennan.

'Mr Morrison will see you now,' she said without deigning to add 'Mr Brennan'. She pointed down the corridor leading off from the reception area. 'Second door on the right.'

'Thank you,' Brennan said, forcing a smile. He set off down the windowless corridor that was lit with imitation art-deco sconces. Brennan found the door with Morrison's name on it and knocked, hoping to strike a note somewhere between timid and boisterous.

'Come,' called a headmasterly voice.

Brennan opened the door and advanced into the room. Morrison was still reading a file on his desk, belatedly looking up to acknowledge Brennan's presence.

'Sit down, Mr Brennan.'

'Thank you for seeing me, Mr Morrison.'

'I gather you were rude to one of my staff on the telephone,' Morrison said, peering at Brennan over the rim of his spectacles.

'Yes, I probably was.'

'You've no apology to make?'

'She must have had worse, given her obstructive telephone manner.'

'I'm sure. But she takes it all in her stride. I keep hoping that she's going to throw a tantrum and quit. I inherited her from my predecessor, you see, and she never lets me forget how brilliantly he worked.'

'You mean you're *glad* that I was rude to her?' Brennan asked with a frown.

'I'm ecstatic, Mr Brennan. It's the main reason I agreed to your coming in. I thought a man who can stand up to her must have something sensible to say.'

Brennan smiled and shook his head.

'I'm sorry, I was expecting a similar response from you to the one that I got from her.'

'She sees it as her job to protect my official dignity by keeping as many people as possible at arm's length. But it's a coroner's job to meet the public. So how can I help you with . . . ' he looked down to check the name on the file, 'David Southwell?'

'Well, I've recently had contact with the solicitor who represented the late Mr Southwell's interests at the inquest. And from his account, I thought there were a few discrepancies.'

'Really? Tell me.'

'In the first instance I was intrigued about the site of his death. I'm investigating, as a journalist, another matter concerning the MoD, and I wondered why Southwell's death was more or less brushed under the carpet by them?'

'From my notes, I can see that we had

346

MoD policemen and a personnel officer at the hearing — that doesn't seem to me like an attempt to cover up Mr Southwell's death.'

'I wasn't there, so I couldn't say. But what bothers me is how the MoD police found out that Southwell was there. I was told that the train driver simply called the civilian police, but that MoD police quickly attended the scene afterwards.'

'Perhaps the civilian police alerted them?' said Morrison, making his first note.

'Yes, perhaps. But, with respect, shouldn't the precise sequence of events have been established?'

The coroner scanned his file on Southwell again, scratching at an unshaven patch below his chin.

'You mean that you're suspicious that the MoD police didn't find him first?'

'Exactly so. And what bothers me more is that there are two surveillance cameras in the area of that platform. Surely the MoD police on duty would have picked up a body hanging from a shelter? I mean, what were they doing otherwise?'

'I see. I have to confess that I didn't know about the cameras, and that they weren't brought to my attention. So you think there's a possibility they may have picked something up?'

'I don't know the scope of the surveillance, but it just seemed to me when I went to the station that it could have happened. That Southwell's body was spotted but that the MoD police delayed their response in some way.'

'Why would they do that?' asked the coroner.

'It's the first instinct of the military mind, to refer upwards, seek advice. Perhaps they were told just to leave him there because it was close to, but not actually on MoD property? Perhaps they were playing cards and didn't see the events on the platform?'

'Events?' asked the coroner, with a distinct furrowing of the brow.

'Since Southwell died, two men have been looking into his life. They got into his home under false pretences and ransacked the place. His solicitor's office was broken into and his personal file on Southwell was stolen. Then, last night, there was another development that may be related. After I'd had a meeting with an MoD scientist, I was abducted by two men and left on Salisbury Plain. They threatened that if I didn't cooperate with them, the same would happen to me as happened to . . . well, they didn't mention Southwell's name, but I felt that was who they meant. I think that they were after something that Southwell might have had. I also think that they might have murdered him.'

'I'm beginning to regret that you got past my guard dog of a secretary, Mr Brennan,' Morrison said as he made more notes. He laid down his pen and stretched back in his chair.

'I'm sorry to drop this on you, but it would have been irresponsible of me not to report these matters, I think,' Brennan said in a determined tone.

'Except that it is all speculation, Mr Brennan. In my experience, professional burglars often study the 'Deaths' columns in papers to find vulnerable properties. And if there *was* something suspect in Mr Southwell's background, I would imagine that the MoD Special Branch, perhaps even the security services, would be looking into it. I seem to recall that he was a loner who drank a lot. That's the classic profile of a spy or double agent, isn't it?'

'Now who's speculating?' Brennan said, smiling ironically. Fortunately, Morrison picked up on the irony and smiled back.

Brennan continued. 'I know how the security services operate, Mr Morrison. They put me in jail a few years back for crossing them. The two men I encountered last night had all that cold professionalism, but they were harder, more desperate. I don't know what else I can say that could make you reopen the inquest.'

'You haven't come up with enough to make me do that, Mr Brennan. But let me see if I can get my hands on any surveillance camera footage that might be relevant. That was a conspicuous lapse on my behalf and I should do as much as I can to make up for it.'

'Do you have the legal authority to get them to hand it over?'

'Yes, I do. I can create quite a stink if they don't play ball, too.'

'Perhaps you should send your secretary up to Abbey Wood and let her do the asking?'

The coroner laughed, stood up and offered his hand to Brennan, who shook it gratefully, happy to have met someone in public office who would actually admit to a mistake and then also do something to correct it.

'I'll leave you my card if I may, Mr Morrison. My investigation will go on, so anything new that you find would be of great help to me.'

'I'm afraid it would need to be heard in open court first — but, if I do pick up anything that relates specifically to your inquiry, there are ways and means of getting information to you.'

'Thank you, Mr Morrison.'

Brennan left and walked back down the corridor with a rare spring in his step. He even gave the secretary a wink and a smile as he passed her.

'You've got a damned good boss there, you know?' he said, without stopping to see if she reacted. Brennan's ebullient mood lasted as far as the steps of the coroner's office. Pausing to switch on his mobile phone, Brennan saw the 'message' symbol come up on the tiny screen. He dialled the answering service and held the phone to his ear, expecting to hear Janet's voice telling him the bad news. Instead he heard a familiar male voice saying, 'Hello, Brennan, it's your logistics pals here. Hope you got home all right. You have till tomorrow night to deliver. We'll call you at midday to arrange a venue. Don't let us down.'

'Piss off,' Brennan said under his breath as he switched the phone off again.

* * *

Brennan had already had it in mind to go to London anyway, but the combination of events on this particular day forced his hand. He took a taxi round to Temple Meads station and just caught the 3.15 train that

351

would get him to London a couple of minutes before five o'clock — always assuming that it ran to time. Brennan had treated himself to a first-class fare — now well over £100 for a return ticket — on the basis that Mark Beattie's little gravy train was about to run into the buffers so he might as well enjoy himself while he could.

Seated among the professional mobile-phone classes, Brennan looked a touch out of place with his bruised face. But while his fellow travellers twittered about spreadsheets and told their wives what time they would be back for dinner, Brennan's three calls were of a more serious nature. He called Her Majesty's Prison at Erlestoke; Tim Williams's Public Relations Agency; and, finally, Tommy Preston, his old cell-mate, who now resided in the luxury of a service flat at the White House Hotel near Regent's Park.

As a result of his calls, Brennan was able to get a prison visiting order to see Joe Fletcher the following day — it helped that the governor's secretary remembered Brennan himself from his six-month sentence there. He also secured an appointment that evening for a drink with Tim Williams in their old watering hole on Whitehall and a dinner date at the hotel with Tommy for seven-thirty. He did not ring his wife.

By the time he'd finished his calls and been served coffee and biscuits by a hostess with a trolley, Brennan had become quite drowsy. So from Chippenham all the way through to Paddington, he dozed intermittently despite the trills of the phones and laptop computers all around him. Waking with a start as the train stopped at Paddington, Brennan instantly felt refreshed, the aches and the fatigue brought on by his night on Salisbury Plain having ebbed away.

He took a taxi down to the Whitehall pub that he and Timmy Williams used to frequent in what seemed like another life. Though it was a warm early-autumn evening, the pub had no more than a dozen punters in it, most of whom looked as though they'd been there all afternoon. There wasn't a single lobby correspondent or political *apparatchik*, as far as Brennan could tell. The parade had moved on to the briefing rooms of New Labour's Millbank Tower or the designer wine bars on Horseferry Road. Brennan ordered a pint and sat at the bar in a mood of what he could only think of as 'nostalgic depression'.

Ten minutes later, as Brennan finished the pint, Williams sauntered in, wearing Raybans and a white silk suit, the ultimate spin-*meister*. He nodded to Brennan and joined him at the bar.

'What's that, Frank — pint of Old Hack's Bitter?' Williams teased.

'Something like that. Whatever it was, I won't have it again.'

'How about sharing a jug of Pimm's with me? We can find our old table in the back room.'

Williams ordered, then followed Brennan through to one of the booths at the rear of the main bar. A thousand government secrets had changed hands here in the late 1980s, as journalists and civil servants got pissed together on a regular basis. Brennan felt the undertow of pretence as he and Williams sat down for a conversation that would not feature the free flow of information.

'I hear you're still banging on at your story, Frank, despite my reassurances,' Williams said, a vague hint of impatience in his tone.

'You shouldn't believe all that MI5 says about me. My documentary career is over.'

'Good. It didn't suit you, Frank. You're a gumshoe, a *schlepper*, a man who walks the mean streets of Wiltshire alone,' Williams said, dissolving into a self-regarding chuckle.

'Maybe so, but I can still save your job,' Brennan replied with a sneer.

A barmaid delivered a jug of Pimm's, filled with wilting fruit, and two glasses. Williams waited while she poured out two measures.

Once she had gone, he leant across to Brennan and poked a finger in his chest.

'I'm not putting up with any more bollocks from you, Frank. You're a has-been, a dinosaur. You didn't adapt to the new rules and very soon you'll be extinct. So don't tell me my job's in your hands because I don't believe you.'

'I'll give you one more chance to be nice to me, Tim, and then I'm leaving. If you level with me over what happened at that farm, I can warn you about something unpleasant that's coming your way.'

'Sorry, no deal.'

'You sure? It's a Ministry of Defence matter.'

Brennan thought he saw Williams twitch slightly.

'You're bluffing, Frank.'

'Call it, then.'

Williams sipped his drink and then lowered his Raybans, leaving them to hang across his chest on a brightly-coloured spectacle cord.

'I need to see something. Give me the flavour of it.'

'A suicide that wasn't. How do you feel about that, Timmy? Interested?'

'Not enough.'

'Well, now *you* have to give *me* something if you want to know more.'

'I said I wasn't that interested.'

'Your client is going to be seen in a very poor light when this comes out — neglectful at best, conspiratorial at worst. And when they see my name on the story they are going to ask you — you especially — why you didn't stop it. 'We thought you had Brennan on toast', they'll say to you.'

'Give me a name.'

'No, you give me the truth first. *Then* I'll give you a name.'

'What you saw that night was not quite an exercise, although it became one. There was no danger to the public. There is no story in it. Never was.'

'I'm afraid I need to know what killed the cattle, and how.'

'You were going to give me a name, I believe?'

'Yes — it's 'David'. How's that for starters?'

'You really think you're still big-time, don't you, Brennan?'

'Big enough. What killed them? Where did it come from?'

Williams took a long slug of Pimm's.

'I can't even trust you to keep my name out of it these days, can I?'

'I'm open to persuasion.'

Williams leant forward.

'It was anthrax,' he said in a hush. 'But it wasn't weaponized.'

'What the fuck does that mean?'

'It had nothing to do with the military, nor with Porton Down. The field had been a site for some Second World War germ-warfare exercises. The stuff had been in the ground for decades. The old farmer recognized the symptoms his cattle had and panicked. Called us rather than the police.'

'Why the airlift to Boscombe Down, then?'

'How did you know they went there, Brennan?'

'Because I'm nosy. Why was there a security sweep at Porton Down a few days later?'

'Frank — you're making things up again . . . '

'Why was the herd replaced in the same field if the ground was contaminated?'

'That's all you're getting, Brennan.'

'You, too,' Brennan said, standing up. 'You had your chance, Tim. In the old days we could have sorted this out in ten minutes.'

'You'll get ten *years* this time if you print anything, Frank. We're not as tolerant as the Home Office.'

'Nor as bright,' Brennan said as he left.

Out on Whitehall, the rush-hour traffic was virtually at a standstill, with four rows of cars, vans, lorries and buses all packed together in a noxious mass. The diesel fumes hung over the road in a near-visible cloud. Brennan set off towards Trafalgar Square in search of a taxi that was not snarled up in the Gordian knot of traffic. Sweating, panting people brushed past Brennan, running unnecessarily for stationary buses. A *Big Issue* seller waved a magazine in front of his face, and now the siren of a police car began to wail from somewhere inside the lava-like stream of vehicles.

'Fuck this for a game of soldiers,' Brennan wheezed to himself as he looked for sanctuary. And then he remembered 2 Brydges Place, the little club behind the Coliseum. He couldn't remember whether or not his membership had expired, but was fairly sure that they wouldn't turn him away, given his extensive custom in the past. Brennan crossed the Strand and made his way up the rather unpleasant alley where the club's entrance was situated. He pushed open the door and climbed the dark, narrow staircase. Entering the bar area, he saw that all the tables had been laid out in a line, covered in white linen tablecloths upon which several dozen glasses stood, with champagne bottles resting in large plastic containers crammed with ice. The first trays of a buffet

358

were also laid out on one of tables. Brennan nodded to the youth behind the bar.

'There was no need to lay all this on for me.'

The youth frowned at him.

'Are you a member, sir?' he asked.

'Sure.'

'And are you invited to this party?'

'Not exactly. Whose is it?'

'Stuart Gill — you know, the newspaper mogul.'

'*Mogul*'s pushing it a bit. He used to sub my copy fifteen years ago.'

'Well, it's his party, so I'm afraid you'll have to leave.'

'But I'm a friend of his. Can I just stay until he comes, and say hello?'

The young barman considered this.

'I suppose so. Then it's up to him, really.'

'He's a pussycat. I'll have a glass of champagne, please. And I'll pay for it, mind.'

Brennan installed himself at the window table in the next room, with a view out towards the Strand. It was just after six o'clock. He'd expected to be longer with Williams, although the brevity of their meeting had come as a relief in the circumstances. Brennan felt sure he'd come out of it with more than Williams had. He imagined the PR guru getting his secretary to access the MoD's central personnel computer with the search words 'David' and 'suicide'.

In contrast, Brennan was convinced that Williams, though lying to him in the main, had admitted some fragments of the truth while inadvertently acknowledging others by omission. Williams hadn't mentioned the younger Gudgeon, even though he must have known that he worked for DERA. And the deployment of troops and a helicopter wouldn't have been justified by the discovery of anthrax spores in the ground. Both Gudgeons, senior and junior, would have recognized this as a case for the Ministry of Agriculture — unless, of course, they knew that the anthrax was derived from another source. Brennan began to relish the prospect of cornering Gudgeon for his account of the night.

'Frank! What the hell are you doing here?'

Brennan looked up from his drink. It was Stuart Gill standing at the top of the staircase, pausing to recover his breath after the short climb. He was both fatter and better dressed than Brennan remembered him, a classic combination resulting from his increasing elevation in the print and media world.

'Just popped in for a drink, Stuart. How are you?'

'I'm *extremely* well, old son. What happened to you? Been beaten up by the wife?'

'I wish it was that simple.'

Gill made no move in Brennan's direction, and Brennan was disinclined to get up from his table for a display of false *bonhomie*. The physical distance between the two former colleagues might have been small, but the difference in their status was now immeasurable.

'What you up to, then?' Gill asked, wiping his brow with a handkerchief.

'Oh, the usual stuff. Nothing you'd be interested in.'

'They've put me in charge of the cable television operation now,' Gill said, preening. 'It's the future. You know, delivering an electronic newspaper straight into the home —news, features, gossip, sport, showbiz — the lot.'

'I don't think I heard investigative journalism on that list, did I?'

'It's not right for the medium, Frank. The punters don't want to be grabbed by the lapels as soon as they get home from work. They want the televisual equivalent of a large vodka and tonic.'

'Where do the topless Swedish twins fit into that scheme?'

'They're the ice and the lemon, old son,' Gill said with a chuckle. 'Look, I'd love you to stay for a drink . . . '

'But?'

'Well, I've got a few American investors on their way over. I chose here because they like sort of Dickensian premises, you know.'

'I could do a good Bill Sykes at the moment,' Brennan said as he stood up and finished his drink. 'Don't worry, Stuart. I won't hang around to embarrass you.'

'I knew you'd understand, Frank.'

They shook hands as Brennan passed.

'Give me a bell sometime, we'll do lunch. Got my own table at The Ivy now,' Gill said as he moved instantly away to survey the progress of his buffet. Brennan made his way down the staircase and out into the alley. A tramp was stretched out asleep on the other side of the entrance. Brennan wondered whether Gill had booked him from a specialist agency to impress the Yanks, or whether he was real and in imminent danger of being dragged away by Gill's chauffeur.

Brennan caught a taxi heading up Charing Cross Road, and fifteen minutes later walked into the air-conditioned coolness of the bar at the White House Hotel, where a cocktail pianist played American standards. Tommy Preston was seated to one side — away from the Venetian-blinded windows but facing the door. He wore a grey cashmere suit and red silk tie, and stood as Brennan approached, holding his arms open for an embrace. The two men kissed each other on respective cheeks, and then Tommy turned away and signalled to a waiter.

'*Obrigado!*' he called, getting an instant nod from the waiter. Tommy gestured for Brennan to sit in one of the bar's high-backed armchairs, opposite his own but subtly angled so as not to block Tommy's view of the bar's entrance. It was the habit of a lifetime, keeping one eye on the door, but not nearly as necessary now as it had been during the gang wars of the 1950s and 1960s. If any of his former rivals arrived to get him now they would almost certainly be preceded by a Zimmer frame. The waiter arrived in short order.

'Mis-ter Preston,' he said virtually curtsying with deference.

'This is my friend Mr Brennan, Luis. You look after him the same way you look after me, right?'

'Of course, Mis-ter Preston. What can I get you, sir?'

'A glass of champagne, please,' Brennan said with a restrained smile. He didn't want the waiter thinking he was an old gangster too.

'Luis!' barked Tommy. 'Bring him a half-bottle rather than over-charging him for two bleedin' glasses.'

'Yes, Mis-ter Preston.'

'And Luis, *frigo*, okay?'

'For yourself, Mis-ter Preston?'

'Similar, *por favor*,' Tommy said pointing at his glass of brandy.

'Looks like you've got the bar under control, Tommy,' Brennan said admiringly.

'Well, if you don't let them know how you want things to be straight up, that's when they start taking liberties. How are you, son?'

'OK, Tom. Yourself?'

'When we was in the 'hospital' together, I made you promise you'd never lie to me. And now you just have.'

Brennan shrugged.

'Your face has a got at least a dozen stories written all over it, and you come here and tell me you're OK? What am I? Bo-Peep?'

'I'm working. On an investigation.'

Tommy eyed Brennan sceptically. He pulled up the left sleeve of his jacket to reveal half a dozen expensive-looking watches strapped to his arm.

'This is what I'm doing at the moment. They're all *schneide*, of course, but it keeps the bills paid. Now you tell me the truth about where your face has been.'

The waiter returned with the drinks, obliging Tommy to stage an operatic silence, as though great affairs of state were under discussion to which no underling should be privy. Finally, as the waiter retreated, Tommy lowered his hand as a signal for the conversation to resume.

'I'm being chased by two firms,' Brennan said, adopting Tommy's argot for simplicity. 'MI5 and a couple of heavy-duty chancers, possibly ex-military, possibly arms dealers of some sort.'

Tommy nodded, acknowledging his acceptance of this as the truth.

'Right, we shall have to get you some help then, won't we? Do you have a 'when' or a 'where' yet?

'No, but the 'when' will be soon.'

'Good. You pick both, then. Get them on your territory. No dark alleys, no underground car parks, no lay-bys on small roads, although these *are* your territory, come to think of it. What I mean is, you meet them in public so they can't get too busy. Then you get yourself (a) an edge and (b) a way out. You never go in nowhere not knowing how to get out, right?'

'How do I get an edge?' Brennan asked.

'Well, the Secret Police or whatever won't like being out in public view. And the 'chancers' won't like the law being around. So you get them both to come to the same place at the same time.'

'And then what?'

'Then you duck, son.'

14

Brennan caught the 11.30 p.m. train from Paddington, having managed to get himself pretty well slaughtered over dinner with Tommy Preston. They'd drunk a bottle of champagne, two bottles of Rioja — these in memory of Tommy's sojourn on the Costa del Crime — and had finished off with several brandies. They'd also each smoked a Cuban cigar, with Brennan buying a third for the train journey home. Now, as the train lurched out of Paddington with its collection of late-night travellers, most of whom, like Brennan, appeared to be drunk, he lit up the cigar and basked in the contentment of security that Tommy had always conjured around himself. It wasn't just the fact that he'd been a hard man all his life and had survived to tell the tale, but also the sense of relish and style with which he still lived that life. He could be potless most of the time, but he'd always have a smart suit left and a couple of Gieves & Hawke shirts to keep up appearances. He would always find money from somewhere when he needed it most — he'd even sold one of his fake watches to the maître d'hotel of the restaurant that night. And he was always good company, no matter what the circumstances. Tommy was a top geezer, and Brennan felt immeasurably reassured to have him on his side.

Emboldened by the reunion, not to mention the several litres of drink, Brennan decided he was in the mood to make a few late-night calls on his mobile phone. The smoking carriage was otherwise deserted, so he could be free with his words. First he rang Mary Ashton, expecting to hear opera in the background when she answered. But the recorded message was still in the way.

'Hello, Mary, this is Frank, again. I need the answers to a few questions. Who were your two male visitors last night, and why did you put them on to me? What are they after and what do they think I have that is so important to them? This is very important, Mary. Call me back at any time. You may be in danger, so you need my help. Keep yourself safe, Mary, and stay cheerful. I'll sort it all out for you. Goodnight.'

Brennan left the phone switched on as he restoked his cigar. Despite the euphoria brought on by the evening with Tommy, he knew in his bones that something unpleasant was likely to happen in the next twenty-four hours, something from which words and attitude wouldn't be enough to protect him. He felt sure that the two men who had abducted him were professional life-takers who wouldn't hold back if he messed them around. Brennan wondered, briefly, about turning the whole business over to the police. But then, they probably wouldn't believe him anyway. Better to follow Tommy's strategy on the basis that it had kept him out of serious harm's way for the fifty-odd years of his criminal career. Brennan's phone rang, so suddenly that he had to double-check that he was alone in the carriage before realizing it was his own.

'Frank Brennan,' he said, expecting it to be Mary. It was Janet.

'Is that the same Frank Brennan that I'm about to divorce on the grounds of a long separation?'

'It's only been ten hours, Jan,' Brennan pleaded.

'During which you called me how many times? Where are you?'

'On the train. Coming back from London. I've been to see Timmy Williams. Then I had dinner with Tommy Preston.'

'A good one, by the sound of it. Well, had you called me or responded to my message I might have been able to save you the trip. You're out, Frank. Mark's cancelled the film.

Or your involvement in it, to be precise.'

'Hardly a surprise. He thinks Joe Fletcher's guilty, doesn't he?'

'On balance, yes. But he also thinks you're barking up a forest of wrong trees.'

'And where do *you* stand on this?'

'I agree with him, I think. You've been straying off in too many directions. The investigation lacks focus.'

'It won't tomorrow,' Brennan snapped.

'Too late, Frank. Anyway, Mark's been very honourable about it. He's paying you the next two and a half grand as a gesture of thanks for your work.'

'In return for the rights to the material, I bet?'

'*You*'ll have to ask him that. I'm not your agent. OK, I'm going to bed now. There's a parcel for you from your girlfriend on the kitchen table — probably the underwear you left at her place last night.'

The phone went dead. Brennan switched it off and tossed it onto the seat opposite. He pulled on his cigar several times, sending plumes of blue smoke up into the luggage rack above. It was just like the bad old days on the newspaper, when he'd had a story to chase to the accompaniment of the discordant sound of marital grief. Brennan smoked, dozing intermittently, all the way to Bath, where he brushed the traces of tobacco ash from his clothes and reclaimed his phone before stepping out into the cool night air. A few drunks sang their way along the platform. Brennan scooted past them to try and get to the front of the taxi rank outside the station, but he was being absurdly optimistic about the availability of cabs at quarter past one in the morning. The rank was deserted. He waited for ten minutes, staring up the long stretch of Manvers Street for a sight of an illuminated cab roof-light. He set off for Bath Abbey where the rank was usually more populated, passing several ragged bundles of rough-sleepers in doorways, the hidden underbelly of Bath's Georgian theme park. Now he felt guilty about giving that *Big Issue* seller the swerve in Whitehall, felt bad about feeling bad about his life. These sombre thoughts and the five-minute walk not only sobered him up but also stiffened his resolve to complete the investigation. 'I ain't no sigh,' he said to himself, adopting the boxing parlance that flecked so many of Tommy Preston's observations on life. 'Sigh and a shrug — mug,' Brennan mused with a chuckle as he climbed into the last cab on the rank.

On the way back to Bradford, Brennan checked his mobile again for messages. But there was no call from Mary, just Janet's from earlier in the evening. Now that he knew the details he decided to delete the message rather than listen to it. If only face-to-face communications could be conducted on this basis, Brennan wondered how much better the world would be. Call-delete-call-listen-respond-delete would be a reasonable representation of a day's contact with Janet. His favourite joke, which naturally she hated, was that while women faked orgasms, men retaliated by pretending to be interested in what women were saying.

'We're here, mate,' the taxi driver said, nudging Brennan from his semi-conscious state. Brennan had indeed drifted in and out of sleep on the journey, his mind a whirl of abstract thoughts. Had he told the joke to the taxi driver or just dreamt about it? Brennan paid the fare and set off down the pathway towards Tory. He'd asked to be dropped up on the Winsley Road rather than down on Newtown, partly because it was an easier and shorter walk to the house from there. Doing the steep climb up Conigre Hill from Newtown would have strained his digestive equilibrium. There was also less chance of an ambush at the top end of the terrace, where the narrow footpaths were both well-lit and overlooked by the bedrooms of other cottages. Brennan had taken this into account because he now accepted that he was genuinely under threat from his two abductors: preparing for anything they might do against him would help him control his fear. He made it down to the house, passing only an old man walking a small dog that had strained on its leash and barked at Brennan despite his size. Brennan would need some of the same spirit for the next day.

Once inside the house, Brennan sagged with relief. He poured himself a glass of mineral water and took off his jacket and tie. On the kitchen table was a squat cardboard parcel, about nine inches high and six inches wide. Janet had not left a note alongside it, obviously preferring to let her sarcasm stay vocal. Brennan picked up the parcel. It was deceptively light. He caught sight of a printed address label above the postage stamps. It bore Mary Ashton's name and address. Brennan tried to recall if he had indeed left anything sexually incriminating at her house the previous night. But the memory of his brief encounter with Mary was fairly clear — no clothes had been removed, no bodily fluids exchanged, no collars had been stained with lipstick.

Brennan fetched a kitchen knife and sliced through the Sellotape with which Mary had sealed all the edges of the box. He opened the top flap and found inside a protective carton made of polystyrene. He slid the rest of the cardboard box off this and saw that the polystyrene packaging divided at its centre. Brennan sliced through the two pieces of tape that held the top half to the bottom and eased the top section off with the blade, as if he were opening a boiled egg at breakfast. With the top off, Brennan could instantly see that what Ashton had sent him was no love token. A stainless-steel flask, not dissimilar to a cocktail shaker, stood upright. Its screw top was bolted into place with four steel pins, and the junction of the top with the rest of the flask had been sealed with a pitch black collar of dense wax. On the body of the flask Brennan could see luminous yellow labels marked with black skulls and the words: 'Deadly Pathogens'.

Brennan stilled his breathing and movement in fear. He moved around the table with his head low, scanning the flask for any other information — storage or safety instructions, or perhaps a tag saying 'Fooled you, Frank — there's only a Martini inside!' But there were just two further warning stickers. Brennan stepped away from the table, keeping his eyes on the flask all the time. Was it timed to open or explode? Had he been careful enough opening the package? How much shaking had the postman given the package on his long walk up to the house? Brennan endured a brief nightmare vision, brought on by his drinking earlier in the evening, of the flask's top popping like a champagne cork with a deadly spray spiralling out after it. Despite his worst fears, though, the flask remained inert. He moved back towards it again, sliding the top section of the polystyrene sleeve back on so that at least the staring skulls were out of sight.

Brennan rummaged around the outer cardboard packing and found a double-folded piece of paper. He opened it out. Mary Ashton's handwritten note read:

I'm sorry to do this to you, Frank. But you're the only person I've got to turn to. I've been a silly girl. Those two men want this flask. If you can parlay a way out for me I'll be yours forever. And please don't take it to Porton, because they'll put me inside for life! Thank you so . . . ooo much! Yours, Mary. PS Keep it in the fridge and it should be fine!

The banality of this postscript confirmed Brennan's suspicions of Ashton's unstable nature. He could almost hear the fake heartiness of the middle-class country spinster in the words, emphasized by the over-extended 'so' and the excessive curlicues of the handwriting. But then, as Brennan realized, it didn't need the services of a graphologist to confirm that Ashton was completely loopy. The woman had sent a package of killer germs through the fucking post — what the hell was she thinking of? Was she so detached from reality that the possible consequences of this act had not even occurred to her?

For a moment, Brennan felt like driving straight down to her cottage and shoving the flask down her overexposed cleavage. But then he calmed himself. He placed the flask and its protective sleeve in the fridge and, as a further precaution, took a roll of masking tape and sealed all the edges of the fridge door. Brennan stood back, panting, admiring his handiwork. And then he began to giggle to himself. He'd failed O-level chemistry by a long way, and here he was guessing that sticky tape had the necessary properties to retard the escape of pathogens.

Brennan drank more mineral water straight from the bottle in a desperate rush to sober himself up and stabilize his mood swings. He was in the middle of a weird and deadly exchange, but he had to stay utterly rational if he was to control the outcome. He made himself a mug of double-strength coffee and sipped it slowly while he weighed up his options. If he took the flask to the police he would be heavily implicated in what he presumed was its theft from the laboratories of Porton Down. Given help from MI5, they could easily construct a serious prosecution case against both Brennan and Ashton.

Equally, he had no idea how to dispose of the flask. Nor was it the sort of task about which he could ask questions at the public library, say, or the local chemist's. And then he saw it: the solution, 'the edge', as suggested by Tommy Preston. Brennan was so excited that he could hardly think about sleep. But when he snuggled into bed and felt the warmth of Janet's body against him, he soon fell into a profound stupor that was to be laced with delirious dreams.

★   ★   ★

'Why is the fridge taped up, Frank?' Janet asked calmly.

Brennan stared blearily at her, trying to assemble a rushed structure of memory but failing.

'The what?'

'Is it a prank, or some sort of marital revenge, to deny me my early-morning yoghurt?'

Brennan sat up in the bed and dragged his

hands over his face, massaging his eyelids open with his fingertips.

'It's for our safety,' he said. 'If I keep it simple, do you promise not to ask questions?'

'Possibly.'

'There's a flask of Porton Down's finest produce in there. Don't know what precisely, but it says 'deadly pathogen' on the label, which is 'disease' to you and me.'

'How the hell . . . ?'

'You said you *wouldn't* ask questions. I'm dealing with it, OK? It's under control. And now that I'm no longer under contract to your production company it is, strictly speaking, none of your business.'

'You mean you let me sleep through the night without telling me that our house contained a germ-warfare agent?'

'Come on, let's be grown up here. The place is full of bleach and slug poison and chemical sprays. I'm happy that the flask is professionally sealed.'

'So your girlfriend sent you this, did she? Not much of an endorsement for your sexual performance, is it?'

'Janet, I didn't fuck her. She's a lonely woman with a nightmare job killing animals with biological agents. Somehow, she's got herself into deep shit . . . '

'And you with her.'

'That's my own fault, not hers. But I've got it sorted out.'

'It doesn't look like it to me.'

'Janet, I want you and Lester to stay away from the house tonight. These two guys know where I live. As I'm in the process of outflanking them, I think you should be well away from the firing line. I don't want any hostage-taking.'

'The military jargon seems to be rubbing off on you.'

Brennan shrugged forlornly.

'I have to start thinking like them if I'm going to beat them, Janet. If I'm right, they probably killed Southwell, so I have to be prepared for them to have a go at me.'

'Have you got help?'

'It's on its way,' Brennan said without looking at her. 'Now just let me get on with it, please. I know how to look after myself.'

Janet nodded, and smiled grimly.

'I'll get you some toast and coffee — it will have to be black, of course, because I can't get into the bloody fridge.'

Janet kissed Brennan lightly on the forehead and left the room. An hour later, Brennan was showered, fed, refreshed and ready to face the day. He'd charged up his mobile, placed the flask in a picnic cool-bag, and was just about to set off for his visit to

379

Joe Fletcher at Erlestoke Prison when the phone in the kitchen rang. Janet had set off for the railway station so there was no need for Brennan to mask his anxiety. He picked up the phone, stiffening himself both physically and mentally for the task of staying in control.

'Brennan,' he said firmly.

'Up and about early, that's what we like to see, Brennan,' said the voice of one of his abductors.

'Eight o'clock, the Farrant Arms, tonight. It's in the first village on the western perimeter of the Porton site. Any problems, ring my mobile — you have the number.'

'Wait a minute, Brennan — we decide the rendezvous.'

'Not so, mate. Eight o'clock or forget it.'

'What about your fee?'

'We can discuss that later. Bye.'

Brennan hung up the phone, then lifted the receiver and laid it to one side. He wasn't sure he'd sounded that convincing as an *arbitrageur* of deadly germs, but that was their problem. He had what they wanted, and as long as he stayed on the move until the evening, they had little chance of intercepting him. Brennan placed the phone back on the hook. It began to ring again immediately but Brennan left it unanswered.

He got out of the house quickly, just in case his abductors were nearby. He tucked the cool-bag into the deepest recess of the car boot, packing objects around it to keep it upright and relatively stable. Then, for the first mile of his drive out of Bradford, Brennan checked for Mercedes saloons in his rear-view mirror but was relieved to see none. Prosperous as this corner of West Wiltshire was, not too many people went in for ostentatious automobiles as there was plenty of peasant envy about, waiting to be translated into the sly vandalism of slashed tyres or snapped aerials. Brennan took the B-road route to Erlestoke as an additional precaution against being followed.

Approaching the gates of the prison, he felt a pronounced *frisson* of dread, not just because of his own time there but also because he was bearing bad news for Joe Fletcher.

'I'll find somebody else as soon as I can,' Brennan reassured the boy as Fletcher sat opposite him in his prison drill shirt and dungarees in the glorified Nissen hut that passed for the visiting room.

'I can't afford fancy solicitors, Mr Brennan. And they've stopped legal aid now, haven't they?'

'It's been rationalized, certainly. But I'll ask around.'

'I've got no chance, though, have I? There'll be all-out war going on now the government's set on banning hunting. The countryside fraternity will have all their mates looking out for them — you know, the House of Lords, the police, the judges and magistrates, and all that network of the land-owning classes. They'll love putting someone like me away.'

'I promise you I'll get a lawyer on your side soon. Have you had any visitors?' Brennan asked, changing tack.

'No. The other lads and the sabs won't come near a prison. They do write to me, though. They're planning a protest march for me in Salisbury. Try to make sure I'm not forgotten.'

'You won't be, Joe.'

'Why did Cochrane quit, then?'

'Some new evidence came to light. Circumstantial but damaging to your case. I don't think he had the stomach for a fight, to be honest.'

'You mean he thought I was guilty?'

'The son of the farmer who was killed by the bomb works at Porton Down. He rears all the animals used in the experiments. In other words, he would be among the prime targets for your movement. It looks like you simply killed the wrong bloke.'

'But I didn't do it, Mr Brennan. I've no idea how to make a bomb. I didn't know anything about this bloke or his son.'

'The prosecution will try to prove that you did. You found Dr Ashton's house. They'll say you were capable of finding Gudgeon on his farm.'

'I'll be well fitted up, won't I?'

'I'll see that it doesn't happen, Joe. Promise.'

Brennan turned the conversation round to prison life, recalling some of the ways he had found to survive the sudden shock of confinement. Of course, in Brennan's case, Tommy Preston's company and outside work on farms had helped keep him stable. Brennan guessed that an animal rights activist would get a hard time from his fellow prisoners and, as a prisoner on remand for murder, Fletcher would not be allowed outside for anything other than exercise in the prison yard. Brennan could see that his attempts to keep things upbeat were fading. So he left, promising Fletcher another visit by the end of the week, this time with a supportive solicitor in tow.

Brennan made his way out of the prison, getting some ironic baiting en route from a couple of the warders who remembered him. Ordinarily he'd have laughed it all off, but he sensed the probability that Fletcher's freedom would in fact be long denied, and he was also keenly aware of the possibility that he might well be joining him on the inside.

Brennan set off for Salisbury on the next of his strategic movements for the day. He called Luke Barrs on his private line and requested a meeting at a place where Barrs could preserve his discretion.

'Just come straight up to the office, Frank. I've got nothing to hide,' Barrs had told him, the sudden lack of caution surprising Brennan so much that, for a while at least, he suspected he might be walking into a trap. The suspicion still dogged him as he waited in the reception area of the *Salisbury Gazette*'s office. He half expected 'Parker', the MI5 operative, to appear at his shoulder and pull out an arrest warrant, but no such thing happened. In fact, he was ushered straight up to Luke's office, where the young man sat with his hands cradled behind his head.

'Are you sure this is all right, Luke?'

'More than sure,' Barrs said confidently.

'Only I've just been to visit Joe Fletcher. So I don't want any of this to rebound on you.'

'It already has, Frank,' Barrs said, with a weak attempt at a smile.

'What happened?' Brennan asked darkly.

'I was summoned to dinner by the proprietor last night. Nothing was said up front but it was obvious that he wants me out of this chair. He kept asking me if it was time for me to move on to a big city paper. Said he wasn't sure that I was clear enough on the major issues of local life, meaning things like Porton Down, the military's presence in the county, the right to hunt and so on.'

'You don't have to answer this, but did you sign up for Parker's mob?'

'I didn't, Frank. I told them I wasn't interested. I presume they had a word in the old man's ear. Odd how power works, isn't it? Subtle but unsubtle at the same time.'

'I'd call it crude intimidation myself. What are you going to do?'

'Work out my notice, and keep an eye on the job adverts in the *Press Gazette*. You were right that time when you told me about journalists having to toe the line or cross it at some stage in their career. I didn't think it would happen to me so soon.'

'I feel responsible for all this now,' Brennan said mournfully, hoping he would receive instant absolution.

'Well, you are in a way — making me decide whether to be a man or not. I'm very grateful to you, Frank.'

'How far does the proprietor's influence

spread, I wonder? He might still be able to scupper your prospects of getting onto a national paper in London.'

'Chance I'll have to take, isn't it? My gut feeling is that he cares only about the local area. But, as you said, there's a network of these guys who all think alike, who don't want the old order challenged.'

'I can give you a few names to contact, good people, you know. Though you'll probably not want to mention me, just in case.'

'OK, thanks. So what was it you wanted to talk about, anyway? I feel in the mood to run 'Joe Fletcher's Prison Diary' just to piss them all off even more.'

'Well, basically, I wanted you to shop me to MI5.'

Luke's face crumpled into a huge frown.

'What for?'

'I've got a meeting tonight in that pub we had lunch in — the Farrant Arms, remember? It would suit my purposes if Parker was led to believe that I was up to something and that he needed to be there.'

'It'll sound a bit odd coming from me now, won't it? Trying to get back on-side after I've already shown them the door.'

'I think you'll find that the security services are only too happy to welcome those who've rejected them in a previous life. It confirms their idea of their own meaningfulness and their sense of superiority. And, just to protect yourself from any more fallout, couch it in the vaguest terms. Don't profess to know what it's about. It's a whisper, that's all.'

'OK. What time do you want them there?'

★   ★   ★

Brennan lunched, soberly, at the Farrant Arms, chatting occasionally to the landlord about horse racing while mapping out the exits and the blind spots that he would need to know by instinct that night. There was a car park at the rear of the pub, which could be accessed by a corridor on which the toilets were situated. There was a simple push-bar fire exit to the far side of the pub where the dining area was, while the main door opened more or less straight out onto the village's high street.

'You booked-up tonight?' Brennan asked the landlord idly.

'Not many in during the week, now the schools have gone back. Why, do you want to make a reservation?'

'I'll have to see. Got a few friends coming over for a drink. They might want to eat, they might not.'

'No problems. Last orders are nine-thirty.'

'They'll have decided well before then,' Brennan said innocently. After lunch, he phoned Tommy Preston from the car park and gave him the precise layout of the pub and directions to it. Brennan then drove the short distance to the main entrance of DERA Porton Down and parked as close as he could without arousing official suspicion. He switched on his emergency hazard lights to give the impression that he was waiting for the AA, then sat back in his seat, watching through his racing binoculars the small movement of traffic in and out of the site. In between, Brennan kept a check on any messages left on his phone, but there was only a stroppy one from the other 'chancer', wanting further clarification on what Brennan wanted as his 'finder's fee'. But, for the first time, they left a contact number, evidently that of a mobile, and Brennan made a note of it. The first link with the real existence of these two individuals — and he could safely think of them as 'arms dealers' now — had been established. Brennan phoned Janet at her office, and she was both surprised and relieved to hear from him.

'What's happening, Frank?'

'I'm on a stake-out. It's all very quiet. Can you trace a mobile phone number for me, find out the subscriber's name or company?'

'I think I can manage that,' Janet said with a hint of sarcasm.

Brennan gave her the number and chatted for a short while about Joe Fletcher's state of mind. Then, suddenly, out of the main-gate of DERA rolled Mary Ashton's Volvo estate. Brennan checked through the binoculars that it was her behind the wheel.

'Got to go, Jan!' he shouted, switching the phone off and then easing his car out onto the main road, remembering just in time to turn off the hazard-warning lights. He tucked the car in well back from Ashton's as it headed back towards Salisbury. He would drive closer in the city where the traffic was more dense. But then, just before the ring road, Ashton turned off and headed down a suburban avenue flanked on both sides by large Victorian houses. As the avenue ran deeper into the countryside, suburbia faded. Ashton kept on, with Brennan dropping back from her again to avoid being spotted. Half a mile on, Brennan saw her steer the Volvo into the drive of a substantial building that looked one part residential, one part bureaucratic. Brennan stopped to watch the car make its progress to the building's entrance, where Ashton parked in a bay. Moments later, through the binoculars, Brennan saw her make her way into the residential wing of the building.

Brennan brought his car slowly up to the drive, where a sign announced 'Downsview Hospice'. He paused while he took in the implications of this, then drove on up to the main entrance, parking his car next to Ashton's. There was no point hiding now. He smartened himself up as best he could and walked in.

A quiet, flower-decked reception area, panelled in light oak, awaited him. At a formal desk, a middle-aged lady receptionist beamed in welcome.

'Can I help?'

'Yes, I'm supposed to be meeting Dr Mary Ashton here.'

'She didn't mention anything,' the receptionist said, frowning.

'Oh, well, she might not have got my message. Is she here yet?'

'She's just this minute gone up to visit her father. You're very welcome to wait here.'

Brennan shuffled in mock embarrassment.

'I'm terribly sorry. It's slightly awkward,' he said, hushing his voice suddenly. 'We've just got engaged to be married, you see, and she wanted me to meet the old man. I said I'd try to make it . . . so here I am.'

'Oh, well, hurry along then. It's Room 23

on that corridor there. And congratulations.'

'Thank you.'

Brennan walked quietly across the reception area and made his way down a carpeted corridor whose large windows gave views out over sweeping grounds. The hush was so intense that Brennan felt he ought to tiptoe. Through one of the windows he could get a better angle on what had looked like the bureaucratic wing of the hospice. But he could see now that it displayed obvious signs of being a small medical centre. Large surgical lights hung from the ceilings of rooms on the ground floor, while rows of test tubes and laboratory equipment could be seen through the windows of the second. Brennan thought, with brief cynicism, that Ashton would feel at home here herself.

He reached the door of Room 23, where a brass-framed holder on the door held a card bearing the name 'Edward Ashton'. Brennan knocked gently on the door, and he heard Mary's voice say 'Come in'. As Brennan eased the door open, he saw her sitting at the bedside of an elderly man, holding his hand. The old man was asleep, wearing a clear plastic mask that was connected to an oxygen pump on a stand.

'Sorry,' Brennan said, holding up his hands in apology. 'I'm very sorry.'

Ashton glowered at him but said nothing. Brennan closed the door behind him. She continued to hold her father's hand.

'This is very low-rent of me, but I need to talk to you,' Brennan said quietly.

'In due course, Mr Brennan,' she said firmly. Brennan noted the sudden return to icy formality. He stood his ground.

'How is he?' Brennan asked lamely.

'He's dying. That's what the word 'hospice' implies, doesn't it?'

'Yes, I know. I meant, how is he at this moment?'

'Going through a bad patch. His lungs are shot to hell. This mask and the oxygen are all that's keeping him alive. Not that living has much dignity or quality.'

'It seems a very . . . respectful place, though.'

'It's the best I could afford,' Ashton said bleakly.

'I think I may have found a way out of this mess for you, Mary.'

'I couldn't risk losing my job, or being arrested . . . '

'I understand. I do. But you'll have to level with me if I'm to see this through. I can't fight anything other than a just war.'

'I needed the money, that much should be obvious. There are violent, brutally medieval people in ugly little parts of the world who want to obliterate their enemies and who don't care how they do it.'

'And there are two men wandering around Wiltshire prepared to pay very well to provide them with the means.'

Ashton looked away momentarily, readjusting the oxygen mask on her father's face.

'Why did they come to you, Mary? The stuff in that flask is not something you can advertise. Not even on the Internet.'

'They didn't come to me. Not directly, anyway. It was all the fault of my ex-husband.'

Brennan looked at her and knew in an instant who she was talking about.

'It was David Southwell, wasn't it? David Southwell. I was fucking right all along. You know he's dead, don't you?'

'Yes — not that I care. It was his own fault. Stupid man, he should have left me in the past.'

Ashton let go of her father's hand and stood up, walking across to the window. Brennan followed her, standing at her shoulder, still talking in not much more than a whisper.

'Let me guess — he knew he was losing his job, so he contacts you to see if you can provide him with some nasties to sell.'

'Almost true. He'd got very pissed one night — a regular feature in our brief marriage — and boasted to these two friends that he could get his hands on pathogens and precursors for biochemical agents. They commissioned him, but he hadn't actually asked me. He just assumed I'd cooperate.'

'And you did, didn't you? You were at the farm that night, making a rendezvous — far from not knowing about it, you were a chief conspirator.'

'I was there but I put a stop to it. I couldn't go through with a handover. Instead of passing it on to David, I junked it.'

'In what way?'

'Nat Gudgeon helped me — we injected the cows directly, and then got his father to call DERA. That scared David off.'

'It also got him killed, because he failed to deliver. And these men have been tracking you down since then. In their eyes, you're a supplier.'

'I was scared, Frank. That's why I sent it to you. To get them off my back.'

'It would have helped if you'd told me the truth — about the original incident, about knowing Nat Gudgeon.'

'I didn't know who you were. I thought you were security to begin with, testing me out, setting a trap.'

'So tell me about Nat Gudgeon — why did you choose his farm?'

'He got the stuff out of Porton for me. It's easier at his end. And it helps that he's in love with me. Infatuated, even.'

She turned to look at Brennan.

'You mean you use him — like you're using me? You said you were doing this for the money. You expect me to be your bagman?'

'It's for him, not for me,' she said, pointing to her father, wheezing away inside his oxygen mask. 'I just want to be able to keep him here.'

'Sell the Volvo. Sell the cottage. Get a bank loan. You don't have to become an international dealer in biological-weapons material. You don't have to risk your job or your life.'

'You don't understand. I want Porton Down to pay.'

Brennan frowned, and took a grip on Mary's wrists.

'What are you on about?'

'They didn't just experiment on animals, you know. My dad was only twenty-two years old when he volunteered. They told him it wouldn't harm him. Sprayed him with tear gas and God knows what else. When he became ill, they refused to acknowledge he'd ever been there. They'd even destroyed his medical records. And what they did to him has been passed on to me. I was the only child in the family. No sisters or brothers — and no kids for me, either.'

'Why the hell did you go and work there then?'

'I said — to make them pay.'

Brennan could see tears welling in her eyes. He pulled her head onto his shoulder and felt her dissolve into shivering sobs. He stroked her neck to calm her.

'It'll be over tonight. Then you pack it in, right? Take yourself to Verona for a month and fill your boots with opera.'

Brennan felt the movement of a nod on his shoulders. Though Ashton had lied to him or withheld the truth, he couldn't help but feel sympathy for her. But if things went pear-shaped that night, Brennan knew that he would only be able to offer her a limited defence.

'I think you'd better let me know what I've got in that flask . . . '

* * *

Brennan parked his car as close as he could to the pub's emergency exit without blocking it. He left it facing the road so that he would have no laborious three-point turns to undertake in the event of an urgent escape.

There were no other cars in that section. Brennan opened the boot and took out the cool-bag as calmly as he could, now that he knew its contents. He wondered to himself how many other blokes across Britain were popping down to their locals carrying a flask containing bubonic plague. He lifted the bag gently onto his shoulder and made his way into the pub via the main door. There was no sign of 'Parker' nor of the two 'chancers'. Brennan took a seat in the dining area, adjacent to the emergency exit, ordered a bottle of mineral water and asked for the menus while he waited for his 'friends'. He placed the bag under the table between his feet. No matter how much water he drank, his mouth remained as dry as a desert. His insides were in turmoil, as though his organs had become wriggling, squirming creatures. He thought about just handing over the flask to the arms dealers and leaving. No fee, no conditions. But he knew they'd be back for more, with the power of blackmail at their disposal. He also knew that he had a responsibility not to allow this medieval death-dealing agent onto the free market. So it had to end tonight, one way or another.

Brennan sipped his water and watched the door. On the dot of eight o'clock, the two 'chancers' walked calmly in, standing for a moment to survey the pub. There was an old couple seated by the bar, the landlord behind it, and Brennan sitting alone in the dining area. They nodded to Brennan, almost approvingly. One of them went to the bar and came back with two glasses of orange squash. Then they both sat down with Brennan, one on either side of him.

'Looks like a meeting of the Temperance Society,' Brennan said grimly, nodding at the drinks. They smiled patiently.

'We don't get you, Brennan,' said the older of the two men. 'Southwell was just desperate for dosh. But you've got a job. So what's in it for you if you don't want money?'

'World peace?' Brennan suggested sarcastically. 'What I really, really want is me and Mary left out of this.'

'We can donate your fee to charity, if you like,' said the younger man.

'Just tell me where it's going,' said Brennan.

They both shook their heads.

'It's not here, nor Europe, that's all you need to know. Wouldn't shit on our front step, would we? Not Iraq, either. It's nowhere our boys could get harmed.'

'How moral,' Brennan said.

'Can we see the goods?' asked the older man. 'My colleague can take the bag outside for a look, and I can sit here and keep you company.'

Brennan's eyes flickered as 'Parker' arrived, accompanied by his two operatives. Brennan thought he recognized them as the two who'd threatened him with a knife in Bradford, pretending to be animal rights activists. They paused by the door, watching Brennan but more intent on weighing up the other two men.

The chancers were quick to pick up on the vibrations. They recognized something about Parker and his men, in an instinctive, feral way. All Brennan could scent was the threat of imminent violence.

'I think this is stitch-up, Mr Brennan,' the older man muttered menacingly.

'Just the underbidders making a last-minute offer, that's all.'

The two chancers stayed still, sensing that an immediate move would trigger a fire-fight. They checked over the opposition. They could see that 'Parker' was hard, probably ex-army. But the two younger ones looked like untested pups.

Nobody moved. There was just a long, thickening silence as each side assessed the other's strengths, deciding who they would target if it came to a tear-up.

'You don't want to die for the sake of this

stuff, do you, lads?' the older chancer said calmly. 'Like we've been telling Mr Brennan — it's going well away. So it's not your fight. Go and have a good night elsewhere.'

'We're not going anywhere,' 'Parker' said firmly.

'Brennan — why don't you stand in front of me?' the older chancer suggested. 'You're going first, whatever happens.'

'I think I'll sit right here,' Brennan said. 'By the way — just a thought, but if a bullet hits this bag, we're all dead men.'

'That's big talk for a man with no gun,' the older chancer said, looking as though he could strangle Brennan with his bare hands.

'He's got a gun,' said a rasping Cockney voice. 'Two of them.'

It was Tommy Preston emerging from the corridor, flanked by two massive heavies, each of whom had pump-action shotguns, one trained on the chancers, one on 'Parker' and his team. Brennan moved his hand slightly to wipe his brow.

'If anybody wants to be a hero, I'm informed it's out of fashion these days,' Tommy said. 'Mr Brennan's my friend, and anyone trying to hurt him is going to lose most of his claret in about two seconds flat. So stay still while he comes away with us. Come on, Frank.'

Tommy nodded. Brennan reached down for the bag and stood up. He moved sideways across the dining-area floor and left the bag there, halfway between the two groups.

'Now you can effect an arrest, 'Sergeant Parker',' Brennan said as he backed away towards Tommy. The older chancer cursed, and then bent and grabbed at his sock with his right hand. He'd just got a snub-nosed pistol out when a blast from one of the shotguns blew him back against the wall. 'Parker' instantly threw himself flat and took out the younger 'chancer' with a pistol he pulled from inside his jacket. A second shotgun blast went up into the ceiling, bringing down plaster and a shower of dust as Tommy dragged Brennan out with him, closely followed by the two heavies.

In the car park there was a Range Rover, doors open, engine running. Tommy and Brennan dived into the rear seats, with one heavy taking the wheel, the other keeping his gun trained on the pub from behind the open car door. The vehicle took off with him still standing on the running board, and he only climbed inside as the Range Rover put distance between itself and the pub.

'How's the sphincter, Frank?' Tommy asked.

'A bit relaxed,' Brennan said.

'Mine, too,' said Tommy, with a grimace.

They dropped Brennan at Mary's cottage at his request, the Range Rover speeding off without ceremony. Brennan felt reassured that her Volvo was there, but was disturbed by the sight of Gudgeon's truck parked further up the road. Brennan rang the doorbell cautiously. There was no answer. He wondered if they might be upstairs making love, but in the silence of the darkening night he could hear no sounds of pleasure. Brennan moved round to the side of the cottage, and for the first time could see that the door of the stone-built barn was open, with a light shining from the ceiling. Brennan advanced slowly towards the outhouse, picking his way across the grass. As he approached the door, he could see that each wall of the barn was lined with wooden shelves, upon which rested row upon row of animal skulls — sheep, rabbits, cattle, pigs, rats — a complete ossuary of the animals Mary had experimented upon.

As Brennan stepped a little closer, his stomach clenched as he saw Mary half-naked and dead on the floor, with twine wound tightly around her neck. Nathaniel Gudgeon's body lay slumped against the wall, a huge, weeping wound in his chest. The shotgun that he had used to kill himself lay across his legs. Brennan backed away and ran into the orchard where he was at once violently sick, slumping to the earth and shouting out loud in distress.

★ ★ ★

The police found Nat Gudgeon's confession back at the farm. He'd blown up his cantankerous father for the love of Mary or, more precisely, for the money that he felt would attract her to him at last. The pathologist reported that Mary had been raped before she was strangled. Joe Fletcher was freed from prison, all charges dropped within hours.

The two dead 'chancers' were quickly identified as recently dismissed members of the Parachute Regiment, looking to make a living out of the world they had previously policed. The security film at Abbey Wood, handed to the Bristol coroner under legal duress, confirmed them as the killers of David Southwell. The MoD police, who had been away from their desk watching a porno film, were sacked without compensation.

Brennan had no heart left to tell his story, either to Mark Beattie's company or to any newspaper. But he handed all his notes to

Luke Barrs, who was able to place the account on the *Independent*'s review-front, a first step on the long march of a career in national journalism.

Once published, the story also destroyed the job of Timmy Williams, whose company lost the DERA account with immediate effect. The subsequent review of security at Porton Down discovered that the employment of such an unstable personality as Dr Mary Ashton had been greatly facilitated by the fact that the records of experiments on her father had been destroyed by a previous generation of administrators who believed that state secrecy had no consequences.

THE END

We do hope that you have enjoyed reading this large print book.

Did you know that all of our titles are available for purchase?

We publish a wide range of high quality large print books including:
Romances, Mysteries, Classics
General Fiction
Non Fiction and Westerns

Special interest titles available in large print are:
The Little Oxford Dictionary
Music Book
Song Book
Hymn Book
Service Book

Also available from us courtesy of Oxford University Press:
Young Readers' Dictionary
(large print edition)
Young Readers' Thesaurus
(large print edition)

For further information or a free brochure, please contact us at:
Ulverscroft Large Print Books Ltd.,
The Green, Bradgate Road, Anstey,
Leicester, LE7 7FU, England.
Tel: (00 44) 0116 236 4325
Fax: (00 44) 0116 234 0205

A GOOD MAN'S LOVE

Elizabeth Harris

Hal Dillon and Ben MacAllister had been deeply affected by the appalling death of their university friend Laurie. Hal journeyed to Mexico to continue his anthropological studies, and there found distraction in his passionate affair with Magdalena. But was he inviting even more heartache? Ben became a wanderer. While working in Cyprus he had met English girl Jo Daniel, and, after a nomadic summer together, they travelled to England to embark on what promised to be a lifetime of marital bliss. But Jo discovers that promises don't always come true.

BLACKBERRY SUMMER

Phyllis Hastings

Debbie converted a wing of the old farmhouse into an Academy for Young Ladies. She hoped this would enable her to make provision for her children's future careers. But she could not foresee the disastrous fire or the regret and guilt she would feel for giving her youngest son to be reared by her twin sister Dolly. Next to the farm, Dolly's wealthy husband Christopher built an imposing mansion in the Gothic style, and planned to run a racing stable, but his schemes were doomed to end in tragedy.

SLAUGHTER HORSE

Michael Maguire

The Turf Security Division is surprised and suspicious when playboy Wesley Falloway's second-rate horses develop overnight into winners. Simon Drake investigates, but suddenly there is a new twist — someone is out to steal General O'Hara, the star of British bloodstock, owned by Wesley Falloway's mother. With a few million pounds at stake, lives are cheap; Drake finds himself both hunter and quarry in a murderous chase where even his closest associates may be playing a double game.

MERMAID'S GROUND

Alice Marlow

It's been five years since Kate Williams' beloved husband died, leaving her with two young children to raise. Now she's built a good life in one of Wiltshire's prettiest villages, and she has her dream job, as gardener at Moxham Court. For the last year, Kate has had a lover, roguishly attractive Justin Spencer, but he won't commit to more than a night here and there. When she takes in a male lodger, Jem, Kate's secretly hoping his presence will provoke a jealous reaction in Justin. What she hasn't reckoned on is exactly how attractive Jem will turn out to be.